Praise for

The EYE of ZEUS

"With twists, loyalty between friends, and its cast's cleverness, the middle grade fantasy *The Eye of Zeus* hits all the right notes."
—*Foreword Clarion Reviews*

"This charming and brilliant novel is superbly plotted and will win over readers . . . Phoebe's voice is dead on and authentic, as are those of her friends. The author's masterful prose and style serve the story instead of merely taking center stage . . . This author and novel are ready for prime time and the big time."
—*Publishers Weekly*, BookLife Prize Critic's Report

"This first installment in Adams' Legend of Olympus series is a nonstop, fast-paced adventure with an engaging, brave, and resourceful protagonist; fans of Rick Riordan's Percy Jackson series, in particular, will likely enjoy it."
—*Kirkus Reviews*

"A great addition to any library collection, with a fiery, smart protagonist readers will love."
—*School Library Journal*

"Alane Adams delivers a sensational twist on Greek mythology with an adventure full of heart, action-packed moments fit for the legends, an emotional journey, and the strength of friendship . . . *The Eye of Zeus* is the perfect adventure that will give children a passion for mythology, a love of adventure, and introduces them to fun twists on classic myths."

—*Readers' Favorite*, five stars

2020 Readers Favorite Silver Medal
Winner—Children-Preteen

THE MEDUSA QUEST

Published by SparkPress, a BookSparks imprint,
A division of SparkPoint Studio, LLC
Phoenix, Arizona, USA, 85007
www.gosparkpress.com

Published 2021
Printed in the United States of America
Print ISBN: 978-1-68463-075-2
E-ISBN: 978-1-68463-076-9
Library of Congress Control Number: 2020919176

Interior design by Tabitha Lahr

LEGENDS of
OLYMPUS: Book 2

The
MEDUSA QUEST

ALANE ADAMS

To Jésus Hernandez

CHAPTER 1

If you think finding out my dad was Zeus made my life a bed of roses, think again. It had been two months since I returned from Olympus and settled into Carl's place in Brooklyn. He had two tabby cats: Franklin, who liked to claw up my favorite sweaters, and Maxwell, who liked to bring me dead things he found on his walks. I liked living with Carl. We had an understanding—I kept my nose clean at school, and he overlooked the occasional singe marks on the ceiling when I let a stray lightning bolt fly.

Point is, things were going smoothly. You could say life was fine. Picture perfect. I finally had a permanent home, decent friends, and didn't hate school. *Much.*

I had nothing to complain about.

Except . . .

Except, hello! I had to live every day knowing my real family was off having adventures in some ancient magical realm that in reality didn't—couldn't exist. I found myself reading every story I could find about Perseus. My brother had grown up to be a next-level hero. Sure, I had saved

Olympus, but I'd nearly destroyed it in the process. Perseus—that scrawny kid I'd defended from bullies in the marketplace—had grown up to cut off Medusa's head *and* saved our mother from an evil king. Not bad for a kid whose own grandfather had tossed him into the ocean in a wooden box when he was only a few hours old, hoping he would drown.

Our mother, Danae, princess of Argos, had been banished by her own father for having my brother, thanks to a prophecy that Perseus would grow up to kill our grandfather, King Acrisius. Personally, I thought oracles did nothing but cause problems. If I ever came across another one, I'd probably let her have it with a lightning bolt.

I'd only met my mother for a few minutes, but for the past few weeks, I'd dreamed about her every night in full color. Me, who'd never been much of a dreamer, couldn't turn off the kaleidoscope of images when I closed my eyes.

They all started the same, with me walking up to the door of that little hut on the island of Seriphos and knocking. She opens the door, and there's a look of surprise on her face, then shock as she realizes it's me, her long-lost daughter, standing right in front of her. She holds her arms out, a single tear sliding down her cheek as she reaches for me—when suddenly a monster leaps out of the shadows and devours her right in front of me.

After the fifth night I woke up screaming, Carl had to reassure the neighbors in the adjoining apartment he wasn't torturing me. We tried everything. Soothing music. A glass of warm milk. A night-light by my bed.

But it didn't stop the dreams.

Finally, Carl put foam padding on the wall so at least the neighbors wouldn't be woken. Some nights I didn't even remember the dream. I would look at Carl over breakfast. He'd be drinking his coffee—eyes focused on the newspaper—but I would see the tiredness and the worry etched in his brow.

"Why?" I asked one morning.

He rattled the pages. "Why what?"

"Why do I keep dreaming a monster is eating my mother?"

He snorted. "What do I look like, a shrink?"

"No." I stirred my cereal. "But do you think it's, like, a premonition?"

"I think it's a bad dream, kid. You went through a lot."

"But what if it is?"

He folded the paper and put it on the table. Maxwell jumped onto his lap, and he rubbed his orange head. "Say it is—what can you do about it? The doorway—whatever it was—between here and there is closed."

My shoulders slumped. "Right. So it could be true."

"It could be you miss her." He laid a gentle hand on mine. "No one can blame you for that, kid."

"Yeah." Hot tears stung my eyes, and I blinked them away. "I better get ready for school."

Riding the subway from Brooklyn to Midtown, I let the rumble of the train soothe me. I wondered for the thousandth time if I'd made the right decision coming back here. Don't get me wrong—I loved Carl. He was the one constant in my life. And Angie and Damian were the best friends I could ever ask for. But they weren't family. A hole in me kept getting bigger—a hunger for something that was mine, to belong to something. A family. Like what Perseus had with our mother.

The train rolled to a stop at my station, but I stood frozen as the doors opened and shut. I couldn't face seeing everyone at school. I knew where I had to go. The only place I ever felt connected to my family. I sent a quick text to Carl. I had promised I would always let him know where I was, and he had promised to cut me some slack when I needed it. He replied, asking if I was okay. I sent a thumbs-up and silenced my phone. The train rumbled on. I changed trains at Lexington Avenue and, twenty minutes later, walked out into bright sunlight. Athens Square Park was across the street. The wrought-iron gate hung ajar, as if it was waiting for me.

I crossed, dodging a taxi, and pushed open the gate. The place was deserted—no kids on the playground, no old guys playing chess. *No two-headed mutant dogs.* Three fluted columns held the same semicircular arch of stone flanking a pair of bronzed statues. The first was Socrates, a balding figure dressed in a toga seated with his hand out, as if he were in the middle of a conversation. He was supposedly a famous philosopher that Damian liked to quote endlessly.

"Hey, Socrates, how's it hanging?" I slapped his hand with mine and moved on to the next one.

Sophocles was a playwright, and he held a mask in each hand. One crying, one happy. "I guess we all wear masks, don't we, Sophy?"

His bronzed face didn't move, and I sighed, turning to search for my sister.

Athena stood on her podium, staring off into the distance, her face serene in the sunlight. One arm pointed outward as if she was reaching for something. I walked over and stood in front of her, then frowned. Someone had scribbled graffiti on her bronze dress. I climbed up on the podium and scrubbed at it with my sleeve, rubbing at the marks until it wiped off. Satisfied, I stood on my tiptoes so we were face-to-face. She was my half-sister, and I liked her more than I cared to admit.

"I miss you," I whispered in her ear. "I wish you were here. I keep dreaming my mother is in danger. I know it's silly, but I'm scared I made the wrong decision. Please, help me."

I waited, but her bronze face didn't shift, didn't soften. She remained still and cold, a lifeless statue, nothing more. I wanted to punch the hard metal.

This had been a waste of time. Talking statues were a thing of the past.

I jumped down and was heading for the gate when another statue caught my eye. I hadn't noticed it before. This one was a bust with just the head and shoulders. I walked over to it, bending down to read the inscription.

"Aristotle. Dude, you got shortchanged. Everyone else got arms and legs."

"I know. It isn't fair. But then again, life isn't fair."

My head snapped up. "Did you just say something?"

The eyes blinked slowly. "Was I not clear?"

"No, you were. It's just—"

Footsteps sounded behind me. I whirled around to find the other two bronzed statues stretching their arms.

"Socrates! Is that you?" the bust figure asked.

"Aristotle. It's been an age."

"And you, Sophocles. Written any good plays lately?"

"Not in centuries."

"How are you all talking?" I asked.

"You woke us up, dear." Sophocles yawned widely.

"Me?"

"I don't see any other daughters of Zeus hanging around, do you?"

"Whoa, whoa, why now? I've been out here loads of times. You've never spoken before."

"Ah, but you never made a request for help," Socrates said, holding up a finger.

"A request?"

"Yes. You're having dreams. Tell us about them." He seated himself cross-legged on the pavement and motioned for me to join him. Sophocles sat on the other side.

"But how do you know that?" I sat, eager to hear more.

"We have ears, you know. You whispered to Athena, but it was as if you were shouting it from the rooftops. Quickly now, we don't have much time."

I filled them in on all the details of my dream I could remember.

"And this monster, what does it look like?" Aristotle asked.

"I don't know—I never actually see it. I usually wake up screaming at that point."

"Let me handle this," Socrates said.

"Oh, not this again." Aristotle rolled his eyes. "The famous Socratic method."

"My method works." The philosopher leaned forward, looking directly at me. "You're having a dream that a monster, unspecified, is eating your mother, and you believe it to be real, an omen."

"Yes."

"Why?"

"Why what?

"Why do you think it's real?"

"Because it feels real."

"Why?"

"Because I'm terrified."

"Why? It's just a dream."

"No, it's not."

"Why?"

Ugh, this guy is annoying. "Because it doesn't feel like a dream."

"Why?"

"Because right before the monster eats her, it's like it switches."

"Switches how?"

"To a cave. I can hear water dripping."

"You didn't mention that before."

"Well, I didn't remember it before."

"You're in a cave you think is real. Why?"

"Because I can feel the stones under my feet. It's cold, and there's this sound."

"What sound?"

"I'm not sure. It's all a blur. This part only lasts a second or so. That's why I didn't remember it before."

"What does the sound remind you of?"

I thought about it. It was just a whisper, a split second before I snapped out of the dream. "A snake."

His face broke into a smile, and he threw his hands up. "There you have it. The monster you're dreaming of is clearly Medusa."

Sophocles began clapping, but Aristotle blew a raspberry. "Lucky guess."

"Wait. Medusa? Isn't she the snake-head lady?" I asked.

"A gorgon, to be specific," Aristotle quipped.

"And you think she's after my mom?"

Sophocles folded his arms. "I think it likely you are having a shared dream with your twin brother, Perseus. It is he who will face Medusa. This has nothing to do with you."

Socrates nodded. "Agreed."

They rose to their feet and walked away.

I turned back to Aristotle's bust. "So my mother is safe?"

He shrugged one shoulder. "Dreams have many interpretations. Perhaps she is, in which case there may be another in danger."

"Another? Like who?"

"Perhaps the person you have crossed dreams with." His face shifted back and became solid.

"Wait. I have more questions." I rapped my knuckles on his head, but he didn't respond. I spun around, hoping to catch the other two before they climbed back on their podiums, but I was too late.

CHAPTER 2

I was on my third slice of pizza by the time Angie and Damian made their way into the pizza parlor owned by Angie's dad. We met there after school almost every day.

"Katzy!" Angie plopped down next to me. "What's poppin'? You missed out on Julia Pukes-bury getting blitzed by a ball right in the face during PE."

Damian sat down across from us. He was busy looking down at his phone, fingers flying as he texted.

"Hello to you, too," I said.

His eyes flicked up, and he smiled absently, then went back to his phone.

"What's with him?" I asked.

"Parental issues."

"What sort?"

Damian never complained about his parents, but then again, they weren't around much. They traveled a lot— some sort of marine biologists out saving the planet.

"They were supposed to be home this week," Angie said in a low voice. "It's his thirteenth birthday Friday, but they're stuck on an iceberg somewhere."

"That sucks." Of course, I didn't point out my parents had never been to any one of my birthdays. What would be the point? I grabbed my soda and took a deep slurp as Damian set his phone down.

"Sorry, Phoebes. Where were you today?"

"I went to Athens Square Park."

Angie's dad set a fresh cheese pizza in front of us, dropped a kiss on Angie's head, and told us not to eat it all in one bite.

"And?" Angie expertly folded a gooey slice before shoving half of it in her mouth.

"And nothing much. Just three statues came to life and told me my brother might be in danger."

Angie's pizza-stuffed mouth fell open, while Damian froze mid-bite.

"Say what?" Angie said after she'd swallowed.

"Are you serious?" Damian asked.

"Yes. I told you about my dreams—they won't stop. Last night was bad. I just couldn't face school today, so I took the subway out to Queens and went to see Athena. I told her about my dream. I didn't expect it to wake the old brainiacs, but, boy, did they have a lot to say."

"And?" Damian prompted.

"And they said I have it wrong. That it's not about my mom. It's a 'twin crossover.'"

"What does that mean?" Angie asked.

"That Perseus is the one dreaming this stuff, not me. That I'm, like, crossing wires."

"Why?" Angie asked, taking another bite.

"Because he's the one in danger."

"They said that?" Damian looked thoughtful.

"Something like that. It was a lot of mumbo jumbo."

"So what are you going to do about it?" Angie dropped her gnawed crust onto her plate.

I laughed bitterly. "Uh, nothing. Remember? I came back here to this wonderful place and left my real family behind."

There was silence.

Angie cleared her throat. "You didn't have to, you know. We didn't make you come back."

"I know." I let out a breath. "I'm sorry. I don't blame you. I just—"

"Don't know if you made a mistake," Damian finished quietly.

"Yes."

"It's only human to miss your family. Statistics show a direct correlation between reported happiness and time spent with loved ones."

"Zip it," Angie and I both snapped. Damian spouted statistics as if they explained everything, but you couldn't quantify *feelings* or *family*.

Damian shrugged. "I'm just saying it's perfectly normal to miss your family. I miss mine all the time." Shadows chased across his face.

"So . . . are they going to make it back in time for your birthday?" I asked.

He tried to smile, but it looked more like a grimace. "No. They're frozen in. Cold snap. The ship can't move. It's okay. I have Hilda."

"She's your housekeeper?" I vaguely remembered him mentioning her before.

"You could say that." He fidgeted in his seat.

Angie and I exchanged glances. It wasn't like Damian to be evasive.

"Damian? What aren't you telling us?" I asked.

"Nothing."

"Nothing? Well, I've never met Hilda, and I have a sudden urge to see where you live." I leaped up from the table, and Angie followed.

Damian stared at us, slack-jawed. "Why?"

"Because we've never been there," Angie said, "and we want to meet this Hilda."

"We can talk about the birthday party we're going to throw you," I said.

"No. No party." He scrambled to his feet. "And she's boring. She's just my housekeeper."

"Then you won't mind introducing us," I said, glad to have my mind off my own problems. One thing was certain: Damian was hiding something, and that was so unlike him I couldn't help wanting to know more.

Angie looked up his address on her phone, and we headed uptown outside Vito's. Damian scurried after us, trying to talk us out of it.

"Hilda doesn't like visitors. She really doesn't get on with people. She will probably call my parents, and they'll ask you to leave."

"Your parents that are stuck on an iceberg somewhere?" I said over my shoulder. "They'll probably be glad to hear you have friends to keep you company."

Angie and I raced ahead, turning down streets until we stood outside the red door that marked the narrow three-story brownstone wedged between two other taller buildings.

I looked at Angie, and she grinned, extending her arm. "After you."

"No, after you."

Damian caught up, wringing his hands. "Please don't ring the bell," he pleaded, but we were already marching up the steps. Angie thumbed the buzzer. A shrill bell rang inside.

We heard a whirring sound, like a machine running, and then the latch clicked, and the door swung open.

Before us stood the oddest thing I had ever seen.

It might have been a futuristic vacuum cleaner if not for the apron wrapped around the middle. A glowing screen the size of a toaster displayed a large smiley face. A long flexible coil extended from the top, with a round camera on the end that swayed in our faces. A pair of mechanical arms with pincerlike hands protruded from her sides and waved in the air. She rolled forward on battery-powered rollers as the camera examined us.

"Um, Damian, what is this?" I asked.

He sighed. "This . . . is Hilda."

The machine whirred, and the face on the screen smiled wider.

"Pleased to meet you," she replied in a synthetic British accent. "Are you friends of Master Damian?"

Master Damian? This had to be a joke of some kind. There was no way Damian's housekeeper, the person who looked out for him while his parents were gone for weeks at a time, was this *machine*.

"Hilda, this is Angie and Phoebe," Damian said resignedly. "I told you about them. May they come in?"

I could tell Damian was hoping she'd slam the door in our faces, but Hilda rolled backward, pulling the door open wider.

"Come in, come in. I've got a fresh tray of cookies coming out of the oven."

We followed Hilda as she zoomed down a hallway lined with pictures of Damian at various ages. The kitchen was modern, filled with gleaming stainless-steel appliances. Hilda used her pincers to pull open the oven and removed a tray. After expertly flipping cookies onto a plate, she plopped it down on the kitchen table.

"Help yourselves, children. Master Damian hasn't had friends over in an age of Sundays."

"Hilda, we're just going to do homework, all right?" Damian asked.

Her round eyes blinked on the monitor, then she waved an arm at us. "You want Hilda to give you space. Of course, Master Damian. Socialization time with peers is essential for development. Just call if you need me." She zoomed out of the room, cheerily humming a tune.

Damian and Angie sat down, diving into the platter of cookies, but I wanted to explore. The area was immaculate, not a speck out of place. I opened the pantry—even the condiments were lined up in perfect formation, like little soldiers.

The refrigerator was the same: water bottles and sodas neatly lined the door, and the shelves were stacked with sealed rectangular containers. "So let me get this straight." I popped open a soda and leaned back against the door. "Your parents leave you alone for weeks at a time with a robot?"

"Shh." Damian looked down the hall. "She doesn't like that word."

"What word?" I whispered. "You mean *robot*?"

He nodded. "She's a Housekeeping Indoor Light Duty Assistance module, hence the name Hilda. My dad built her out of spare parts."

"I thought your dad was a marine biologist or something," Angie said, shoving an entire cookie in her mouth.

I swear the girl had a bottomless stomach.

"No, that's my mom. Dad's a roboticist. He builds the submersibles they use to explore underwater. He's a wizard at making things work. Listen—forget about Hilda—there's something you need to see." Damian dug into his backpack and pulled out a thick book titled *The Complete Works of Greek Myths*. "I checked this out from the library."

"Did they dedicate a chapter to me?" I joked. "I did save Olympus, after all."

Angie snorted. "Not before destroying Apollo's temple and burning down Nemea."

I punched her lightly on the arm.

"This is serious." Damian opened the book to a marked page. "I didn't want to believe it, but now I'm not so sure. See here?" He pointed to a paragraph.

I leaned over his shoulder. "It's talking about that Hercules dude. The one we ran into heading out of Nemea."

"Correct. Killing the Nemean lion was one of his tasks."

"So we did him a favor." I snatched the last cookie before Angie could reach it.

"Not necessarily," Damian said. "Since Hercules wasn't the one who did it, he failed to complete the labor."

Angie frowned, studying the page. "Weren't there twelve trials?"

"Labors, but yes," Damian said.

"Then why does this page say there were thirteen?"

"That's the problem," he said. "History has been changed."

"What do you mean?" A shiver of dread raced up my spine like a stray current of lightning.

"I mean when Hercules failed a labor, they added another one."

"Wait, wasn't he supposed to kill the hydra too?" Angie asked. "Why aren't there fourteen?"

"He failed that one in the original myth because he received help, so there was already another labor added. But you're missing the point. Don't you get it?"

We stared at him blankly. "So he had thirteen trials," I finally said. "What's the biggy?"

He stabbed a finger down on the page. "The pages in this book have changed. And it's not just this one. All the books talk about the thirteen labors of Hercules."

I still didn't see why it mattered. "Did they at least give me credit for the Nemean lion?" It would be cool to see my name in print, but Damian rolled his eyes.

"No. The story says the prince of Nemea killed it with his bare hands."

"But that's total hydra dung," Angie said. "We killed that lion and saved the prince from being eaten."

"Who took credit for the hydra?" I asked.

Damian said nothing, waiting for me to guess.

"No. He wouldn't," I said.

Damian grimaced. "An unnamed child of Apollo used a sun bolt to cut off all its heads."

"Let me see that." Angie grabbed the book, then frowned. "Hey, where did it go?"

"What do you mean?" I asked.

She turned the book around. The page was blank, and then words flickered back onto it.

"Damian, what's happening?"

"I don't know, but it can't be good, and it gets worse. I went looking to see what else had changed."

"And?"

"And it has to do with your brother."

The shiver running up my spine turned to ice. My knees went weak, and I sank down into the chair next to him. "What about him?"

Damian bit his lip.

I grabbed him by his shirt. "Damian, what happens to Perseus?"

The words exploded from him. "Your brother was supposed to defeat Medusa, only he gets turned to stone.

Polydectes ends up marrying your mom and puts your brother's stone figure in the palace as a reminder not to challenge him."

I released him, sinking back in my chair. "No. That can't be. Perseus is a hero, and my mom hated that guy. Damian, we have to fix this."

"We've done enough damage. We can't go mucking about with mythology." He sat back, folding his arms.

"This is my brother we're talking about," I said. "I have to go back and warn him."

"And how are you going to do that?" Angie asked. "You need some kind of portal thingy to Olympus."

"So we'll find one."

"How?" she demanded.

"By asking someone who's been there before."

"Like who?"

"Like the person who brought me here."

CHAPTER 3

Carl had found me on a bench at a bus stop outside Katz's Deli, but the question that had always lingered was, *Who had dumped me there?* I'd always figured it was my loser parents on their way out of town, taking the fastest bus away from me. But now I knew someone had taken me from Olympus through a doorway between worlds and left me there.

At first I'd assumed they'd gone straight back to Olympus—but what if they'd stayed? What if they'd been watching over me all these years?

And I had an idea who that person might be.

The next morning, Angie and Damian waited for me outside Dexter Academy.

There was a crowd at the top of the steps, and a couple of TV reporters with cameras were interviewing Principal Arnold. Next to him stood my arch nemesis, Julia Pillsbury, practically glowing with pride.

I wanted to hate her—really, I did—but after that incident with the hydra in the girl's bathroom, I think she was afraid of me. She'd avoided me ever since.

"What's up with the paparazzi?" I asked.

"It's all over the school," Angie said. "Apparently Julia's a prodigy."

"You mean, like, gifted? In what? Being stuck up?"

"You haven't seen her video? It's got, like, a million views." Angie held up her phone, scrolled to a video, and pressed play.

Julia perched on a fancy chair in a formal living room, dressed in a black dress like the kind you wear to the opera. She held some kind of weird guitar, which she started playing. The notes sounded surprisingly good—as if the music were out of this world.

"It's odd. I've never seen her practice before," Damian said, tapping his chin.

I pushed the phone away. "She's good, but we have more important things to worry about. You guys ready?"

Angie patted the leather satchel slung across her shoulder. "Got this from my mom's closet. It has everything I need."

Damian had suggested we pack some things for Olympus in a bag that might blend in. I'd taken one of Carl's worn leather soft-sided briefcases with a shoulder strap. Damian had a similar satchel.

We trudged up the stairs past the throng of people and headed straight for Miss Carole's office. Miss Carole was the school guidance counselor, but something about her was familiar, like I'd met her before. I'd been to about eight different schools, so it was hard to keep track, but she reminded me of an aide in a class when I was in first grade, and an office clerk about four schools ago. I could have sworn I'd even had a bus driver once with her silver eyes.

Plus, there was that whole episode with Leonard, the basilisk lizard who'd escaped his cage and possibly turned into a hydra and destroyed the bathroom. It had bitten me, and hydra fangs were quite poisonous, but Miss Carole had given me some weird-tasting juice, and I'd felt better immediately.

I could have chalked that up to some powerful dose of medicine, but I'd tasted the same juice in Olympus after Ares stabbed me with my father's lightning scepter and I'd almost died.

Ambrosia. Nectar of the gods.

"Are you sure it's her?" Damian asked. "She might report us—it sounds pretty loony."

I stared at the name on the door. "I know it's her."

"How can you be so sure?" Angie asked. "I thought you didn't remember who brought you here."

"It's right in front of us. Damian, you're so smart I can't believe you didn't see it." I pointed at her name, CAROLE. "If you rearrange the letters—"

His eyes widened. "You get oracle!" He shook his head. "I can't believe I missed that."

I raised my hand to knock when her gruff voice called out, "Come in."

I opened the door, and we stepped inside. Her office was dim and cluttered with files and old books. The shades were pulled down, and she sat hunched over her desk, typing rapidly on an old typewriter. Her graying hair was coiled in a bun on top of her head. It was hard to tell how old she was because her skin wasn't wrinkled much at all, but she *felt* old, as though she'd been around for centuries. She didn't turn around, continuing on with her typing. "Miss Katz, Mr. Rodina, Miss Spaciacolli, what can I do for you?"

"How did you know it was us?" Angie asked.

She hit the return carriage firmly and turned around. "I could hear your thoughts clanging around in your head as you stood outside my door. Sit." She waved us over to the small love seat.

We crammed in knee to knee.

"You have something you wish to ask?" She pinned her silver eyes on me.

"Yes." I decided to get right to it. "Are you the one?"

One pencil-thin eyebrow went up. "The one what, dear?"

"The one who brought me here?"

"Don't you take the subway?"

"Not here today. I mean to this world. From ancient Olympus."

Her eyes flickered, then hooded over. She smoothed her hands over the trim gray skirt she wore. "What is this about?"

"I need to go back."

"Back?"

"To ancient Olympus."

"Is this some kind of joke?" She looked from me to Angie and Damian. "Some kind of prank you kids are playing?"

"No. I'm serious. I know what you did."

"Did?" She didn't even blink. She was so cool I almost doubted myself.

"You gave me ambrosia. After the hydra bit me. Please. I have to get back there. My brother is in trouble."

Her eyes narrowed. "I thought you didn't have any family."

"I don't. I mean, not here, but there I do. Which you know if you're the oracle."

"I see. And you want me to help you go back there."

"Yes."

"Hmm." She looked between the three of us and then picked up the phone. It was the old-fashioned rotary kind. She dialed a bunch of numbers, letting the rotary spin back each time. I waited, knees shaking.

"Yes, this is Miss Carole. I think I have a solution to our situation. Yes, I knew you would understand. Thank you."

"Well?" I asked when she hung up.

"It's all sorted," she said.

I nervously wiped my hands down my uniform skirt. "So you're sending me back?"

"I'm sending you where you need to go," she said cryptically. "Two birds, one stone." She frowned, then added, "I've always disliked that saying. Do you know how hard it is to kill a bird with one stone, let alone two?"

"What do you mean 'two birds'?" Damian asked.

Her silver eyes flicked to his. "It seems we have a situation."

"Situation?" *What have I done now?*

But it wasn't about me.

"An artifact has appeared in human hands. It happens every so often. One of the gods gets careless, and a priceless object falls into the hands of mortals. The effects can be quite powerful."

"Like a weapon?" Angie asked.

"Possibly, but not this time. It's a musical instrument."

Damian snapped his fingers. "Julia's guitar."

"Not Julia's, Hermes's, to be exact," she said in a bland voice, as if it were an everyday thing to be discussing an instrument that belonged to an actual god. "And it's a lyre. We need to get it back from her before it's too late."

"Is the lyre going to destroy Olympus?" I asked.

"No, it's going to give Miss Pillsbury world fame, and it will be impossible to get the lyre away from her when that happens. You should see what it did to that Hendrix fellow." She shook her head. "It's taken me years to get it this close. We have a small window to act where her prowess will quickly be forgotten."

"Wait, you want us to steal Julia's guitar-lyre thing?" Angie asked.

She frowned. "I already told you, dear, it's not hers. It's Hermes's, and yes, he would like it back. For what you're planning, I suspect you'll want him on your side."

"Fine, we'll do it," I said. "There's three of us against one of her."

Her frown deepened. "I must warn you. The lyre is being guarded by her father's bodyguards—you'll have to be clever without drawing undue attention. Meet me at this address with the lyre at three p.m." She wrote down an address on a slip of paper and passed it to me. "Go now. I have a portal to prepare, an opening spell to craft—you can't imagine the paperwork." She went back to her type-writer, rapidly tapping on the keys.

Damian and Angie shuffled out the door, but I paused in the opening. "So it's true then—you're the one who brought me here."

She nodded but didn't stop her typing.

Anger bubbled up inside me. I'd waited a long time to face the person who'd dumped me on a bench.

"You left me at a bus stop. Alone. I was a baby," I added, in case she'd forgotten. "Helpless. Why?"

Her fingers stilled. "I am an oracle. I see things."

"And you saw that Carl was going to find me and not some psycho stranger?" My voice rose, and I clenched my fists, trying not to cry.

She turned to look at me then, her eyes liquid pools of silver. "I saw that it would be difficult but that you would be okay. I did my best. I apologize if you felt abandoned. I found it to be a very strange world. Still do."

My anger collapsed, and I was left feeling hollow.

"You better be going." She turned back to her type-writer. "If you miss this window, the next portal opening to Olympus is in about eighty human years."

CHAPTER 4

"So what's the plan?" I asked as we huddled by our lockers. Down the hallway, Julia was standing next to her locker, surrounded by her adoring fans. The bad news was there were three guys in dark suits standing six feet away, looking every direction up and down the hall.

"She's got some serious protection," Angie whispered. "They've even got earbuds in. They look like CIA."

"Where's the guitar thingy?" I craned my neck. "Damian, you're the tallest. What do you see?"

He stood on his tiptoes. "It's in a case. She's putting it in her locker."

"Perfect. We'll steal it while she's in class."

"What about the three goons?" Angie asked.

"Oh, you know, we'll do that thing." I waggled my eyebrows.

"What thing?"

"You know, the one where Damian's the bait?" I winked at him.

He paled. "Not again. You promised."

"Hey, it's not a hydra. It's just three guys being paid to guard a guitar. Besides, they're going to be a lot more worried about Julia than her instrument. We just need you to somehow endanger her life and make them go running to help her while Angie and I bust into her locker."

We agreed it would go down during gym class. Julia had already been mackereled by a ball this week, so it wouldn't be too suspicious if Damian found a way to knock her out. Of course, it wouldn't be just any ball but one I had enhanced with a dose of lightning.

Mr. Leland, our gym teacher, blew his whistle. "Captain for Blue Team will be our resident musical prodigy, Julia Pillsbury." He gave her the same fawning smile every teacher in school directed toward her thanks to the hefty donations her daddy made.

She sailed forward in crisply pressed gym clothes, taking the blue singlet from him.

"And captain for Green Team is—"

"Damian Rodina," I announced, pushing him forward. "It's his birthday," I added.

"Er, fine," the coach mumbled, tossing him a green singlet. "But Blue Team picks first."

Julia chose a kid named Evan Baker, who happened to have the strongest arm in school.

Damian pointed at me, then Angie on the next turn, and we slipped on the green jerseys.

When everyone was chosen, Julia planted her hand on her hip, a ball balanced in the other as she flicked a glance between the three of us. "I hope you enjoy the taste of humiliation."

"Been to the girl's bathroom lately?" Angie snapped back.

Julia paled but gave a little shrug. "Vandals like you get what's coming to them. Shall we begin?" She looked over at Coach Leland, and he blew his whistle.

"Players, take your places."

We lined up, setting the supercharged ball directly in front of us. We had to get to it before anyone else. That was key.

Damian huddled in the back.

"Wait for us to get out first," I said.

He nodded, shaking his hands out. We stood in front of him, guarding him. Mr. Leland blew his whistle, and everyone charged the line to grab the balls. Some kid tried to grab the supercharged ball, but Angie elbowed him aside and snatched it up, while I grabbed another. I let mine fly past Julia on purpose, making her grin wider as more and more balls began flying. The goal was to get out quickly, but we couldn't make it look too easy. I could dodge the balls easily enough—it was as if they were in slow motion—some kind of demigod side-effect, I supposed. Evan Baker launched a missile at Angie's head, and I shoved her aside, ducking under it. As she hit the gym floor, she carefully rolled the supercharged ball back to Damian's waiting hands.

It was time.

When Julia took another shot at me, I pretended to try to dodge it but let the ball smack me hard in the shin.

She pumped her fist as though she had won the lottery. I hobbled over to the side of the gym as Evan took out Angie next. Balls were flying fast, and without me and Angie, Green Team was losing big-time. We scooped up our satchels and hovered by the exit door as Damian prepared to make his move. There were only a couple defenders left on Green Team, while Blue Team still had a swarm of them.

"Hurry up, Big D," I muttered. He was dancing foot

to foot, waiting for his opening, but Julia was using her teammates as defenders, darting out only when she had a clear shot. Then Blue Team took out our last two teammates, leaving only Damian.

Blue Team lined up, each of them holding a ball. They were going to destroy Damian. He looked nervous, holding the ball in front of him, as if that would stop nineteen balls coming at him.

"On my count," Julia said, elbowing her way into the center of the line. "This is going to hurt, a lot." She cocked her arm back, and the entire row of Blue Team followed suit. "One, two—"

"Three." Damian launched the supercharged ball at her. It zinged across the gym like a lightning bolt and hit her square in the chest, knocking her off her feet like she'd been smacked by a twenty-five-pound medicine ball. She landed on her bottom and slid twenty feet across the gym before hitting the padded wall.

The entire gym went silent. Mr. Leland's whistle dropped from his mouth as he stared in shock. But there was no time to enjoy Julia's distress—I tugged on Angie, and we slipped sideways out the exit. "Help!" I shouted. "Julia Pillsbury needs a doctor."

Instantly the sound of pounding feet echoed in the corridor. We stepped aside as a pair of dark-suited men rushed through the open door, talking into their wrists.

We darted down the hallway and peeked around the corner to her locker. There was still one guard standing by, talking rapidly into his watch.

"I got this," Angie said. She ran around the corner, waving her arms in the air. "Help, help, you have to come help. Julia's bleeding."

She tugged on his arm, but he resisted.

"I can't leave my post," he grunted, trying to pry her off, but she wouldn't let go.

"Did you hear me? Those other two said to come get you. She's bleeding. What is her father going to say if you let her die?"

That got him moving. She dragged him around the corner, turning to flash me a wink.

I headed straight for her locker. I could feel the hum of power, as if the artifact called to me. I raised my hand, calling up a slender bolt of lightning, and the locker door rattled.

I placed it against her lock, pushing harder until the metal grew hot and turned red, and then the lock snapped open.

"What do you think you are doing?" a voice barked.

The lightning fizzled out in my hand as the school principal, Mr. Arnold, waddled toward me, his walrus mustache moving up and down as he pursed his lips.

"That locker doesn't belong to you, Miss Katz."

"Sorry, Mr. Arnold, I was just passing by, and I thought I heard something. I thought maybe Julia was trapped inside. Don't you hear it?"

His mustached bristled. "I don't hear anything except a disturbance in the gym, which I assume you are behind."

"Just listen." I put my head closer to the locker. The lyre inside rattled harder. Principal Arnold leaned his head in, and that's when I snatched the door and yanked it open.

It was childish, I know, but it was all I could think of in the moment. The locker hit the principal square in the head, and he teetered backward, tripping over the foot I extended and landing hard on his backside.

"Miss Katz, you will be expelled for this!" he bellowed.

I snatched the lyre up and took off running, but Julia's goons had exited the gym. They saw me holding the case and took up pursuit. I spun around, but Mr. Arnold was marching toward me.

I was ready to call up a nice fat lightning bolt when Damian called to me.

"Phoebes, over here."

He and Angie were holding open a door to an empty classroom.

I bolted in, and they locked the door behind us.

Furious pounding sounded with shouts of "Open this door!"

"Arnold's going to remember he has a key any second," I said.

Angie was already at the window, pushing the sash up.

"Angie, we're on the second floor," I said.

"It's okay. There's a fire escape." She slipped through, waving for us to follow.

"I'll stay here," Damian said, oddly pale. "Hold them off."

"No, you won't." I gave him a push. "Go on, get out there."

I passed him the case and followed him out the window onto the fire escape. His legs moved in a jerky motion as we made our way down the narrow metal steps, and then he froze at the landing. It ended about ten feet from the ground.

"Jump," I said.

But he stood staring, unmoving.

"I said *jump*." Grabbing his arm, I leaped off, taking him with me. We tumbled on the pavement as Mr. Arnold's head stuck out the window.

"Get back here this instant or I'll have you arrested for larceny!" He continued shouting at us, his voice fading as we raced around the corner.

I unfolded the paper Miss Carole had given me. "We have twenty minutes to get to this address."

"It's rush hour—a taxi will take too long," Damian said. "We'd better hoof it."

"Where is this place she's sending us?" Angie grabbed my hand to see the note.

"Not sure, but I had a foster home around there a few years back. I think there's a school on that block."

We ran, dodging cars and people on the crowded sidewalks until we made it to the appointed address. There was a school there all right, but it was closed. Instead, the playground area was lined with food trucks. The smell of grilled onions and fried food filled the air. Snaking lines of people fanned out in every direction.

Damian scanned the trucks. "How do we know we're in the right place?"

"And where's Miss Carole?" I checked the time on my phone. It was 2:59. "She should be here."

"Hey, Katzy, what exactly are we going to do when we get back there?" Angie asked.

I frowned at her. "Save my brother from being turned to stone."

"That's it?"

"Yeah."

"Are you a complete lunatic?" She was practically shouting, the pink-dyed ends of her pigtails bouncing.

I frowned at her. "What's your problem?"

"Do you even know who Medusa is?"

"Of course. She's, like, some snake-head lady."

She pounded one fist into the palm of her hand. "She's a gorgon, nimrod. You turn to stone just by looking at her."

"Obvi, I'm not planning on looking at her."

As Angie continued to stare at me, I put my hands up. "What?"

"You know she turned a lot of people to stone before Perseus killed her."

I stepped closer, right up to her face. "And according to Damian's new mythology, she turns my brother into a rock. Get it? A rock! I can't let that happen." As they remained silent, my temper rose. "Look, you guys don't have to come with me. In fact, I want you to stay here. You both have a lot going on. Damian, you have to celebrate your birthday with your vacuum cleaner, and, Angie, I bet your parents are sitting by the door waiting for you to come home."

They stared at me with pained looks, and the silence stretched. I knew I had gone too far, but I couldn't stop the words that tumbled out.

"I'll go back to Olympus by myself because, you know, you're both a liability."

"Oh, just shut it," Angie snapped. "You're digging a hole and heaping it on top. Damian's already feeling pretty garbage right now, because it's his birthday in a couple days and his parents aren't going to make it home, so let's not rail on him about that, all right?"

I gulped back my shame, nodding.

"And as for my parents, yeah, they're not perfect. Pops is always working, and Ma prefers to spend time in Miami, but it's complicated, and it doesn't mean she doesn't care. She just—" Her voice stopped, and her eyes grew moist. "She's just got her own problems to worry about."

Guilt flooded me. Angie never cried. "I'm sorry." I touched her arm. "I'm a stupid donkey, and I should just learn to zip it."

She rubbed the heels of her palms across her eyes and took a deep breath. "It's fine. It's just that you're not the only one who has problems."

"I get it. I do. I'm an idiot. Forget I said anything. So about traveling back there—last time . . ." I stopped, trying to think of the right words to describe how awful it had been. Facing a hydra. Nearly being killed by the Nemean lion. The chimera and poor Karisto dying. We'd almost lost Damian two times, or was it three?

"It was brilliant," Angie said.

"I had a great time," Damian added. "And statistically speaking, there are five less monsters to deal with, six if you count the Crommyonian sow."

I gaped at them. "Seriously, you guys are mental." I wanted to burst into tears of joy, because I had never had friends like this in my life. "Fine, we're all going, and we're going to make sure none of us get turned into a rock, including my brother. So, Damian, which truck do you suppose it is?"

"Uh, I think it might be that one." Damian pointed at a sleek black-paneled truck with flames on the side and the name TITAN'S TACOS.

CHAPTER 5

C *ould it be that simple?*
It looked like any other food truck, with a paneled side and a window that propped up to reveal a counter and a griddle inside. There were two guys working. I rubbed my hands together. "Who wants a taco? I'm buying." We got into the line and waited our turn.

"I think we're in the right place," Damian whispered.

"Why do you say that?" I stepped forward as the line moved.

"The lyre case. It's rattling like crazy in my hand."

I looked down and saw the case jump. Excitement grew—I was going back to Olympus. I could hardly believe it! We eagerly made our way forward until we were next.

A guy wearing a Titan's Tacos T-shirt leaned over the counter, holding an order pad. "Whaddya want?"

"We want to go to Olympus," I said.

He looked bored. "It's a free country. Go wherever you want."

"We want to go to Olympus," I repeated. "Miss Carole sent us."

A pulse ticked in his throat. He jerked his head to the side. "This sounds like an order for Tony. Move it. Next."

The guy behind us elbowed his way in, and we moved down to the next window.

Tony was big, his shoulders hunched underneath the sweatshirt he wore. He had a patch over one eye and was calling out numbers, shoveling paper plates piled with tacos into the eager hands of customers.

"Hey, are you Tony?" I asked.

"Number?" he answered in a deep basso voice.

"I haven't ordered."

"Then step aside."

"No . . . I want . . . that is . . . we want to go to Olympus."

"Miss Carole sent us," Angie added.

Tony's upper lip curled in disgust. "The oracle doesn't command us. We're serving out our time nice and peaceful."

"Time? What do you mean?"

He leaned down, resting meaty elbows on the counter. "It was Tartarus or this place. Personally, I'd rather be in that dark hole. Have you seen the size of the sewer rats here?"

"So, what, this is the dumping place for the trash of Olympus?" I asked.

"Hey, who you calling trash?" he asked.

"Sorry. You're like prisoners serving your time," I corrected. "Does Miss Carole watch over you?"

"Yeah, she's like our . . . what do you call it?"

"Prison warden," Damian offered.

"Yeah, there's a new batch coming in tonight. I've still got two hundred more years on my sentence. Never offend a god like Apollo—steal one sun bolt and you pay with your life."

"Are you some kind of demigod?" I asked, curious.

"No, a cyclops. They change us into humans to blend in. I miss being big." He sighed, resting his chin on his palm.

"I thought cyclopes only had one eye," Damian said.

"Oiks, I've had a headache for eighty years." He lifted his patch. "It works perfectly good. It just hurts to look out of it."

"So how does it work?" I asked eagerly. "Where do we go? When do we leave?"

"Look, I don't care whether the oracle sent you or not. This portal is for prisoners only."

"Says who?"

"Says me."

"Do you know who my father is?"

He snorted. "Let me guess. Some high and mighty god, probably Zeus himself."

"Exactly."

"If I had a drachma for every one of his brats I've met over the years, I'd be richer than King Midas."

"But not that many here, asking to go back, so what's it going to take?" Everyone had their price.

His single eye narrowed. "Daughter of Zeus—have you any special talents?"

"You mean like this?" I held up my hand, and a tiny lightning bolt no bigger than a pencil appeared.

His eyes widened. "Can you make it bigger?"

"Can you get me a ride?"

A smile lifted one corner of his lips. "Come around back." He closed the window with a snap.

We shuffled to the back of the truck, but Damian put a hand on my arm.

"Miss Carole told us to wait for her."

"What does it matter? She's late and we're here."

A lock slid to the side, and the back door opened. Tony held a hand up, stopping us. "Lightning bolt first."

"Wait—why do you want it?" I asked.

"The truck's running low on fuel. I have to charge it up, then I'll take you to the portal."

The door blocked the view of onlookers, so I called up a nice fat lightning bolt. Tony pulled on thick leather gloves to grasp hold of it.

"Wait here." He slammed the door in our faces.

"I have a bad feeling about this, Katzy," Angie said.

"It's fine. Just hold on."

The truck rattled. Then vibrated. Then the muffler let out a backfire so loud it sounded like a boom of thunder, scattering the people in line.

The truck shimmered in the air, and I realized I'd made a huge mistake.

"Wait!" I lunged forward, trying to grab the door, but it vanished into thin air. People milled about, mumbling about the truck, then, being New Yorkers, moved on about their business.

Miss Carole arrived out of breath. "Sorry I'm late. Where is the taco truck?" She looked around, and then her eyes snapped back to me. "You didn't give Tony lightning, did you?"

"You didn't tell me not to."

Her silver eyes flashed fire. "I specifically said to wait for me."

"We did. It's just you weren't here."

"When Olympus is destroyed, it will be your fault."

"Hold on, who is going to destroy Olympus this time, and why is it my fault?"

"Did you or did you not slay the Nemean lion?" she demanded.

"Yes. To help save Carl."

"And that lion was to be one of Hercules's labors."

"Yeah, Damian explained that to me. He was given an extra one. So what?"

"So what? Your actions have changed the entire framework of Greek mythology."

"Change is good," I said flippantly, tired of always being blamed for every little thing that went wrong.

Her face turned grim. "No, in this case change is bad. Very, very bad. The order of events has changed, and Hercules's third and fourth labor are now a double billing. He's to steal apples from the Garden of the Hesperides *and* slay the dragon Ladon that guards it."

"But he did just fine the first time," Damian said. "Stealing the apples was one of his easiest trials, and he killed the dragon with a single arrow even though it wasn't part of the trial."

Miss Carole held up a finger. "But now it has been made into a labor that has two possible outcomes—pass or fail."

"So if he fails, they'll just give him another one," I said. "I need to worry about Perseus."

She swiveled grave eyes toward me. "Princess of Argos, you are not listening. Hercules can't fail. I've had a terrible vision, one in which Ladon destroys Hercules."

"So?" I didn't see how one less of my father's many offspring was really going to matter.

"So?" Anger sparked in her eyes. "Hercules is the most famous of all the Greek myths. If he doesn't rise to become an immortal hero, people will lose interest in the great myths, and if that happens, the gods themselves will disappear into the mists of the unknown."

"Wait, wait, wait." I cast my mind back to Athena's words the first time I'd met her as a statue. "I thought that place ran on its own timeline in a never-ending cycle?"

"Correct. The immortal gods live on in a world out of time that spins on its own axis, ever unfolding and starting anew. But the magic that keeps the axis turning is dependent on people's faith in their immortality."

"The pages in the mythology book," Damian said with a snap of his fingers. "That's why they went blank for a moment."

"So, all because I helped save Olympus, it's my fault this is happening?" Why was I not surprised? Everything always pointed back at me.

Miss Carole seemed to age in front of us, lines etched deep in the grooves around her mouth as she said, "Hercules must complete his labors without receiving assistance or the consequences will be catastrophic. Olympus will disappear, and you, Phoebe, won't even exist."

The last words were a blow. *Not exist? What does that even mean? Am I going to disappear?*

"Uh, Katzy, we got bigger problems," Angie said. "That black SUV's driven around the block twice. I think they might be looking for us."

"But how would they find us?"

"Maybe there's a tracking device in the case," Damian said.

We set it down and opened it. Damian ran his fingers along the red velvet lining, then tore back the fabric, revealing a black case the size of a matchbox with a blinking red light.

He pried it out and threw it under another food truck, but it was too late. The black SUV stopped in the middle of the street, and the three goons from school stepped out.

"We should run," Angie said.

"I got this," I said, cracking my knuckles.

"No," Damian said. "You can't use your powers out in the open."

"You want these guys to catch us? Or do you want to get away?"

"Get away."

"Then let me do what I do best." I looked to Miss Carole, and she nodded permission.

I closed my eyes, holding my hands out. I wasn't looking for a lightning bolt. Damian was right—too many camera phones. But a sudden tornado? Totally explainable.

In my head I saw the spinning. The winds moving in sync. Around and around in a circle. Up and up in the air. I saw the truck spinning, spinning.

Flinging my arms to the side, I shouted the words that formed in my head. *"Anemos trovilos!"*

Energy hummed through me, tingling in my blood like a swarming nest of ants and knocking my teeth together.

"Oh my," Miss Carole said. "That is something."

I opened my eyes, shocked to see a massive black funnel cloud tearing down the street straight toward the black SUV. It tossed taxis aside, sending people running.

Oops. I hadn't expected it to be quite that big.

"We gotta go." Angie dragged me backward, but I resisted, transfixed by the sight.

The men had started toward us, but now they stopped, turning at the sight of the dark funnel. It was louder now, howling, whipping trash cans and newspaper racks in the air. A kiosk went spinning down the road, and then it was on them. It sucked up their SUV, spinning it up in the air and them with it. I watched them go round and round as though they were on the spin cycle in a washing machine, and then Angie and Damian dragged me away from the school to a side street that dead-ended into the main school building. Miss Carole unlocked a small powder-blue car that had seen better days. Bad news was we would have to drive back toward the avenue where the tornado was currently growing larger by the second. We tumbled into the back seat, and she gunned the engine.

The oracle eyed me in the rearview mirror. "Phoebe, dear, I don't suppose you can turn down the tornado?"

"Sorry, they didn't cover that in my demigod training. I only know how to start it."

"No matter," she said serenely. "We'll just have to outrun it. Buckle up."

We hastily strapped on our belts as the car lurched forward. The tornado was moving, heading for the inter-section. She put the pedal all the way down, and the engine backfired before catching. The tires spun on the pavement, and we barreled into the intersection. She threw the wheel into a hard left. We squished against Damian as the tires slipped, fishtailing. The world went dark as the edge of the funnel consumed us. I could feel the rear tires lifting off the ground, trying to suck us backward, and then they caught just enough to propel us forward, and we escaped the suction, racing ahead of it.

"Is it ever going to stop?" Angie craned her neck back to look at it.

"I might have overdone it," I said.

"Turn here," Damian said. "I live just over the next street. We can lie low there."

"Not for long," I said. "Julia's dad will have the police after us."

"Long enough to think of our next step," he said.

Miss Carole left the car double-parked, and we raced up the steps. Hilda met us at the door, a perplexed look on her screen. "Master Damian, the school called! They say you stole something valuable!"

"It's okay, Hilda." He ushered us in. "I'll explain

everything." We headed for the kitchen, and she followed, waving her robot arms in the air.

"But, Master Damian, I am your guardian. Your parents will think I've failed in my duties. They'll decommission me."

Damian put his hands on her shoulders. "Hilda, it will be fine. Trust me, okay?"

Digital tears streamed down her screen face, but a wobbly smile appeared. "I baked fresh cookies."

"Perfect." He smiled at her. "I'm sure we can all use one."

We sat around the table.

"We need to find another portal," I said.

"But how?" Angie asked.

"I don't know." We looked hopefully at Miss Carole.

She shook her head. "I'm afraid I don't have the tools to open a portal alone. The taco truck contained a powerful talisman from Olympus that I add this to." She drew out a jar of metallic powder and set it on the table. "Tony must have been hoarding it, waiting for the right moment. I should have never trusted a thief with such a valuable position, but he's been so well-behaved."

"What is it?" I lifted the jar, feeling a vibe of power from inside, as if it was magnetic.

"It's mined from Mount Olympus itself. It's the dust that spreads magic throughout the ancient world we live in. I need both the talisman and the dusts of Olympus to create a portal, and a source of power."

"What if we used another talisman," I said, thinking fast.

"It would have to be powerful," Miss Carole said.

"You said Hermes's lyre was powerful." I patted the case on the table.

Her eyes widened, then sparkled with excitement. "Yes. It is possible. We would just need a source of power."

"Like this?" I called up a glowing lightning bolt. It vibrated in my hands, humming with power.

Her brows knitted. "It's a start. But we would need a way to concentrate and direct it. The great craftsman Daedalus himself built a special power converter we camouflaged in the taco truck."

"Hilda," Damian said suddenly.

Our eyes turned to him.

"What about her?" I asked.

"Hilda has a core power source. It's not exactly off the shelf." His eyes slid sideways, which meant he was being evasive.

"Damian, what is it?"

"It's a tiny—I mean very tiny—nuclear reactor. It's how they power the submersibles. Did I mention my parents work for the government? My dad borrowed a tiny bit of uranium and . . . I really shouldn't talk about it."

"It's perfect," Miss Carole said. "Phoebe, you insert the lightning bolt into this Hilda when I say the word."

"Master Damian?" Hilda's voice sounded uncertain, and a big question mark took up her screen.

"It's okay, Hilda," he said, going over to her. "You know I wouldn't let anything bad happen to you. We just really need your help right now."

"Will it stop Damian from being in trouble?" Her screen face frowned, and she clasped her pincers in front of her, as though she really cared about Damian's problems.

He nodded. "It will help a lot of people. Listen, I might be gone for a few days, but I'll be back. Just tell my parents—"

"That Master Damian is away on a field trip, like last time?"

He smiled. "Yes. And thanks, Hilda. You're the best."

Her cheeks turned red on the screen. She rotated back on her wheels to face us. "Hilda is ready."

I held the lightning bolt in my hands, but I wavered, looking at Damian. "What if I fry her circuits?"

"What if mythology ends forever?" he said. "You won't exist. None of this would have happened."

I gulped back the fear and raised the bolt. This had to be the best part of being a child of Olympus. I loved calling up lightning. Sometimes I went on top of Carl's building during a storm and unleashed lightning up into the sky. It was the only time I really felt like myself.

I squared my feet up, looking into the scared face of Damian's beloved machine. "Okay, Hilda, this isn't going to hurt because deep down you're a machine and you can't feel pain."

"Anything for Master Damian," she replied, her machine face settling into one of resolve. My heart kicked in my chest, and I began to understand why Damian thought of her as more than just a robot. She had a heart to her. She seemed to care, which made no logical sense but felt genuine.

I looked at Damian. "Are you sure she's not going to . . . you know . . . go nuclear on us?"

"No," he said, looking queasy. "So please be gentle."

Oh, great. There was just the smallest chance I could turn this machine into a nuclear reaction that would likely level a few city blocks. My hand shook, and I took a steadying breath and then placed the tip of the lightning bolt to her screen. Her entire frame jolted.

"Oh my!" Her machine eyes grew wide. "That tickles."

I pressed harder, sinking it in deeper until with a *gloop*, the bolt sucked out of my hand and disappeared.

Miss Carole stepped forward with the jar of Olympus dust and began sprinkling it around the room, murmuring words I couldn't understand.

"Join together with the artifact," she said.

Damian clutched the lyre. We each had our satchels strapped across our chests. I hooked my arm in his, and Angie grabbed his other arm. We stood in front of Hilda.

At first nothing happened, and then a light came on, a blinking cursor, and she started to hum. Faster and faster, she shook and shimmied, vibrating side to side.

"What's happening?" I asked.

"The portal is opening." Miss Carole sprinkled more dust, filling the room with sparkling particles that danced in the air. All of my senses were tingling, as if my blood were on fire. I wanted to launch lightning, cause a thunderstorm, fly in the clouds.

Hilda vibrated louder and louder, and then parts flew off—first her wand eye, then her left arm—and then her screen cracked.

"What's happening to Hilda?" Damian cried. He tried to move toward her, but our arms were locked in his.

The lyre in the case vibrated, jumping so hard Damian dropped it. The case broke open, and the strings on the lyre began to play a screeching melody that hurt our ears. Wind howled in the kitchen, sending things flying. Hilda stood there, her screen glowing brighter and brighter as the music swelled.

Miss Carole stood with her arms flung wide. Her lips were moving, but I couldn't make out the words.

Hilda began whistling like a teakettle, and then Damian's kitchen bent. I mean it literally warped; the refrigerator was bending inward, the table stretching outward.

"I don't like this," Angie said.

"Hilda!" Damian shouted, trying to break free.

"Hold him," I said to Angie, leaning down to grab the lyre out of the case.

Once my hand touched the neck, there was a surge in energy. Hilda glowed brighter and brighter until she was like an incandescent bulb. Miss Carole had the same light beaming out of her eyes. The light encased us, surrounded us, and then suddenly, it went out.

CHAPTER 6

My bones felt as if they'd been put through a meat grinder. Everything hurt. I didn't want to open my eyes, afraid of what I might see. Someone elbowed me, and I grunted, sitting up. Damian and Angie were piled across my legs. Angie rolled off, and Damian got on all fours, looking around unsteadily.

"What happened?" he asked. "Where's my kitchen? Where are we?"

"Your guess is as good as mine," I said. "It all went a little wonky at the end. Who knows where that bucket of bolts sent us."

Damian glared at me. "For the last time, Phoebe, her name is Hilda."

It was too dark to see anything. By the feel of it, we were in some kind of cave. I shook my hand out and called up a small lightning bolt, then immediately wished I hadn't.

"Nobody move," I said softly.

"Why?" Angie said. "I want to stretch. I'm—"

"Shh." I gripped her leg tightly and pointed upward.

She tipped her head back and started to scream. I clamped my hand over her mouth until she calmed.

"Are those—?"

"Bats. Big ones."

"Don't they, like, drink blood?"

"The largest bat is known as *Pteropus giganteus* and is found on tropical islands near Sri Lanka," Damian whispered. "Some bats do drink blood, but mostly they like insects, frogs, and lizards."

"So these could be bloodsuckers," Angie said. "Brilliant. I'm so glad I came back."

"They're sleeping right now, so if we're really quiet, we can sneak past them," I said. "Damian, follow me. Angie, bring up the rear."

I stood, quietly gathering my satchel. Damian grabbed Hermes's lyre. It had a red strap he slipped over his head. It was impossible to know which way led out, so I chose a direction at random, figuring when I ran into a wall, we would be able to turn, but we got lucky. After twenty paces, we saw a dark opening. All we had to do was keep walking quietly, and we would be out of this bat-filled cavern.

Behind me Angie whispered, "Phoebe, I've got to—" And then she sneezed. Like the loudest *ahhhhchooo* in the world. We froze. There was a moment of suspended silence, and then the air exploded with the sound of flapping wings and high-pitched screeches.

"Run!" I dropped the lightning bolt, and we fled for the opening, but the bats were all over us in an instant, in our hair, biting at us, flapping in our faces.

I clenched my fists, concentrating. A wind gusted through the tunnel and then grew stronger, sending the bats backward.

We stumbled over rocks as we made it into the tunnel. Behind us we could hear the bats regrouping as my wind died down. A circle of light emerged ahead.

"Keep going," I said. "We're almost there."

We raced out into the open air as the bats flooded out behind us.

Bad news.

The cave emptied out of the side of a cliff.

If Angie hadn't grabbed me by the back of my shirt, I would have pinwheeled right off the ledge to the ground hundreds of feet below. We dropped to our knees, huddling, as the bats flew over our heads, pouring out of the mouth of the cave.

When it finally quieted, we stood and took stock of the damage.

Angie had bite marks on her face and arms. I hadn't fared much better. Damian had them on the backs of his hands where he'd covered his face.

"If I get bat rabies, I'm going to be so mad," Angie said.

"So what do you think?" I asked Damian. "Are we in the right place?"

Below us was a valley covered in low stands of trees and rolling hills.

"Look." He pointed at a distant structure. "That looks like a temple."

"Greek?"

"It's hard to say. I don't see any familiar landmarks. No sign of Mount Olympus, but we could be on a different island."

"Seriphos?" I asked hopefully.

"Don't think so. It was more mountainous."

"How do we get down?" Angie looked over the ledge. "There aren't any trails, and I'm not going back into that cave."

"We could walk along that ledge." I pointed at a narrow crevasse.

"That's not a ledge. That's suicide," Damian said, looking suddenly pale.

"Not if we hold on to the crack above and jump the last part." I wiggled my fingers into the crack to test it.

"You want us to parkour our way across?" Damian asked.

"You have a better idea? Should we go back inside that cave? Wait for the bats to come back?"

"No, it's just . . ." He hung his head, mumbling, "I'm scared of heights."

"Is that why you wanted to stay back in the classroom?"

He shrugged. "Seemed safer than going out the window. I'd rather face Python again than step out on that crack."

"Wait, then how come you could fly around on Albert?" Angie asked, referring to his pegasus from our first trip to Olympus.

"Albert made me brave," he said simply. "You know how a pegasus can understand what we're saying? They can also sense what we're feeling."

"Listen, we don't have much choice here unless you're planning on sitting out this adventure. All you have to do is follow my lead and don't look down. I'll go first."

Slipping the lyre strap over my head, I jammed my fingers in the crack that ran along the cliff wall. I stepped out, testing one foot on the ledge. It wasn't wide—maybe three inches—but it was solid. I stepped out with both feet, inching my way across toward another outcrop about fifteen feet away. I made it safely and stepped down, heaving a breath of relief.

"Now you, Damian."

"No, Angie first." He was breathing fast, his eyes wide as he stared at that crack.

I nodded at Angie.

She stepped out, taking the first three steps quickly. On the fourth, her foot slipped.

"Angie!"

She pulled herself back up and flashed me a grin. "I'm good." She made it the rest of the way and leaped across the small gap to land next to me.

"Now you, Damian."

He looked over his shoulder, back at the cave entrance. "What if there's a nice road in the back of that cave that leads down?"

"What if the man-eating bats come back?" I asked.

He sighed, straightening his satchel. He put one hand out. It was shaking badly. He gripped the crack and stepped onto the ledge.

"That's it," I said. "Just don't look down. Keep going."

He took another tentative step. I could see sweat beading on his forehead.

"You got this, Big D," Angie said.

He took another step. A small smile crossed his face. "It's not so bad." He stepped again, but suddenly the ledge under his foot crumbled and broke away. His feet dropped, and he was left dangling by his hands.

"Damian!" I screamed, wanting to leap across the divide and grab him. He scrambled his feet against the wall and managed to lever himself back on the ledge.

He stood there, leaning his head against the wall.

"Come on, D, you have to keep moving," I said.

"No, I'm good. You guys go ahead."

"We're not leaving you here," Angie said.

"And I'm not moving, so just go on. I'll figure something out."

"By the time that happens, this place might not survive. You heard the oracle. We don't have a lot of time."

He sighed, shaking his head, but he moved an inch closer. Then another.

"You're almost there, Damian. Your legs are long. Just one long step to the right."

He stuck his leg out. We grabbed his trousers as he let go, stepping fully onto the edge.

He collapsed back against the cliff in relief.

I slapped him on the shoulder. "Now we just have to do that, like, ten more times."

It took two hours, but we finally made our way off the cliff onto solid ground. Damian dropped to all fours, hanging his head, taking in deep gulps of air.

"You did it, D!" I plopped down beside him, clapping him on the back.

He rummaged in his bag, then pulled out a bottle of water, tilting it back and gulping it down.

I opened my satchel and pulled out the gold-trimmed tunic the king of Nemea had gifted me, along with the supple leather boots that still fit like gloves.

Angie put on her golden headband. She looked like my sister Athena.

We ducked behind some bushes and changed, leaving our gym clothes behind. We grinned at each other in our familiar garments. Damian's tunic was a little short because he'd grown another inch.

"I miss sun-brain," Angie said. "Do you think we'll run into him?"

"Macario's probably too busy trying to impress Apollo." I rubbed my hands together. "So, first thing's first. We find a boat, get to Seriphos, locate Perseus, and, you know, help him slay Medusa."

"No, first we have to find Hercules and help him with his labors," Damian argued. "Without him knowing we're helping."

"Herk-A-Jerk can wait." I was itching to get to my brother and maybe see my mom. I ached for that hug I never quite got in my dreams.

"Phoebes, did you even listen to Miss Carole? If he doesn't defeat this Ladon, it's all over. We won't even miss you because you will have never been born."

"Well, that's stupid."

"You realize how ridiculous you sound right now," Angie said. "We can't just go barging after Medusa unprepared. We need things like an almond sword to cut her head off."

"Adamantium," Damian corrected.

"Yeah, that. And we need a magic bag to put it in." At my open-mouthed stare, she said, "What? You think I didn't read up on this stuff after we got back? I know all about snake-head lady and how Perseus killed her, and we don't have what we need. Period. Tell her, Damian."

"She's right. The sword is a scimitar—the blade is curved. Perseus also had Hades' Helmet of Invisibility, which he got from some nymphs, and winged shoes to help him fly, which he got from Hermes along with the sword. Then he visited three old women called the Graeae, and they gave him the location of Medusa. Oh, and most importantly, Athena gave him her shield Aegis to reflect Medusa's image."

"So he didn't have to look at her and get turned to stone," Angie said. "Face it, Phoebes, we can't just go running off half-cocked."

I threw my arms up. "Fine, we'll find this Hermes guy and trade him his lyre for the shoes and the sword. Then we'll round up Athena. I'm sure she'd be delighted to help her favorite half-sister."

"Perseus isn't due to battle Medusa for years," Damian said with a frown. "Right now he's just a kid like us."

"So?"

"So I'm just saying, it's going to be harder to convince him to go along with us given that he's only twelve, and Polydectes hasn't challenged him to go after Medusa yet."

"Then we'll slay her ourselves," I said.

"That will mess up Perseus's myth of becoming a hero," Damian shot back. "We can't interfere with the major story lines."

I surrendered. "Fine. We can't do anything until we figure out where Miss Carole and your mechanical nanny sent us. We might as well start walking."

From the cave entrance above, we had spied a dirt road snaking along the center of the valley. We started trudging through the trees.

"Damian, I don't suppose you know where this Ladon monster and the apples he's guarding is located?" I asked. "It might help narrow down where we are, if Miss Carole sent us to deal with that first."

"It's called the Garden of the Hesperides. I think it's in North Africa."

I shot him a glance. "Africa? You're joking, right?"

"No, the northern part is easily within reach when you sail on the seas here. The Argonauts visited on their journey, but I don't remember exactly where. Sorry," he said, "I've been distracted lately."

"You're not, you know, worried about your parents, are you?" I asked.

"No. The stuff they do is dangerous, but my mom knows what she's doing. I just wish they were home more."

A rumbling growl made us stop.

"What was that?" Angie squeaked.

We backed away as a creature stepped into view, stalking forward on thick strong legs. It had a lion's body, but its face was freakishly human, like a Neanderthal's face had been transplanted. It had a broad forehead, flattened nose, and widely spaced eyes under a thick golden mane. Its teeth were canine with two fangs curving down. Most horrifying, its tail ended in a trio of barbed tips that waved in the air. It let out a low growl that sounded like a lawn mower starting up.

"Damian, what is it?" I asked.

"I'm not sure, but I'm guessing it's a manticore," Damian said. "They pretty much like to eat anything that moves."

"Great, we're back five minutes and we're already in mortal danger," Angie said. She reached into her bag and pulled out a large hunting knife.

At my look, she said, "What? I came prepared this time."

The lightning bolt flashed in my hand before I even thought it. "Stay behind me," I said. "I'll take care of this mutant beast."

But just then, another manticore stepped out of the bushes, followed by another.

Crud.

I waved the lightning bolt around. "You guys get ready to run. I'll cover you."

"Are you crazy?" Angie waved the knife in front of her. "You can't handle three of these things by yourselves."

"I can't put you and Damian in danger."

"When are we not in danger around you?"

Damian ignored the beasts and calmly unlooped the lyre from around his neck and sat down cross-legged.

"Damian, no time for a concert," I said as the nearest manticore snarled, baring gleaming white fangs.

The other two manticores circled closer, their tails curved over their backs so the barbed tips were pointed at us. Sweat ran down my back. If I was lucky, I could take out one of them, maybe two, but three?

Suddenly one of the barbed tips on the nearest beast's tail shot out a stinger headed straight for my heart. I managed to swat it away with the lightning bolt. Angie hit the ground as two more stingers shot straight for her head from the manticore closest to her.

And then Damian began strumming the lyre, and the sweetest sounds came out. Even though he didn't know what he was doing, the lyre took care of turning his awkward strums into something so beautiful it brought tears to my eyes.

The manticores stopped snarling and swayed slightly. A distant look came over their eyes.

"Keep playing," I said. "It's working."

Damian strummed harder, his fingers flying over the lyre as if it were controlling his movements, and the beasts slowly lowered their heads, lying down on the ground, resting their chins on their paws, before beginning to snore loudly.

We grabbed him by the elbows, lifting him to his feet. He continued to play softly as we stepped backward out of the clearing, and then we turned and ran.

When we were a safe distance away, we stopped to catch our breath.

"Damian. Those manticore things, where do they come from? Maybe it will help sort out where we are," I asked.

"No idea. Sorry I'm not a walking Roomba."

Ouch.

"I didn't mean—"

"Yes, you did. Hilda was my friend. She took care of me, and you treated her like she was just a machine."

"Because she kinda is."

Tears spilled out, running down his cheeks. "No, she was more than that. She was my friend. And now she's been destroyed, and I'm never going to get to tell her thank you for everything she did for me. I don't expect you to understand."

"No, I don't," I said honestly. "But I'm sorry I hurt your feelings. Forgive me?"

He nodded, scrubbing the tears away.

"Good, because we really, really need to figure out where we are."

Before he could answer, a voice cut in.

"Ho there, fair travelers, what brings you to these parts?"

A young man with an impish face leaned against the trunk of a slender tree. Blond glints with a hint of gold ran through his hair. His fine tunic was trimmed in silver with a set of wings embroidered on the chest. His smile was friendly but sly, his green eyes probing and calculating.

I called up a lightning bolt, but it fizzled out in my hands.

"No need for dramatics, dear," he said. "Clearly we are family."

"I've never met you," I said.

He bowed slightly. "Hermes, at your service. I believe you have something that belongs to me." His eyes went to the lyre strapped to Damian.

Damian started to take it off as Hermes stepped forward, eagerly reaching for it, but I stepped between them. "Not so fast. We're not just going to hand it over."

Hermes's green eyes narrowed. "You know I could just take it."

"And I could make your life miserable," I said, calling double fists of lightning.

He sighed. "What is it you want, sister?" The word *sister* was said in a snide tone.

"I want you to give us the things we need to slay Medusa."

One eyebrow went up. "Slay the gorgon? Are you quite mad?"

"Yes, probably. We need Hades' helmet that makes you invisible, some winged shoes—I think the ones you're wearing—and what else, Damian?"

"A scimitar of adamantium sharp enough to cut off her head. It was used to kill Argus, a hundred-eyed giant. And a bag powerful enough to contain her head."

I looked back at Hermes. "Right. Those three—four things, and then you can have your stupid lyre back."

He stared at us, his eyes coolly assessing, and then he tossed his head back and laughed. "Aren't you a bold one? Father really went to town with you. Who is your mother? No, don't tell me—a sea nymph."

"My mother is Danae, princess of Argos." I couldn't keep the note of pride from my voice, but he frowned.

"As I recall, she gave him that welp Perseus."

"Yup. He's my twin brother."

His eyes lit up. "You're the daughter of Zeus who nearly destroyed Olympus. I heard about you. I was out of town when all of that happened."

"So are you going to help us?"

He folded his arms. "Well, why would I?"

"Because you helped Perseus."

He looked perplexed. "When? I've never even met him."

"Way back when. Damian, explain it."

"Phoebe was sent away to the human world, which is where we're from. And in the human world, these stories happened thousands of years ago. So according to the legends we've read, you were willing to help Perseus when he was older. You gave him the items he needed to slay Medusa."

Hermes shrugged. "I've got nothing against that gorgon, so why would I get involved? I might help him if our father asked, but I haven't heard from Zeus in ages. I hear he's taking a vacation after that fiasco in Olympus you were responsible for, so my answer is no."

I was speechless. I had no idea how to answer that. "Maybe you should help him because he's your brother and it's the right thing to do."

"You're my sister, and I see no reason to help you." He idly picked at his nails.

"Fine, I'll just incinerate this stupid lyre. We're tired of carrying it around." I held a lightning bolt over the instrument in Damian's hands and started to bring it down when his voice rang out.

"Wait."

I stopped.

"Give me a reason as to why I should risk crossing the gorgons and help you."

"Something's gone wonky with the whole Greek myth cycle."

"What do you mean?"

"I mean Hercules was supposed to have twelve labors."

"It's thirteen now, I hear," Hermes said. "Something went wrong with that lion of his."

"Yeah, I might have killed it."

He looked doubtful. "I heard it was a Nemean prince."

"They lied."

"So?"

"So the order of his labors has been changed and a new one added. His next one was supposed to be . . . what, Damian?"

"The Cerynitian hind. A very fast deer he chases."

"But instead he's been tasked with killing a dragon named Ladon when he steals apples from the Hesperides."

Hermes gave a little shrug. "Ladon isn't so scary. All hiss and no bite. I'm sure Hercules is up to the task."

"According to an oracle we know, Hercules might die."

He scoffed at that. "Oracles don't know everything, and one less child of Zeus running around is no great loss. Besides, I thought you were here to help your brother slay Medusa."

"We are," Damian said. "But Hercules's heroism made him a symbol of mythology. A story to be repeated over and over again, generation after generation. Without him, the people in our world lose interest in the old stories."

"So?"

"So if that happens, *poof*, you and I don't exist," I said.

Hermes looked between us, assessing our faces for the truth. "It sounds an unlikely outcome," he said, but there was a hint of uncertainty to his voice. "I wish I could help, but I've got to run." He held his hand out for the instrument.

"Not before we get what we need," I said.

"Look, I don't have Hades' little helmet or that scimitar my father gave me."

"Where are they?"

He sighed, folding his arms. "The Argus Slayer was lost in a card game to someone with more heads for cards than I."

"Who? What was his name?"

He waved a hand "I can't recall, but the helmet was an interlude I won't soon forget." His eyes sparkled with the memory. "Some lovely nymphs promised to watch over it for me. Good news for you, they reside in the Garden of the Hesperides and tend to the sacred apple tree. Sounds like you can kill two birds with one stone."

Two birds, one stone. There was that phrase again. Excitement seized me.

"What about those winged shoes of yours?" I asked.

"These old things?" He tapped the toes together. "Surely these aren't of interest."

"Oh, I'm interested," I said. "If you want this lyre back, I'll be taking those shoes off of you."

Hermes's eyes grew cold, but he toed off his shoes, kicking them to the side. "Take them."

Damian went to pass him the lyre, but Angie held his arm back. "I don't trust him. Make sure they're the ones we need."

"You don't trust the word of a god?" he said haughtily.

"No!" we all said in unison.

I tugged off my boots and put the shoes on. They were a size too big but otherwise okay.

"Now what?"

"Now just click them together three times."

I tried it, but nothing happened.

Hermes grabbed for the lyre, but Angie blocked him.

He sighed. "Fine. I can't give you my winged shoes." He clicked his heels, and a pair of silver sandals appeared on his feet. Wings fluttered from the ankles like living things. "I need them to return to where I was. But I'll make a deal with you. You round up all the things you need, and when you have them, if you're still alive, you can swap my lyre for these shoes. Deal?"

"Deal," I said. "Where do we find you once we have the items?"

"Oh, I'll find you. Just play a melody on my lyre." His eyes slid over it longingly, and then he rose off the ground, saluted us, and started to zoom away.

"Hey," I called after him. "Can you tell us where we are?"

He spun, floating in midair. "Just outside the pearl of Greece. Athens," he added at our blank looks. "Just over those hills." He pointed to the west and then, with a nod, zoomed off.

Athens. The capital of Greece. And the city named for my sister. Which meant maybe she was close by.

We set off at a quick pace under the blazing sun. Before long, we broke through some brush and stood at the edge of a ravine.

Before us was an incredible sight.

A temple with massive white pillars perched on the top of a hillside. Beneath it, a large city sprawled in every direction. A red clay road packed with horse-drawn carts led into the city.

"What's that temple on the hilltop?" I asked.

"The Parthenon," Damian said, looking awestruck.

"I thought it was called the Acropolis or something," Angie said.

"Acropolis refers to the hill it's on. It means high city. The actual building we see looks exactly like the real Parthenon. It wasn't built until around 500 BC, but a version of it existed in mythology."

We picked our way along a path that led down from the hillside toward the city. Insects buzzed, and the sun was hot, but it felt good to be home again.

Damian told us all about why Athens was named for Athena. She and Poseidon had vied for the honor of having the city named after them. Poseidon had gifted the Athenians with water, but Athena had gifted them with an olive tree, and they had chosen her.

"Hey, Damian, when you were reading about my brother, why did he fail?"

"What do you mean?"

"I mean what was different about this time?"

"I don't know."

I pulled up, using my tunic to wipe the sweat from my brow. "Think, Damian. Use that brain of yours. The first time Perseus had the Helmet of Invisibility so she couldn't see him, winged shoes so he could fly, a wicked sword to cut her head off, and a shield to reflect her image."

"But he got turned to stone, so he must have looked at her." His brow furrowed. "So it had to be—"

"Athena," I said. "For some reason she didn't give him her shield. We need to find her and fast."

"Why wouldn't she help him?" Angie said. "She's one of the good guys."

"Something must have changed," Damian said.

"What would change to make Athena not want to help my brother?"

"I don't know, Phoebe, but it can't be good."

CHAPTER 7

We entered through the gates of the city, following the throngs of traffic flowing in. We blended in easily enough. No one seemed to think it odd to see three kids walking about in their finest tunics. It must have been a market day—there were colorful stalls set up everywhere selling bolts of fabric and jars of spices. Cured meats hung from hooks. Angie bought us some kabobs with some left-over drachmas she had, and we made our way down packed cobblestone streets.

"Check that out." Angie pointed at a small garden area with an arch inscribed with ALTAR OF THE TWELVE GODS. We wandered among the marble busts. Angie stuck her tongue out at Ares's grim, unsmiling face. I stopped at my father's, putting the back of my hand against his cheek. The stone was cold, but it still made me smile. Next to him stood the bust of his wife, Hera. She looked angry, her eyes glaring at me as if she could see me.

"Hera wasn't fond of Zeus's many offspring," Damian said.

"Not to worry. I'm not planning on visiting Olympus any time soon."

We moved on. When we passed by an open-air amphi-theater packed with Athenians listening to two men on the stage arguing about properties of law, the skin on my arm prickled, and I stopped.

Angie bumped in to me. "Do you mind?"

"Something's wrong."

"What do you mean?" Damian asked.

"I feel something weird. Like my spidey senses are tingling."

Angie rolled her eyes. "You know that's not a thing."

"Um, you know I'm a demigod, right? Maybe it is. Come on, I think we need to go this way." I dragged them down an alley with plaster walls on either side.

At the end was a table with three spinsters sitting at it. Gray hair was piled up on top of their heads. The first one was racking thread on a broken loom that wobbled and creaked in her hands. The second was threading a needle through fabric. The third waited with scissors clutched in swollen claw-like hands.

The Fates. The spinsters responsible for sewing the outcomes of what happened here in Olympus.

"I've never seen such poor work," the middle one grum-bled, jabbing her needle into the fabric.

"I'm doing my best," the first one cried, working the loom faster. The air was filled with the sickly creaking noise as the loom bucked in her hands.

The third one snapped the air with her scissors as she waited for something to cut.

Crud, we have to get out of here. I tried to step back, but their heads suddenly swiveled up, and their gazes locked on me. The pull grew stronger, as if I were being sucked in by gravity.

"Come closer, daughter of Zeus, so we might show you

your fate," the scissor-wielding spinster said, crooking the scissors at me.

"Wait here," I said to Angie and Damian, walking forward on shaky legs. The last time they'd given me my fate, I'd wrecked their loom trying to escape the Erinyes. It wasn't likely they'd forgiven me.

"You see what you have done?" The middle spinster shook the piece of fabric she was holding at me. It had gaping holes, and the threads were loose and poorly woven. "You have wrecked the loom of the Fates. How are we to determine the outcomes with this tangled mess?"

I shifted on my feet. "Sorry, really, I am, but in my defense, the Erinyes were after me. Maybe people should decide their own fates."

Scissor-hands snipped her blades at me. "You don't understand, daughter of Zeus. We don't decide the fates. The loom shows us what is meant to happen. When you broke the loom, you changed what it shows us."

A premonition ran down my spine like a drip of ice water. "What does that mean?"

"It means things are not meant to be this way, but we must record what unfolds from our loom."

"And?" My heart was thumping so hard I thought it might bruise my ribs.

"And someone you care about may meet a very untimely fate," the one sewing said with a sly smile. Her fingers flew as she jabbed the needle in and out in a blur.

I snatched the fabric out of her hands. It was the face of a woman with snakes writhing on her head. A boy knelt at her feet, looking up at her.

"See here how things can change?" scissor-hands crowed, her double-chin jiggling with laughter. "The one known as Perseus shall be nothing more than a lump of granite."

They chanted in unison, "Dead he will be. Wait and you will see."

I wanted to destroy them all with a single swing of my lightning bolt, but I tried to hold on to my temper.

"Please, I want to fix things. Perseus means a lot to me. Tell me what I can do."

"Until we get a new loom, we can only sew what we see," the first one said with a sniff. "Now be gone before we sew a fate even worse for your dear sister, who this very moment is in grave danger from those she trusts."

Athena.

I hurried back to where Angie and Damian waited anxiously.

Angie took one look at my anguished features and grabbed my arms. "What's wrong? What did they say?"

"Athena's in danger from someone she trusts. Damian, where would she be?"

He chewed on his knuckle, thinking. "Maybe by the tree she gave to Athens? It's planted in front of the Parthenon." He nodded toward the broad set of marble steps that stretched all the way to the top of the hill.

We climbed them, taking them two at a time, and arrived at the top out of breath. There were scattered buildings, but the majestic temple in the center towered over the others. Thick white columns curved outward, making it look slightly bowed.

"That looks just like the real Parthenon," Damian said in awe.

Near the steps of the temple, a group of women knelt in a semicircle around a large olive tree, their heads bowed. They were dressed in matching gray smocks that covered their arms and went down to their feet. Hooded cloaks masked their features. They were murmuring in unison, chanting some kind of prayer. None of them moved as we wove among them, edging closer to the tree.

"Is this it?" I asked Damian softly. "The tree my sister planted?"

He nodded. "I would think so."

"Then she must be around here."

"Phoebe, these are her acolytes. The Athenoi. They worshiped her—it doesn't mean Athena is here."

"The Fates said someone she trusts betrays her. Athena!" I called out. "Where are you?"

The chanting cut off like a cord had been unplugged on a jukebox. One of the acolytes rose next to me, throwing her hood back. She looked like an avenging angel with dark hair scraped back into a ponytail and ice-blue eyes that held a lethal power. She looked vaguely familiar, as if I'd met her before, but I was fairly certain I'd never laid eyes on her.

"Do not disturb the prayers of the devoted." Her voice was like a whip, threatening a lashing to anyone who defied her.

"Buzz off. I'm looking for my sister. Athena, where are you?" I called louder.

Three more acolytes stood and faced us, the same flat look in their eyes, as if killing us would be their pleasure. My spidey senses were firing on all pistons now. Something was wrong. Really wrong.

"You need to leave now," the acolyte repeated.

"Or what?" I said, calling a lightning bolt to my hand.

Her eyes flared, and instantly, a long blade was in her hands, and she threw her cloak back, revealing black leather armor underneath. As one, the entire group stood. Weapons appeared in their hands, gleaming knives they pulled out from under their cloaks. Only one acolyte was left kneeling closest to the tree, head down in her hands.

Athena. It had to be.

"Damian, Angie, head for my sister," I said, nodding at the huddled figure. I held the lightning bolt over my head, preparing to swing it, but one lightning bolt wasn't going to cut it.

Think, Phoebe. Rain? No. Sleet? No. Hail is good, but we need something to cover our escape.

That was it!

Clutching the lightning bolt, I thrust it at the sky and cried, "*Omichli*!"

Instantly something cold licked at my ankles. From beneath my feet, a gray mist rose up, quickly spreading. The dark-haired acolyte lunged at me, bringing her sword around. Hatred blazed from her eyes, and for a moment, I wondered what she had against me. I blocked her blow with the lightning bolt. It sent a jolt up my arm, shattering the bolt in two. She brought her weapon around again, but the cloud of mist engulfed us, and I ducked, running in the direction of Angie and Damian.

It was chaos as the acolytes bumped into each other, screaming in frustration. I dropped to my knees and crawled as fast as I could until my shoulder hit the tree.

"Phoebe, is that you?" Angie's voice whispered.

"Yes."

A hand gripped my shoulder, yanking me up. We made our way around the edge of the Parthenon, keeping the wall to one side. Angie and Damian had Athena's arms over their shoulders. I ran smack into a pillar, almost knocking my teeth out.

"Can you ease up on the fog?" Angie said.

"No, Angie, I don't exactly know how to control it."

My hair was damp, and my clothes stuck to me. It had gone from a hot day to a frigid one. The cloud bank swallowed up the entire top of the Acropolis. We were still moving, hoping to find the stairs down, when the earth tilted, and we found ourselves falling.

We'd gone right off the edge of the top. We rolled and tumbled down a grassy knoll, twenty feet or so, before coming to a stop at some prickly bushes.

The good news was we were out of the cloud. Fingers of mist trailed around us, but we could see.

"Angie, you're bleeding!" I grabbed her arm, turning it over.

A gash about three inches long seeped blood.

"It's fine. I just cut it on a rock when we fell." She tore off a piece of her tunic and wrapped it around the cut.

We sat Athena up and leaned her against a tree. I pulled her hood back from her face and nearly gasped. She looked terrible, not at all like the imperious goddess I had seen two months earlier. Her face was gaunt and gray, her eyes sunken in her head. Her hands were cold and clammy. I patted her cheek, shaking her gently, and she opened her eyes, blinking owlishly at me.

"Phoebe, is that you?" Only it came out *Phweebee, ish that you*? Her pupils were dilated. Something was very off about her.

"Yeah, it's me, sis. What's wrong with you? What's happened?"

"Phoebe of Argos," she said, smiling, only the Argos came out like *arghooosh*.

"Athena, what's wrong with you? I've never seen you like this."

Angie smelled her breath, then reared back. "She's been drinking."

"I don't dwink." Athena wagged a stern finger at her. "I keep my body pwure."

"Well, someone's been spiking your ambrosia then," I said. "Those acolytes of yours must be feeding you something."

"The Athenoi are very devoted to me," she said. "They would never harm me."

"They didn't seem so fond of us," I said. "They pulled some nasty-looking weapons on me." And that dark-haired one had seemed determined to end my life. "Did you see that acolyte with the sword?" I asked.

"Not clearly," Angie said.

"It was odd—I'm sure I've never seen her before, but her features seemed familiar. I think it was her eyes."

"We should be moving," Damian said. "The fog is lifting. We're still in plain view."

"We can't go back into the city," I said. "We'll strike off through the trees until we find a safe place to sober her up."

Athena was able to walk if Damian and I put our arms under her. Angie carried the lyre, and we made fairly good time. After an hour's walk, we heard the distant tinkle of a stream. We sank down gratefully in the shade of a low willow tree. Angie scooped up handfuls of water, and I splashed my face.

Athena was fast asleep where we'd left her.

"I know how to handle this," Angie said. "Take her by the arm."

I grabbed Athena's arm, and we dragged her over to the stream.

"She's not going to like this." Angie took her by the back of the head and dunked her face into the icy water.

It took a moment, and then Athena reared back, roaring in anger.

Angie let her sputter and shout and then pushed her head back under.

She kept Athena there another few seconds before lifting

her out. This time Athena was threatening to curse Angie's unborn children and turn them into sows.

Angie ignored her and dunked her head again, holding it under longer this time.

"Don't you think that's enough?" I said nervously, but Angie didn't look fazed.

"She's not ready yet."

This went on another three times until finally, Angie let her go.

Athena swayed on all fours, head hanging down. Her stomach heaved, and then she crawled over to some bushes. We could hear her retching.

"Now she's ready," Angie said.

Athena sat back against a tree. Wet strands of hair clung to her face. But when she opened her eyes, they were clear.

"Phoebe, what are you doing here?" She looked around, and her brows drew together. "And where is here?"

"We're outside of Athens. We had to get you away from your fan group."

"The Athenoi are devoted to me."

"Well this bunch seemed devoted to keeping you out of your mind," I said. "I thought they worshiped you."

"They do," she said, then her face tightened. "They're fools."

"Fools? You're an epic hero. You fight battles and save the day."

"Me, fight battles?" She laughed bitterly. "I don't have my shield or my helmet or my sword. I can't fight battles anymore."

"What are you talking about?"

"You remember after we defeated Typhon and sent him to the depths? That was a good day, but things didn't go well after that."

"What happened?"

"I don't know—I can't remember. My head is filled with these thoughts . . ." She put one hand to her head. "I woke up one day, and I knew I was not deserving of being a warrior, and I got rid of my things."

Shock made me gasp. "Athena, why would you do that?"

"Because it's true. I wasn't there for you, was I, when you needed me? I keep hearing that voice in my head reminding me. I can't make it stop. And why should it? It's true."

"You were there when it mattered," I said, gripping her arm. "Don't be so hard on yourself."

She cupped a hand to my face. "I regret not taking you under my wing, blaming you for everything that went wrong." And then she burped, and a sour odor came out. She groaned, putting her head in her hands. "I don't understand. Everything is so blurry. You shouldn't be back here."

"I had no choice. Perseus is in danger."

Her head came up. "Perseus? But how?"

"I know you don't like to know the stories of the past, but there's one about him. He becomes a hero. It has to do with—"

"Medusa. I know. Our father does share things with me. I'm to help him when he comes of age, but Perseus is still a child, like you. He's not due to battle her for years."

"The myth has changed. Tell her, Damian."

"The books we have tell a new story—that Perseus is turned to stone by Medusa."

Athena frowned. "But that can't be."

"It can," I said. "He must have looked at her. In the original story, he had your shield to reflect her image."

Her eyes turned stricken. "The shield I threw away. So this is my fault."

"No. It gets worse. The oracle who took me to New York had a vision about Hercules."

Her eyes grew puzzled. "Hercules? What about him?"

"He failed his first two trials thanks to me, so he's been given a new one, and somehow the order changed."

"How?"

"I don't know, but his next feat is now a double. He's to steal some apples from the Garden of the Hesperides *and* kill Ladon."

Athena's face brightened. "Ladon is not immortal. Hercules is strong and capable—he can easily defeat the dragon."

"But his confidence is down," Damian said. "Thanks to us, he failed to kill the Nemean lion and the hydra. He may be having doubts about himself."

"The oracle had a vision that the dragon kills him," I said.

"But that would be terrible." Her eyes clouded. "Hercules is a symbol of heroism. Without him—"

"It's bad," I finished. "The gods are no more. Olympus is gone. Look, now that we have you back, you can go help Hercules while I find Perseus and help him."

But Athena shook her head. "No. I must retrieve my shield and helmet. I remember throwing them away, but I can't remember where. Only someone powerful could bewitch my mind like that. I must find out who's behind this while you and your friends go to Hercules's assistance. If Hercules fails, this oracle you mention may be correct. Olympus may very well end."

I bit my lip. "But Perseus?"

"Will wait," she said. "He's not due to battle Medusa for some time."

"But things have changed. What if he goes sooner?"

"Polydectes would have no reason to send him now. If you say he's older when he faces him, that won't have changed."

"What if we killed two birds with one stone?"

Her eyes narrowed. "What do you mean?"

"To slay Medusa, Perseus had to collect some items. He had to visit three old ladies . . . what were their names, D?"

"The Graeae."

"That's right, and they're where?"

"In the far west."

"They live at the base of Mount Atlas," Athena confirmed.

"And the Garden of the Hesperides is . . . ?"

"In the far west," she said slowly. "An island in the middle of Lake Tritonis. It's not far from Mount Atlas."

"So after we save Hercules's butt, we could visit the Graeae and ask them nicely for the location of Medusa. We ran into Hermes on our way into Athens. He said the nymphs who watch over the garden just happen to have in their possession—"

"Hades's helmet," she said. "That is fortuitous."

"It's almost like someone planned for us to cross paths," I said.

Our eyes met, and I saw a dawning suspicion there, but she didn't comment. "You will need transport. A way to travel over water a long distance. A ship will take too long."

I looked at Angie and Damian, and our faces all lit up as the same idea came to us.

"Where exactly is Athens?" I asked Damian.

"South of where we left them."

"But do you think they went home?"

He shrugged.

"I'll bet they're still hanging around," Angie said.

"Who?" Athena asked, looking confused.

"Our rides," I said with a grin.

We walked until we came to a wide clearing. I put my fingers to my lips but Damian stayed my hand. "We'll need to boost it. Can you call up a wind? Something to carry it."

"Can I call up wind?" I snorted, then spun in a circle with my arms out, almost dancing at the idea of using my powers. Wind sprang up around us, lifting my hair and blowing it in my face. Damian whistled, then Angie, then me. The notes were lifted and carried away by the wind.

I stopped twirling and took a deep breath. "Do you think it will reach them?"

"I have no idea," he said, looking anxiously at the sky.

"They'll come," Angie said.

We stood like that for several minutes, none of us willing to look away.

Athena sighed. "Does someone want to tell me what we're waiting for? Oh." The last word came out as a gasp as a sudden gust of wind made the trees around us sway. Then the sound of beating wings filled the sky, and a high-pitched whinny reached my ears. Two, then three, then four winged horses circled over our heads before landing with loud thuds in the clearing.

I raced over to the tall silver one with white-tipped wings and threw my arms around her neck. "Argenta. You came." She whickered softly at me.

Damian did the same with his, a golden pegasus with black wings and a black mane, whom he'd named Albert after his grandfather. Angie's was a charcoal gray named Nero. The fourth one, Zesto, was a deep russet color with streaks of yellow in its mane. It tossed its head, coming over to nuzzle me.

"Sorry, Zesto, Macario's not here. I hope you'll settle for the goddess Athena."

The pegasus's eyes widened, and it snorted, then bowed its head to her.

"You never cease to amaze me," Athena said to me, running a hand over its snout before leaping onto its back. "I will meet up with you as soon as I am able. In the meantime, be well, sister." She stuck her hand out and clasped my forearm. I grasped hers back, and then with a kick of her heels, Zesto took three running steps and leaped into the sky.

I grabbed hold of Argenta's mane and pulled myself up onto her back. When we were seated, we looked at Damian.

"Which way?"

He looked up at the sky, eyeing the sun. "If we head southwest, we'll run into the continent of Africa eventually."

"How far?"

"I don't know, Phoebes. Jeez, I'm not a walking atlas, you know."

"No, the walking Atlas is bronze and in New York City," I joked.

That got him to smile. "Fine. My best guess is it's hundreds of miles. Best I can say."

"These beauties will need to rest and refresh."

"There're lots of islands scattered about in the Mediterranean. We're bound to find one that has fresh water."

"Then what are we waiting for? Let the quest begin!"

CHAPTER 8

The first few hours of our flight felt euphoric. The wind whistled past us as the winged horses soared over the sea. I loved being back in Olympus—so much so I wondered if I should stay when this was all over. Damian would probably disapprove. Too much chance of me altering the course of events, but part of me wanted to. I felt free here—at home. I had tons of extended family, and I could use my powers without fear of being labeled a freak.

As the day passed, we snacked on granola bars Damian had stashed in his bag. The hours dragged on, and we napped as our pegasuses kept flying. Around sundown, I sat up, wincing at the cramps in my legs. Angie pulled up next to me.

"I gotta go." She was bouncing up and down on Nero.

"Me too." My bladder was ready to burst. "Damian, any sign of an island?"

We scanned the blue water, searching for any dark spots. We'd passed several small islands earlier, although none had been inhabited.

"Look, is that smoke?" he said.

A thin black plume rose from a small green dot in the sea. It was a small island, no bigger than a pair of football fields.

"Maybe it's inhabited," I said.

"By someone who can cook," Angie added. "I'm starving."

"What if it's inhabited by someone unfriendly?" Damian asked. "Remember what happened when we let Arachne feed us?"

"Yeah. She turned us into cotton balls and tried to feed us to her baby spiders—but Arachne's nowhere near here. What are the odds this person is like her?"

"I've got to get off Nero, or I'm going to pee my pants," Angie said.

"Okay, but I don't like it," Damian grumbled.

We circled over the island, searching for any obvious dangers like giants or nine-headed monsters. It was kidney shaped with tall leafy cypress trees covering most of the ground. A small waterfall ran down the side of a cliff into the sea. Goats speckled the hillsides, roaming among the crags to chew on grass. A strip of white sand lined the sheltered belly of the island while the outer side was lined with steep cliffs and a rocky shore. Smoke rose from a small thatched-roof cottage built out of rocks. There was clothing hanging on the line but no other signs of life.

"Let's set down on that beach," I said, pointing at the strip of sand near the cottage. The pegasuses glided down and landed with soft thuds. I slid off Argenta, groaning at the ache in my legs.

Angie rushed into the bushes, and I followed. Afterward we went to the edge of the sea and took our boots off, dipping our toes in. A warm breeze stroked my face. The sun was a blazing ball of orange fire as it dipped below the horizon.

"Do you think my mother is watching this very same sunset?" I asked Angie.

"Maybe. Probably."

We turned as Damian joined us. "Africa is in the direction of the sun," he said. "Probably another day's ride before we reach it."

"The pegasuses can handle it," I said confidently. "But we need food."

His face got that worried look. "We need to be careful, Phoebes. What kind of person would live on a deserted island like this?"

"We know it's not a lady with six arms. Nothing ventured, nothing lost, right?"

"Just our lives," he said with a sigh. "Fine, but I'm not bringing Hermes's lyre with us. It's too valuable." He slipped the strap around Albert's neck for safekeeping, along with his satchel.

I stroked Argenta's nose. "Go find some water and something to eat. We'll call you when we're ready."

The pegasuses disappeared into the trees, and we walked along the sandy beach, following our noses toward the smell of smoke mingling with something tantalizing.

"I smell food," Angie said, eyes lighting up. "Something delicious."

The sound of a woman singing floated toward us, and then the cottage came into view. Twilight had settled in around us, and the windows were brightly lit. A breeze blew the curtains, and we glimpsed a slender woman with long black hair moving around the cottage, coming into view at different windows. She sang as she set dishes down on a table.

"What is that song?" I felt it pulsing in my veins. "I could swear I've heard it before."

"Whatever it is, it's almost as beautiful as the smell of that meal." Angie licked her lips.

Conch shells lined a narrow path that led to the door, which was made of driftwood lashed together. A wind chime made of seashells tinkled softly. A riot of different-colored blooms climbed the walls, scenting the air with jasmine. From the eaves overhead, glowing yellow eyes appeared, and something hooted loudly. I almost zapped it with a lightning bolt, but Damian grabbed my arm. "Relax, it's just an owl."

He raised his hand to knock, but the woman sang out, "Come in, dear travelers, come in." She held the last word in a soprano note so high it made the wind chime rattle.

The bird kept its beady eyes trained on us, its head turning as Damian pushed open the door and we stepped inside.

Colorful rugs covered a floor of packed earth. A small fire burned in a hearth made of smooth stones, probably harvested from the rocky shoreline. A low couch was placed in front of the fire. Off to the right, a lumpy mattress on a wooden platform took up a corner of the hut. Gauzy white fabric draped down from the ceiling like mosquito netting.

A slender woman stood by a small stove made of stacked stones. In the center opening, glowing chunks of charcoal warmed the pot on top, which she was stirring with a large wooden spoon. She wore a finely woven gown the color of seafoam. When she moved, the dress seemed to float around her. Her face was framed by long tresses that tumbled down her back and formed a widow's peak on her forehead. Luminous violet eyes probed us curiously. She had high cheekbones like you might see on a runway model and full lips painted a deep red. She was young, probably no more than twenty or so. She carried a golden loom under one arm, and she idly racked thread on it as she welcomed us.

"Come in, children, come in! It's so rare I have visitors. Please make yourself at home."

Here's the weird thing—her words came out like lines from a musical, as if she was singing every word to that tune we'd heard outside. It was kind of annoying, but I bit my tongue and said, "I'm Phoebe. This is Angie and Damian."

"I am Calypso!" she sang with a wide smile. "And my humble home is yours. Please join me. I was about to eat dinner when I saw you pass by overhead, so I added some more to the pot."

We were too hungry to argue and too polite to ask her to knock off the nonstop sing-song voice. There were four chairs tucked around a small wooden table made of weathered planks of driftwood. She set down bowls made of coconuts cut in half and ladled some stew into each of our bowls. We dug in using crude wooden spoons.

She didn't join in, just sat with her loom and began racking thread. A sturdy bag made of goatskin dragged along behind her wherever she went, feeding out the line of thread.

"This is delicious," Angie said as she shoveled in stew.

"Yes," Damian agreed, neatly spooning his in. "Many thanks."

"What are you doing out here in the middle of nowhere?" I asked between bites. "Did your ship capsize?" That would explain why she didn't seem to own anything other than that loom.

"Are you being punished?" Angie reached for another serving of the crispy flatbread from a basket in the center of the table.

"Punished?" Calypso laughed, a long trilling sound like notes on a xylophone. "I live in paradise. It's so beautiful here. I'd love for you to *staaaaay.*" She plucked a string on the loom as she said the last word, holding it for a long moment. Pain jabbed me right in the middle of my brain, as if the word drove a needle in, and I had to shake my head to clear it.

I took a couple more spoonfuls, but my hunger was replaced by a growing knot in my stomach. The sunset had gotten me thinking about my mother, which made me worried about my brother and how soon we could help Hercules and get on with the business of saving Perseus.

"You're distracted, dear," Calypso said to me, her fingers never stopping their movement on the loom. "Tell Calypso what's on your mind."

"Nothing. I'm just worried about my brother."

"Oh dear. Family troubles?"

"No, not yet. It's just something that might happen."

"Well, then that's a worry for another day," she said. "Nothing to trouble your heads today. Not if you *staaay.*" She plucked a strand on the loom, and again, the word penetrated deep into my brain, winding itself around every synapse as it repeated over and over like a distant echo.

A log snapped in the fireplace, and I gasped in air. Angie and Damian looked around dazedly. Outside the window I could see the moon over the water. When had the moon come out? And why did my bones ache as though I'd been sitting for hours?

Calypso kept threading strands through the loom. "You were saying, dear? About your brother?"

I blinked, trying to clear the fog in my brain. "Nothing. I just . . . I have things to do, places to go. I just wish I could fast-forward time."

"Fast-forward? Why, when it's so much nicer to slow things down?" This time instead of plucking a note, her fingers strummed the loom, and soft notes tinkled, spreading drowsiness deep into my bones.

"What are you making?" I fought back a yawn.

"A wedding dress," she said with a shy smile.

"Who's getting married?"

"I am."

"Who's the lucky guy?" Angie asked.

I pictured a dashing sailor she'd met when his passing ship had been caught in a storm, but her violet eyes drifted over to Damian.

Damian dropped his spoon, looking completely baffled, and I burst out laughing.

"Damian, she's joking. She's not talking about you."

"He's a handsome enough boy," she said. "Given enough time, I'd say he'd make a fine husband."

"Like when he's thirty," I said through a big yawn. "Which is a long time from now."

Calypso smiled secretly. "Time has a way of slipping away, doesn't it?"

Something about the way she said it penetrated the fog in my brain, sending warning bells off. I shoved my chair back. "I think we should be going."

Problem was, when I stood, my legs were like blocks of wood—as if I had been sitting for hours. Surely we had only been there a half hour max? My eyes fell on the pile of fabric next to Calypso's chair. It had tripled in size. That didn't make sense. And where was all the thread coming from? Surely that small leather bag couldn't hold all that?

She rose, stroking soft notes out of her loom that soothed the edges of my brain like warm milk. "I insist you spend the night. You must be exhausted, and it's dangerous to be outside after dark. You girls take my bed. I'll sleep on the couch. The boy can sleep on a rug by the fire."

Blood began to flow into my feet, and the pins and needles were excruciating. "He'll sleep by our bed." I winced as we limped over to the lumpy mattress. I was starting to wish we'd just stopped and watered the pegasuses and kept going. There was something odd about Calypso, even though she'd been nothing but friendly.

"Damian, have you ever read about someone named Calypso in your books?" I whispered as Angie and I crawled under the covers. The air was warm, and Damian lay on his back on a rug at the side of the bed, with just a thin cover on him.

"I don't think so." He yawned. "If I did, I can't remember." His eyes drifted shut. Next to me, Angie was already snoring.

I lay back, staring up at the thatched roof. Across the foot of the bed, I could see Calypso on the couch, the light of the fire touching her loom as she continued to weave.

Does she never sleep?

I was determined to stay awake to keep an eye on her. Outside, an owl hooted three times.

Hoot. Hoot. Hoot.

And as though a switch had been thrown, I sank into a deep dark pool of sleep.

CHAPTER 9

When I awoke, I thought for a moment I was back home and the subway was rumbling past Carl's building, and then I realized it was the sound of Angie snoring in my ear. I shoved her off and opened my eyes, blinking against the dazzling sunlight streaming in through the windows. It was long past morning. I stretched, feeling a lethargy as though I'd been in bed for days.

"Is it time for school?" Angie muttered.

"No, dumbhead, it's time to get off this creepy island."

She yawned, sitting up. "Why do I feel like I've been in bed a week?" She stretched. The bandage she'd wrapped around her arm fell off, and she frowned. "Hey, where'd that cut go?"

I grabbed her wrist and turned it over. The red gash she'd received when we'd fallen off the Acropolis was gone. Only a faint red line remained.

"That should have taken days to heal. Something's wrong." I threw back the covers. "We need to find Damian. Now."

I stepped out of bed, but my knees buckled, and I crumpled back onto the mattress. "My legs are Jell-O. Get up. Try to walk."

Angie scooted to the edge and tried to stand but collapsed on the ground, rolling over on her back to stare up at me. "It's like my legs turned into noodles."

"Or we've been in bed for days, long enough for your cut to heal."

She blinked at me. "But why would we sleep that long?"

"My guess is Calypso enchanted us somehow. She kept going on about slowing time and having us stay. We need to find Damian. I think he's the one she wanted." I held on to the bedpost and hauled myself up. It wasn't as bad after a few moments of standing, and I took a step. I grabbed the post again as my legs wobbled. I waited until blood began to flow and my limbs regained some strength, then helped Angie up. We clung to each other, taking one tiny step, then another.

We hobbled over to the kitchen table and sank down into chairs. There was a jug of goat milk. Suddenly ravenous, I grabbed it, swallowing down several warm mouthfuls. It was slightly sour but not bad. I passed it to Angie. She finished it, then wiped her mouth with the back of her hand.

"I'm ready," she said. "Where is this sea witch, and how do we get Damian out of her clutches?"

I would have happily blasted Calypso with a bolt of lightning, but when I held my hand out, there was barely a spark. I didn't have enough strength yet to call on my powers.

"We have to be careful not to be enchanted again." I thought back to our time with her. "She sings a lot. Have you noticed?"

"Yeah, really annoying. I mean, it was beautiful, but it gave me a headache."

"But it was when she played those notes on her loom that I . . . did you feel it? Like a needle in your brain."

"Yeah, I did. So we snatch the loom. We just need to block out all her racket. How are we going to do that?"

I looked around the table. There was a small plate of dried figs. I tore one in half and rolled the pieces between my thumb and forefinger, then popped one in my ear, then the other. "Say something."

Angie mouthed words, but they were so muffled I couldn't make them out. I gave her a thumbs-up. She quickly jammed her ears full of fig and then cracked her knuckles, mouthing, *Let's do this.*

Cracking the door open, we peered around the edge. Calypso sat on the beach under the shade of a coconut tree. She had her loom on her lap and continued to work on it while she talked to Damian. Something she said made him laugh, and her face lit up as her fingers worked faster.

Taking one plug out, I whispered, "We need a plan. She's got Damian under her spell."

Angie wrinkled her nose, thinking. "What if you pretend you woke up and sit down close to Damian. I'll come up behind her and grab the loom when she's distracted."

We put the figs back in, and I stepped out into the bright light. Angie ducked out the side window, keeping out of sight. I brushed against the shells on the wind chime. Calypso's eyes flickered toward me, but she kept talking to Damian in her sing-song voice. I pulled my hair over my ears to hide the figs and walked stiffly across the sand, doing my best imitation of someone enchanted, and sat down next to Damian. His eyes were blank and he stared off into the distance. I could make out faint notes of the song she sang, but it was muffled, like hearing music underwater. Enough to tug at me but not pull me under.

"What a beautiful song," I said woodenly, staring out at the sea. "It makes me want to stay here forever."

Out of the corner of my eye, I could see her face light up. She strummed her fingers across the loom. "Stay, my darling, stay forever. Stay until the sun doesn't rise or set. Stay until the gods cease to exist. Stay, stay, stay."

Even though the words were muffled and faint, my eyes grew heavy, my body crying out for sleep, but I clenched my hands in the sand, digging my nails into my skin, and shook my head to clear it. One of the pieces of fig fell out, but it worked. Damian was not so lucky—a thin stream of drool hung down from his open mouth.

"Actually, I think we should be going," I said suddenly.

Calypso hit a chord that twanged in my brain like a sharp jab.

"Why would you want to leave?" she sang.

"Because we have places to go," I said. "Remember, Damian?" I took his arm, flinching at how cold he was.

"But I like it here. I'm going to stay, stay forever."

"See? He likes it," Calypso crooned. "He wants to staaaaay."

I steeled myself against the sound of the word, imagining fingernails on a chalkboard, and shook Damian. "Come on, Big D. We need to leave right now."

He turned toward me then, and a big goofy grin crossed his face as he recognized me. "Phoebe! Are you coming to the wedding?" He turned puppy-dog eyes on Calypso. "Isn't she beautiful?" he gushed. "She's going to be my wife one day. I love her."

"Yes, dear boy," Calypso crooned. "Calypso is all alone."

"She's alone," Damian echoed. "I should stay. I love this place. I love her."

I wanted to seriously barf, but I did something better. I slapped Damian hard across the face.

His eyes grew round with shock, and Calypso cried out, but at that moment Angie pounced, wrenching the loom out of her arms. She screamed, lunging for it, but Angie tossed it over to me, and this time when I twitched my fingers, I managed a nice-sized lightning bolt.

"Don't move, don't speak, don't sing. Just sit there and be quiet or this loom is toast and you're next."

She hesitated and then folded her arms crossly but didn't say anything.

Damian flung himself between us, dropping to his knees to beg. "Don't hurt my love!"

Seriously, he was starting to get on my nerves. I nodded at Angie, and she put her fingers to her lips and whistled for our rides.

"Un-enchant my friend right now," I said. "And if you so much as try to sing a note, I will shove this lightning bolt down your throat before you can sing *do re mi*."

"Fine." Her voice was low and husky. "Leave if you must. But give Calypso back her loom."

"Why should I give it back?"

She eyed it greedily. "Because it keeps me young, and besides, I have something you need. The boy told me everything. You're the daughter of Zeus that nearly destroyed Olympus."

"Hey, I saved it in the end," I reminded her.

"But you'll destroy it all over again if you don't fix the things you've changed. You need to face Medusa. The gorgon's head can't be held in just anything. It needs powerful magic to contain it or any who carry it will perish. Do you know her blood is so poisonous that if even a drop falls on you, agony will be your fate?"

"So what do you propose?"

"I'll trade you my bag." She tossed me the·leather goatskin she dragged around with her. "It has powerful magic—it can hold more than meets the eye. Take it and leave my loom . . . and the boy," she added coyly.

I snorted. "We're not leaving Damian, lady."

She shrugged and gave a tiny laugh. "It was worth a try. Alas, I will have to wait for another hapless traveler to pass by." She patted Damian on the cheek and then snapped her fingers.

He blinked rapidly, then looked around. "Is it time to go?"

"Yes, Damian." I held my hand out, and he gripped it, getting up to stand on wobbly legs.

Our winged rides landed in the sand next to us, looking well-fed and refreshed.

I held on to the loom as Angie helped Damian up on Albert, who still carried Hermes's lyre. She leaped onto Nero, her bag strapped across her shoulders. Argenta lowered her wing, and I climbed on.

"My loom!" Calypso stretched out her hand eagerly.

"Sorry. Changed my mind."

She lunged for me, but Argenta reared up, flaring her hooves and driving Calypso back before launching herself into the air.

"Give it back!" Calypso cried, frantically running down the beach after us. "I'll grow old and ugly without it. I beg you!" But the pegasuses quickly gained altitude, and we swiftly left the island behind us.

Angie rode up next to me. "Why'd you keep it? Not that I mind."

"And have her enchant the next sucker that passes by? No thanks." I shoved it inside Calypso's magic bag, amazed at how it disappeared inside. The bag hung lightly across my shoulders as if it weighed nothing. I had forgotten my own bag back at the little hut, but I wasn't about to return for the toothbrush and change of clothes in it. "Let's get to Africa, shall we?"

Damian looked confused on the back of Albert. "Explain it again—why we were there?"

"You were in *looove*." I burst out laughing at the look of horror on his face.

"I was not," he said hotly.

"Damian had his first crush." Angie made *kissy kissy* noises.

"No, I didn't. Did I? I can't remember. It's like my head's packed with cotton."

We teased him mercilessly as the winged horses carried us closer and closer to our destination. The horizon before us beckoned. Soon we would deal with Hercules and his dragon problem, and then?

Then we would find my brother.

CHAPTER 10

With the pegasuses rested and fed, we made good progress until dark clouds rolled in and the temperature dropped.

"Can't you do something about that, Katzy?" Angie shivered on Nero as heavy drops of rain splatted on our heads.

"Sorry, I can't control weather caused by Mother Nature."

We dipped lower, but the blast of sea spray made it worse. The wind picked up, buffeting the horses, and making it difficult to see in the stinging spray of water.

"How do you know which way is west?" I shouted to Damian. The sky was an endless canvas of black clouds.

"I don't." His head turned every which way. "I can't make out where the sun is."

"Why is nothing ever easy?" I shouted in frustration.

"We need to look for land. We can't keep flying in this," Angie called.

"We could be close. We have to keep on." We couldn't afford another episode like Calypso—it had cost us precious days.

As it was, we didn't have much of a choice because there was no sign of land. We held on grimly, urging the pegasuses on. Argenta's flanks heaved under my legs as she struggled to keep going.

"Look!" Damian shouted. "I see land."

Ahead of us, a dark mass rose up.

"Is it Africa?" I asked.

"It looks big. Let's hope so."

Spurred on by the sight of land, the pegasuses thumped their wings harder, and soon we soared past rocky cliffs, but strangely, the power of the storm increased once we made land, making it impossible to set down.

Instead of sea spray, sand and grit swirled in the air, and I lost sight of the others. We flew blindly, pushed and tossed by the wind. Suddenly Argenta whinnied loudly as one wing was bent backward by the sheer force of the wind. We tumbled in the air, spiraling downward as she tried mightily to balance. I managed to leap off her back as she hit the ground, rolling over and over. When I finally stopped, I coughed, spitting out a mouthful of sand, and leaped to my feet.

"Argenta!" I screamed.

Miraculously, the winds settled, and the swirling clouds of dust cleared. I wiped the grit from my eyes and raced to the silver animal that lay still on the ground. Scattered feathers lay on the sand.

I put a hand to her flank. She was still breathing. Relief flooded me. "Argenta, are you all right?"

One sapphire eye opened, and she whinnied encouragingly. She tried to get up, but her front legs buckled.

"Just rest a minute." I stood, taking a look around. An ocean of red sand stretched as far as the eye could see. There was no sign of Damian or Angie. The sand was hot even through my boots. Now that the storm had passed, the sky was clear, and the sun blazed down.

Argenta whinnied, trying to rise again. This time she gained all four legs. She stood with her legs splayed, her head hanging down. Her right wing hung limply. I ran my fingers over it, testing the joints.

"I don't feel anything broken. Maybe you sprained it. Can you walk?"

She tossed her head, signaling she could. I had long since stopped wondering how it was these majestic creatures understood us.

"Good. See that dune over there?" I pointed to the highest dune around. "If we climb to the top, maybe we'll be able to see something."

We took off trudging through the sand. My clothes quickly dried and sweat rolled down my back. Following the edge of the dune, we slowly made our way toward the top. My feet sank into the soft sand with every step, making it a hard go. When we finally crested the top, I caught my breath.

Sand as far as the eye could see.

I turned in a circle, searching every direction for any sign of life, my friends, water, but there was nothing but endless rolling dunes. I let out the breath I'd been holding, feeling weak in the knees. We wouldn't last long in this heat. We needed water and shelter fast.

I leaned into Argenta, wrapping my arm around her neck. Her body trembled with pain and fatigue.

"It's going to be okay," I whispered, needing to hear it even if I didn't quite believe it. I scanned every inch of the horizon until my eyes burned. Everything looked the same.

Something flew overhead. It was a large colorful bird of some kind, flapping ungainly wings as it looked down at us. Then it continued on in a straight line.

I followed the direction it took, and sudden hope made my breath catch. Was that a black dot in the sand? Like a pile of rocks? I could have sworn it hadn't been there a moment ago. I blinked to make sure it was still there, that I wasn't imagining it. Maybe there would be shade. Or even better, water. The bird had to drink, didn't it?

"Come on. Let's go that way." I kept a hand on Argenta to steady myself as we walked along the ridge toward the distant speck. My head throbbed, and my tongue was like sandpaper. I wondered how Damian and Angie were faring, if they had landed safely, if they were okay.

Argenta whickered, and I rubbed her neck. "I know you're worried about your friends. So am I."

My face felt flushed, and the top of my head burned. My arms had already turned a shade of red that was going to hurt later. The sun was at its highest point when the speck of rocks turned into something recognizable. The rocks formed an opening in the side of a dune.

"It's a cave," I said. "We can shelter inside and get out of the sun."

As we got closer, the sand dune loomed even bigger. Oddly, there was nothing else around like it, just this pile of rocks forming the opening, as if someone had built something under the sand.

We stopped inside the entrance. A cool breeze wafted across my heated skin, bringing goosebumps. I could have sworn I smelled water. I had never in my life thought water could smell so sweet. Argenta's ears pricked up as we stepped farther into the mouth of the cave. Smooth sand gave way to solid rocky ground. The sides were chiseled out of stone, as if someone had used dynamite to create the tunnel.

"Listen." I paused. Argenta stopped, and we heard it then. Gurgling water.

I grinned at her, and we hurried forward.

The tunnel opened up to a giant cavern two stories high made from the same chiseled granite. A round opening at the top let in sunlight that shone down on a cistern—a pool of water in the center of the room surrounded by rocks. Water bubbled up into the pool from the center, as if there was an underground source.

I fell to my knees at the edge, ready to dunk my head in, but I bumped against something solid, like plexiglass.

Argenta had the same problem, neighing in frustration as the water stayed out of reach.

"What the . . . ?" I put my hands in front of me and touched an invisible shield keeping us away. I jumped up, running my hands up and down, checking all the way around the cistern until I arrived back at Argenta.

The water was right there, but we couldn't get to it.

Sometimes I really hated this place.

I looked at Argenta. "I don't suppose you can fly up and drop inside and scoop some up for us?"

She glanced back at her right wing, which still hung limp, and whinnied mournfully.

Frustrated, I sat down, and Argenta folded her front legs, settling down next to me. At least the stone was cool. I could hear the water gurgling, and it made my thirst insane. I would have given anything, *anything* to have some of that water.

"That's a dangerous offer to make in this world," a cool voice said.

I sat up, wondering if I was dreaming, but there across the cistern sat a slender young woman perched on the edge, her bare feet splashing about in the water.

Maybe the shield was down! I quickly reached out my hand and bruised my knuckles on that invisible force. I tried to rein my temper in. "Who are you?"

"I am Erate, a water nymph, and you have trespassed in

my home." Her face had a fey quality with luminous eyes and ears that tilted upward to small points. Her sleeveless tunic revealed tattooed images covering her arms and legs. *Are they moving?* They crawled around her skin as if it were a living canvas.

I tried asking nicely. "Please. We're thirsty. We just want a drink, and then we'll be on our way."

She gave a little shake of her head. "No one drinks from my pool. It would be impure."

I licked my cracked lips, feeling desperate. "I don't care about me. Just let my pegasus have water. She's injured."

Her eyes glittered with sudden interest. "You would sacrifice your life so that the winged one might live?"

Something was off here. This nymph was hiding something. I could feel a power vibe coming from her, like when I was in the presence of Zeus or Athena. "Who are you really?"

A flicker of irritation crossed her face. "I told you. I am a nymph."

"Then why won't you let us drink? You have plenty."

She reached down and trailed her fingers in the water, deliberately torturing us. "You didn't answer the question."

"Of course I'd do anything for Argenta," I snapped. "But I kinda have to save Olympus and my brother, so if you could just lower the force field, we'll have a few sips and be out of your hair."

She smiled then, only it was sharp as a scythe cutting across her face. "Quite the hero, aren't you?" Behind her a peacock strutted out of the shadows, its tail spread wide. She ran an idle hand over its head. Was this the bird I'd seen flying overhead? Could peacocks even fly?

I was still trying to grasp why a peacock was here when I realized the round eyes on the peacock's tail were blinking at me.

That's right—real eyes, not decorations.

"I'm not a hero," I said, turning my attention back to this annoying nymph. "I'm just trying to fix my mistakes. Why won't you let us have some water?"

"The water is not for drinking. It shows me things."

"Things? Like what?"

"Whatever I want to see." She dipped her hand into the cistern, and the inked images on her arm melted, running together down her arm onto the surface of the water. The ink mixed with the water, and then it was as though someone had turned on a movie camera. On the surface, an image appeared of me being buffeted by the wind as Argenta battled to stay up.

"How did you—"

"I can see many things."

"Can you show me my brother?" I asked suddenly. "His name is Perseus."

She swirled her hand in the water and more of the tattoos dripped from her skin. Another image appeared. It was dark, but I could make out some bars. I leaned forward. "Is that a prison?"

The image brightened, and I gasped. My brother was in chains, crouched down on a layer of straw, leaning against a stone wall.

"Why is he in prison?"

She said nothing, just swirled her hand, draining more ink into the cistern. The image shifted to show me standing among a crowd of boys. Perseus stood next to me.

"Wait, those are the boys that chased me. The big one said he was King Polydectes' son." I raised my head. "Are you saying this is my fault?"

She shrugged. "I am not the one who decides blame. I merely see things."

"Well, where is he? Where is this prison? I need to break him out."

"He is already out." She waved her hand again. This time Polydectes stood in Perseus's cell. Perseus listened intently, then nodded his head in agreement and was escorted out. Polydectes stood alone and then laughed, pleased with himself.

My blood ran cold.

"Don't tell me . . ."

The surface went blank, and the water nymph rose. "I cannot tell you anything. But now you have seen."

I didn't need to be told. I knew.

Perseus was on his way to face Medusa.

Thanks to my visit to Seriphos, the past had changed. Perseus had fought with the king's son, which gave Polydectes the perfect excuse to throw him into prison and send him to his death as a way to atone.

My brother was going to get turned to stone, and it was all my fault.

"Please," I begged the woman. "Can you show me one more thing?"

She hesitated and then shrugged. "What is it you desire?"

"My friends. Where are they?"

"Are you sure you want to see?" Her luminous eyes glinted with malice, as if she was enjoying this. The peacock strutted behind her, emitting a high-pitched shriek.

I nodded, and she dipped her foot in. Tattoos slid down her calf into the water. Angie and Damian appeared in some kind of sand bowl. Their two pegasuses were at their side, eyes rolling with terror. The camera, or whatever it was, panned left, and I saw why.

"You don't have much time if you want to rescue your friends." She laughed, and I heard that leashed power again. Something was very off about this nymph.

The walls of the cavern rumbled, and a rock fell from the ceiling. The peacock cried out again, and then they vanished. The cistern vanished, as if it had never been there. More rocks fell. The place was coming apart.

"Run!" I said to Argenta.

The pegasus scrambled up, and I leaped onto her back. She raced down the tunnel as rocks fell all around us. One grazed my shoulder, bruising me, but then light beckoned, and we emerged outside.

Behind us, the cave collapsed, buried under the weight of the sand above, leaving no trace it had ever existed.

"What just happened?" Had any of it been real? Or in my feverish state of thirst, had I imagined it?

A faint cry reached my ears. *Angie.*

"Come on," I said, urging Argenta on. She couldn't fly, but she could gallop.

CHAPTER 11

rgenta's hooves thudded in the sand as we raced toward the sound of Angie's scream. I heard Damian shout, and then we crested a dune and pulled up. Below in the bowl of sand, my friends were surrounded by the strange lion creatures we'd encountered our first day back outside of Athens. They had my friends surrounded. Damian had Hermes's lyre over his head, waving it like a bat. The pegasuses flashed their hooves, driving the wild brutes back, but they were inching closer.

The lightning bolt appeared in my hand without my thinking. I cocked it over my shoulder and then threw it like a javelin, aiming for the largest beast. It hit the creature square in the side, and the beast howled in rage as its mane caught fire, sending it rolling in the sand and roaring in pain.

The other two turned and saw me at the top of the hill.

"Katzy!" Angie shouted. "About time."

"Sorry I'm late." I twitched my fingers, quickly drawing two more lightning bolts in my hands. "Wait here," I told Argenta. She tried to follow, but I blocked her. "You won't be any help, and you might get in my way. Please."

She tossed her head and planted her feet, ready to charge down the hill in an instant.

The two remaining manticores stalked toward me as I took long steps down the soft sand until I reached the bottom. They spaced apart, distancing themselves to make it harder to strike them.

I'd seen some weird creatures in this place, like the chimera, but the manticore was in the running for Most Ugly. It was those troll-like faces that were almost human, all wrinkled skin and saggy jowls. They looked too dopey to be terrifying, but when their jaws opened and I caught sight of three rows of teeth, my spine tightened. Okay, so maybe a little scary. I had almost forgotten about its barbed tail when two barbs came shooting at me. One nicked the side of my tunic, barely missing me, and the other disintegrated into my bolt.

"Is that all you got?" I twirled the lightning bolts in my hands like batons. I'd had a lot of time to practice up on Carl's roof.

The beasts snarled in tandem, making my eardrums throb.

"Damian, if I kill this thing, it's not going to grow five more heads, is it?"

"No, it just likes to eat people. No superpowers. Those barbs are poisonous though."

"Good to know," I said as the closest manticore launched another spike from its tail. I dropped into a squat, and it went over my head. That was two barbs down. There was only one left.

"Any suggestions? Or should I just go full-on Phoebe Katz on them?" The two manticores had their attention solely on me and my twin bolts of lightning power.

"I tried playing the lyre, but it didn't work this time."

"Then Phoebe Katz it is."

I took a deep breath and let the magic that flowed in my veins gather and bubble up, spinning the bolts faster and faster until they were a blur. The manticores growled nervously, looking at each other. They coiled their haunches, ready to leap on me, at the same time I flung the twirling bolts at them.

Like Fourth of July pinwheels, the bolts spun across the open space. The first neatly lopped off the head of one manticore, but the other beast dodged the second bolt, trying to bat it away with its tail only to lose the tip, which made it howl in pain. Before I could draw another bolt, the manticore launched at me, tackling me to the ground with its front paws on my shoulders. Pain blossomed as its talons dug into my skin. Its mouth opened, and it brought its head down to bite mine off, I presumed, only it stopped mid-bite with a shocked look on its face, as if it didn't know what had just happened. My hand clenched the lightning bolt I'd jabbed deep in its side, right into the center of its heart.

The manticore's tongue flopped out of its mouth, and it collapsed, smothering me under it.

I could barely breathe, and manticore drool ran down my neck. I frantically pushed at the body, and then Damian and Angie grabbed me by the ankles, hauling me out from under it.

I sat up, sucking in air and wiping slobber off my cheek with the edge of my tunic.

"Are you guys all right?" I asked.

Damian and Angie squatted down. "We're good," Angie said. "The pegasuses are a little battered, but I think they'll be okay."

"Where were you?" Damian asked.

"Looking for you. And then I ran into a water nymph."

"A water nymph?" Damian looked puzzled. "Out here in the desert?"

I told them about the strange cave and everything I'd been told. "We have to find Perseus and fast. He could already be on his way to Medusa."

"It's going to take him a while to make his way, and he has to go to the Garden of the Hesperides, so we're bound to cross paths," Damian said, calm as always.

"What if he doesn't go there?" I asked.

"But that's what Athena told him to do." Damian stopped himself. "Wait . . . if Athena didn't go talk to him—"

"Then he doesn't know about the Helmet of Invisibility or Hermes's winged shoes or her shield, which means he could go straight to the Graeae to find out where Medusa's lair is. Damian, we have to go there."

"We will. After we help Hercules."

I wanted to pound the sand in frustration. With each minute that passed, I felt as though I was letting my brother down. What if he was heading toward the gorgon now? What if he was outside the cave?

"Stop it, Katzy," Angie said. "It's not going to help worrying about it."

"I can't help it," I said. "If I hadn't come back, none of this would be happening right now."

"You can't undo that. All we can do is carry on. We're on the right path."

A little bit of my tension eased. "Okay. Damian, any ideas as to where we are?"

Damian was studying the two dead manticores. "How many barbs did the manticore fire at you back in Athens?"

I thought about it. "One, as I recall."

"They shot two at me," Angie said.

Damian's frown deepened. "When the manticores first circled us, I noticed three barbs were missing from their tails. Each one holds three."

"So?"

"So don't you think it odd that three more manticores attacked us today with the correct number of stingers missing?"

"You think they were the same ones?"

"Don't know," Damian said, "but it's odd." He stood, turning. "Hey, where's the one Phoebe set fire to?"

The place where it had rolled was empty.

"It must have crawled away while we were talking." On a sudden whim, I picked up the shorn tail, tugged out the remaining barb, and put it in the bag along with the loom. "Okay . . . Damian, any clue where we are?"

"The storm blew us east of where we wanted to go, but before we landed, I saw a tall mountain off to the west."

"And?"

"And it could be Atlas Mountain, which means the Garden of the Hesperides is that direction." He pointed.

"Atlas—that's where those gray ladies are that know where to find Medusa?"

He nodded.

A little bit of anxiety eased. "Good. Then that's where my brother will go. Let's get on with saving Herk-A-Jerk so I can find Perseus and stop him from turning into a rock."

Our noble steeds were grounded thanks to the damage to their wings, but they were able to carry us on their backs and didn't seem to mind the soft sand. We headed west, following the line of the sun that beat down on us like a hot stove. I tried calling up a rain storm to ease the heat, but the best I could do was a wimpy cloud that spat two drops and then evaporated in the sun.

As the hours passed, Angie's nose took on the color of a tomato. I balanced Calypso's bag on my head, trying to keep the sun off, but the thirst was driving me mad. My tongue felt drier than a piece of beef jerky, and I couldn't even swallow.

Damian suddenly stopped, pointing. "Look, there's the mountain I saw."

I blinked, trying to see through the desert heat. He was right. Rising out of the distant horizon was the tip of a dark mountain.

"According to my calculations, the Garden of the Hesperides is due north of it."

"How far north? It's kind of a big empty desert. If we get lost, I don't know how long any of us will last out here without water."

"It's not clear where the gardens are, but according to Hermes, they're on Lake Tritonis, which means there'll be water."

"So we find this lake, we find the garden, we save Greek mythology." A weariness seeped into my bones. *No pressure.*

"Phoebes . . . what if Hercules isn't there?" Damian asked as we continued on.

I pulled up Argenta. "What do you mean, not there?"

"What if he doesn't show up?"

"Why wouldn't he?"

"Because everything's changed."

I bit the inside of my cheek for courage. "He's going to show."

"How do you know?"

"Because he has to, that's why. We have to fix things or game over."

"What's your point, Damian?" Angie asked. "Why are you being negative?"

"I'm not," he said defensively. "I'm just . . . never mind."

"What?" One thing about Damian, he was usually right about whatever was bothering him.

"Nothing is going according to plan."

"Hey, we have a magical bag to carry Medusa's head." I held up the leather satchel. "And a loom in case we need to knit a scarf. Not so bad."

That got him to smile. "Fine. He'll be there. But don't expect him to cooperate."

I sighed. "Why do I even bring you along?"

"Because I'm usually right."

Our misery grew as the hours dragged on. There was no escaping the sun, and the single bottle of water Damian had packed in his bag was long gone. Even when the ground began to firm and the sand petered out, it wasn't much better walking on baking earth. A fly landed on my arm, and I swatted it away, and then another landed on my nose.

"Hey, get lost." I waved it off, but two more joined the party.

Argenta tossed her head as large flies with blue-black wings settled on her neck. She yelped at the same time I did when one of the flies bit my arm, leaving a stinging welt.

"Guys, I think we have a problem." Damian had turned on Albert to look behind us.

I followed his gaze, and my heart dropped at the buzzing black cloud in the sky. "Is that rain?"

"No, it's alive and it's coming for us."

The pegasuses took off in a dead run, racing across the baked earth, but the cloud of flies was persistent, gaining on us. I turned to look over my shoulder and saw the back end of Argenta was covered in the things. The pegasus didn't complain, racing on steadfastly. More of the nasty pests landed on me. The rushing wind blew them back, but they crawled under my tunic and bit down on my tender flesh. I thrashed, trying to stay on Argenta's back as we bounced along, but slapping at them made me lose my balance, and I went flying off. Hitting the dirt hard, the air went out of me, and I couldn't breathe let alone get up. The flies were on me in an instant, and I frantically waved them away. Panic flooded me. They were crawling everywhere: on my face, in my ears, down my back.

"*Aarrgh*!" I screamed, clenching my fists into the dirt.

More and more flies settled on me until I couldn't even see my skin. I had to do something, or these flies were going to keep biting until there was nothing left of us. *Think, Phoebe.* I pushed aside the pain and the horror and focused on my powers. The rage helped. I imagined a storm, a really big dust storm, and the ground rumbled. Red earth lifted around me and swirled in the air. I didn't need any words to call up my powers—my rage served as a conduit to the earth, growing as the stinging flies bit the flesh on the back of my knees. The ground rumbled again, and this time my powers raised a cloud of dirt, spinning like a cyclone, gathering speed, and sucking the insects into it.

One by one they peeled off my skin, clinging as long as they could until torn away by the force of the wind. I got to my hands and knees, then my feet, shaking out my tunic and brushing out my hair. The wind was roaring so loud my eardrums hurt. The feathers on the pegasuses ruffled, but our winged friends stood their ground, heads down, letting the flies peel off them until finally we were clear of them. I punched my fist in the air, sending the cyclone spinning across the desert, far away from us.

Angie and Damian lay facedown on the ground, moaning.

"Angie, are you all right?" I rolled her over. Her face had welts all over it. One eye was swollen closed. Damian had it just as bad.

"Gawd, I hate this place," Angie said, sitting up and shaking her pigtails out to make sure there weren't any left behind. "It was way easier fighting a nineteen-headed hydra than that pack of flies."

"Those weren't just any flies." Damian's right cheekbone was swollen, making his face look gargoyle-like.

"What do you mean?"

"There was a pestilence the gods would send—they called them gadflies."

"You're saying someone sent those things?" Outrage made my blood boil even as my skin was on fire from the stinging bites.

He nodded. "Someone doesn't want us helping Hercules."

"What if it's both?" I asked.

"What do you mean?"

"Remember what Athena said? Someone spiked her nectar, so she threw away her shield—the very thing my brother needs to not turn into a rock. Maybe the same person is behind it."

"That's not good, Phoebe," he said. "If you're right, someone very powerful wants us to fail. We could be in a world of danger."

"What else is new," Angie grumbled.

We remounted the pegasuses and continued on. We were all miserable. The bites itched and throbbed. My skin was on fire from being in the sun all day. And my thirst . . . I would have cut off my right arm for a sip of water. The sun finally went down, and the temperature dropped, becoming tolerable. The moon slowly rose, illuminating the bare landscape around us. We might as well have been on the moon for all the signs of life. The pegasuses carried on, but their heads were low.

"I wish I had an extra-large soda," Angie rasped.

"With double ice," I added.

"I'd settle for a garden hose," Damian said, "and just pour it over my head."

Argenta stumbled and then righted herself. I looked down at the ground. "Hey, there's shrubbery." It was the first sign of a living thing, other than gadflies and manticores.

The animals picked up the pace, and we sat up, anxiously searching the darkness for any sign of water.

Angie stopped. "Wait, do you hear that?"

We listened. Crickets. Unmistakably singing their nightly song.

Crickets meant more bushes, which meant water nearby.

Ahead of us dark outlines of trees appeared, and then a flicker of light sparkled on a body of water.

"Please don't be my imagination," I whispered through cracked lips.

"Last one in is a rotten hydra's egg!" Angie spurred Nero on.

Argenta didn't need any prodding. We raced across the hardened earth past bushes that grew thicker onto grass, then past trees, until we were at the edge of a large lake. The pegasuses didn't stop—they ran straight in, burying their noses in the water. We dropped down, immersing ourselves in the coolness, scooping up handfuls of the fresh water until I thought my stomach was going to burst. Then I lay back, floating, letting the cool water soothe my burned skin and take the sting out of the bites. I pressed my fingers to the tender spot where the manticore's claws had pierced my skin around my shoulders. The crusted blood rinsed away, leaving three small puncture wounds. *Could have been worse*, I thought. *Could have been my whole head.*

Damian stood up, shaking water from his head. "Now that felt good." He reached down, digging into the mud, and pulled up a handful, rubbing it on his arms. I tried it, and immediately the stinging felt better.

We sloshed onto shore, slathering mud everywhere, then lay back on the grass. Damian rustled in his bag and pulled out three more granola bars. They were squished, and the chocolate chips had melted, but it was the best thing I had ever tasted in my life.

I stood and went to Argenta, running my hand over her wing. She shuddered a bit as I rubbed the joint where her wing met her shoulder. The good news was nothing seemed to be broken. "You just need to rest." I let her go back to grazing on the thick grass that grew along the shoreline. Turning, I looked out over the water. In the center of the lake, a dark land mass waited. There were no lights, no sign of life.

"Is that it?" I asked as Damian joined me.

"I think so. I mean, I can't be sure."

"It has to be," Angie said, joining us. "Why else would someone send those gadflies after us unless we were getting close?"

"True."

"Let's get some sleep," Damian said. "We'll figure a way onto the island in the morning."

We nestled down in the soft grass. The mud dried on my skin, caking off in chunks, but the stinging was gone. I stared up at the stars. They were unfamiliar to me, a different sky than I was used to seeing. I'm sure Damian could have pointed out all the constellations, but he was too busy snoring.

"You awake, Katzy?" Angie asked softly.

I turned on my side. She was staring up at the sky "Yeah, what's up?"

"Nothing. I'm just thinking."

"About?"

"My mom."

Oh. Angie never talked about her mom. "She's in Florida a lot," I ventured.

"Yeah. It's not a vacation though."

"What do you mean?"

Her eyes closed, then opened. "She's got issues."

"Oh." I waited to see what she would say.

Her voice, when she spoke, was raw. "There's a clinic there. She's getting help."

I thought a moment. "Is that why you knew what to do with Athena?"

She nodded, her eyes bright.

"I'm sorry."

"It's okay." She sniffed. "She swears this time it will stick."

"That's good."

"Yeah. She says it every time, but maybe this time it will." She sounded wistful. I ached to make it better for her, but I didn't know what to say.

"You okay?" I finally asked.

"Yeah."

"Wanna talk about it?"

But Angie's eyes had drifted shut, and she was asleep

I watched her, wondering what it was like to have a mother, even one that had problems. I'd never known that feeling. I rolled onto my back, staring up at the stars. Somewhere out there my brother was making his way toward me. All I had to do was be in the right place at the right time, and I could save him.

And then, maybe, my mother would look at me and be proud.

I went to sleep on that thought.

CHAPTER 12

Something loud snapped, waking me. I rolled over. The sun was just making its way over the horizon, spreading pink and yellow across the sky. A morning mist shrouded the island where we hoped to find the Garden of the Hesperides. I'd spent half the night scratching at my gadfly bites, and my eyes were gritty from lack of sleep. Angie and Damian were both out cold. Even the pegasuses had laid down, exhausted by the long ride across the desert.

I sat up warily. Something was moving in the bushes. Maybe the manticore I'd set fire to was stalking us. Shaking Angie awake, I put a finger over my mouth. She nudged Damian. He sat up as I got to my feet, drawing a lightning bolt.

"Show yourself, whoever you are."

The bushes rattled louder as crunching footsteps sounded. I gripped the bolt like a baseball bat, ready to swing it, when a strapping young man emerged, dusty and bleeding from scratches across his chest. Long brown hair was tied back in a ponytail, revealing an angular face and square jaw worthy of a movie star. A manticore barb stuck out of his right arm. He fell facedown at our feet and didn't move.

Hercules at last.

I let the lightning bolt die out, and we quickly rolled him over. His bow and quiver were slung over his shoulder. His chest was bare except for leather straps that criss-crossed it, holding several weapons in place, including a heavy golden sword at his side. He wore a thigh-length loin cloth that revealed well-muscled quads, as if the guy ran a marathon every day.

"He's got one of those manticore stingers in his arm," Damian said. The swelling on his face had gone down, and he no longer looked like an ogre.

"Well, pull it out," I said.

When he hesitated, Angie shoved him aside. "I'll do it." She gripped it and slowly eased it out. The shaft was about six inches long and thick as a pencil. The barbed tip caught on his flesh. He groaned, and then it slid free.

I put my hands on his skin. His body was flushed and hot. "We need to cool him down."

It took all three of us to drag his hulking body into the water. Damian held his legs, and Angie and I kept his head above the surface. After a few minutes, his eyes fluttered open.

I waved at him. "Hey there, Hercules. Welcome back."

"Am I dead?" He blinked at us. "Is this the underworld?"

For a son of Zeus, he wasn't very bright. I pointed upward. "See that big yellow thing in the sky? That's the sun, so definitely not the underworld."

He closed his eyes. "Leave me then. I'm not fit to live." His face sank under the water.

"Oh, no you don't." Angie and I hauled him back up. He tried to fend us off, arms flailing at the water, but even though he was big, he was weak from the manticore sting. We managed to drag his upper body onto shore.

He began to sob then, great heaving sobs that shook his whole body.

"Oy, knock it off," Angie said. "You're giving me a headache."

The sobs petered off, and he accepted help when we hoisted him by the shoulders and walked him over to a grassy patch, where he collapsed. "Who are you?" He eyed each of us with suspicion. "Guardians of the sacred garden?"

"Not exactly," I said.

His eyes narrowed. "But you know my name?"

I tried flattery. "Come on, everyone's heard of the great Hercules. You're pretty famous."

"I'm not famous at all." He frowned, squinting at me. "I've seen you before." His eyes widened. "You were leaving Nemea as I arrived. You were there too," he said, looking at Angie. "And you," he said to Damian. "It's you three who have cursed me. I was supposed to be a great hero, but when I got to Nemea, there was no lion to slay. They said the prince struck it down before my arrival, but a servant told me it was a daughter of Zeus and her friends." He sniffed the air. "Hah, I can smell the lightning on you. Deny it all you want, but it was you."

"It's not what it looks like," I said, but his eyes flashed angrily.

"No? Then how come when I went to the swamps of Lerna, it was only to find the rotting carcass of the hydra? Are you saying that wasn't you?"

I flushed guiltily. "Sorry, it wasn't personal. We had our reasons."

His handsome brow furrowed. "Reasons? Like what? What did I ever do to you?"

"Nothing. We're family—we both have Zeus as a father. I'm just trying to save my brother. My real brother," I added.

"Am I not real?" He thumped his chest with one fist.

"No, you're just, like, half, and there's a lot of you out there. I have a real brother named Perseus."

"Never heard of him," he scoffed.

"That's because like you, he's not famous yet. But one day he will be. If he doesn't get turned into stone," I muttered under my breath.

Hercules rose, swaying slightly. "I think I'll be leaving now."

"Where are you going?" I asked as we scrambled to our feet.

"You've stolen my first two trials. I can only assume you are here to steal the next two, so I might as well give up now." He unstrapped his sword and let it fall in the dirt, added his bow to it, then started to walk back into the brush.

I jumped in front of him. "You can't give up. Come on, you're Hercules."

"She's right," Damian said. "You have to complete these tasks or terrible things will happen."

"Terrible things have already happened," he said with a pained look. "And I have made no progress to atone for them. It is time I surrendered to the Erinyes and allowed them to serve justice and throw me into the pits of Tartarus so I suffer for eternity."

"Hold on—no one's calling up those Erinyes," I said. "You can't give up."

"I already did." He stepped around me and walked away.

"Coward," I called.

He froze. "What did you call me?"

"You heard me. Herk-A-Jerk's a coward. That's why you didn't kill the Nemean lion. You were probably too scared to go into that arena, so you waited till we took care of it."

He spun around, an outraged look on his face. "I did not. I'm not a coward."

Angie jumped in. "Really? Then how come you were too busy hiding in the bushes to help us kill the hydra?"

His face turned red as he glared at us. "Hiding? I wasn't even there. I had to return to the city of Tiryns to receive my new labor. By the time I arrived in Lerna, the hydra was a rotting corpse being pecked over by carrion birds."

"So you're not a coward," Angie said.

"No, I told you that."

"Then why are you running away?" I asked.

He blinked, looking between us, and then his shoulders sagged. "Because I can never atone for what I did. Not really."

"Come on, what could you have done that's so bad?" I punched him lightly on his good arm.

"Er, Phoebe." Damian cleared his throat as Herk started to sob again. "It was pretty bad."

"What do you mean?"

"The story is that he was enchanted and murdered his own family."

Yikes.

"But if he was enchanted, it wasn't his fault. Herk—come on—we all make mistakes. Look at me, I almost destroyed Olympus. Things happen, and the only way to make them better is to fix things. We need you to get back on track."

He whirled on me. "Why do you care so much? And don't say it's because I'm your not-real brother—I won't believe you."

"Look, we have it on good word from an oracle that, in fact, you do become a great hero," I said.

A flicker of hope made him step closer. "What oracle?"

"Her name is Miss Carole," Damian said. "When you complete all your labors, your story inspires people for generations to come. If you give up now, then there will be no great hero to inspire the legends. No one will remember any of this ever happened. The gods themselves could just vanish into the mists of the unknown."

His eyes grew wide with astonishment. "All because I quit?"

Damian nodded.

Hercules slumped down on a fallen log. "That's a lot to think about."

"Look, we're not here to steal your labors," I said. "The nymphs have something we need to save my brother. We'll help you any way we can and then be on our way."

He stared up at me suspiciously. "Do you mean that? You won't steal my labors away for yourself?"

"Pinkie swear." I stuck my small finger out.

He frowned at it, then wrapped it in his much larger one. "Pinkie swear." His stomach let out a loud rumble, and he sighed. "I could eat half an ox right now."

"Damian, got any more granola bars in that bag of yours?"

He rustled in his satchel and pulled one out. "Last one."

"Let Herk-A-Jerk—I mean my brother Herk here have it."

Hercules eyed the bar in wonder, sniffing it before tasting it, then shoved the whole thing in his mouth. "By the gods, that tastes delicious," he said with his mouth full. "What do you call it?"

"Peanut butter chocolate chip granola bar," I said.

Hercules stood, stretching his arms out, then took a length of leather and tied it around the wound on his bicep. He strapped his sword on and checked that all his weapons were in place, then slung his bow and quiver of arrows around his shoulders. When he was done, he struck a pose with his hands on his hips, looking every inch a demigod.

"Let the third and fourth labors of Hercules begin," he announced. With that, he dove into the water and started swimming toward the island.

CHAPTER 13

We quickly gathered our things and made to follow Herk, but Argenta pranced into the water, prepared to swim across with us. I stepped in front of her. "Not you, Argenta. You have to stay here with the other pegasuses. Your wing is still healing."

She pushed forward, backing me up, but I held my ground. "Please," I added, resting my forehead against hers. "I need you to get better. We'll be fine."

With a snort, she backed away, going back to the tender grass and pulling up great clumps of it, eyeing me with disdain.

Damian waited at the edge of the water, chewing on his thumb as he stared at the island just visible through the wisps of fog. He had that nervous look about him, like when we were up on the cliff and he'd frozen.

"Don't tell me you can't swim," I said. "Your parents are marine biologists."

A flush colored his caramel skin. "I can swim. I . . . it's just . . . I don't like deep water." He gingerly followed me in until we were waist deep.

"I'll be right here." I had Calypso's bag across my body so we would have something to store the apples and helmet in once we stole them.

"And I'll be here," Angie said from the other side. She had her hunting knife strapped to her thigh. With her golden headband and belted tunic, she looked like a goddess herself. "If you need something, just holler."

Hercules was already several lengths in front of us. Damian took a deep breath and then lowered himself into the water. He swam like a frog, keeping his head high and gulping in great gasps of air with every stroke. The sun grew higher, and the mist shrouding the island slowly lifted. Thick green foliage came into view, growing right up to the edge of the water, as if even the plants were warning us to stay away. There was no sign of a beach, and the water remained deep all the way up to the edge of the island.

Hercules levered himself up and stomped on the thick plants, breaking off the stalks to make a small landing area. With one arm, he reached down and hauled us up by our scruffs as though we weighed as much as a sack of flour.

We wrung out our clothes and put our boots back on, then followed Hercules into the interior of the island. Rubbery plants with broad green leaves grew underfoot, and tall skinny trees vied for sunlight. Green vines tangled themselves around the trunks, draping down from branches and making the way forward difficult. Hercules used his sword to clear a path.

"I get the feeling they don't get many visitors," Angie grumbled. One eye was still swollen from the gadfly bites, and red spots covered her face, as if she had a case of the measles.

"Hey, Herk, how do you know we're going the right way?" I asked.

"I never get lost," Hercules said over his shoulder. "It's one of my gifts, and it tells me we are approaching the garden. We must be quiet—we don't want Ladon to warn the nymphs of our approach." He moved on, hacking at the vines blocking our way.

"Damian, I don't think you've told us much about this apple-tree-guarding dragon," I said softly.

A funny look came over his face, and he laughed nervously. "Huh, that's funny. I thought I did."

I stopped, grabbing him by the arm. "Spill it. What has it got, nineteen heads like the hydra?"

"No." He gulped. "But it's funny you mention it. They're related."

"And?" Angie said.

"And it has a lot of heads." Damian held up a finger. "Doesn't grow them back though, so that's good. I'm not even sure it's a real dragon—it has a snake body that coils around the tree. I can't wait to see it."

"Damian, how many heads?" I pressed.

"Er." He bit down on his thumb.

"I swear if you don't tell me right now—"

"A hundred, okay?"

I blinked, trying to take that in. "But we can still kill it, right?"

He checked to see if Hercules was listening, but wonder boy was hacking at an impenetrable wall of vines.

"Hercules killed it with a single arrow he shot over the wall," he said quietly.

I relaxed. "Okay, then. He's got his bow, so we'll be fine."

With a final slash, Hercules cut through the mass of vines and stuck his head through. "I see the wall of the garden ahead," he announced.

We stepped out of the jungle into a clearing where, thankfully, the vines and shrubs thinned out to a few scattered trees. Before us, a solid line of plastered stone ran in a curved direction, encircling whatever was inside. I could make out a massive tree somewhere in the center. Glints of gold sparkled among its leaves.

The golden apples Herk needed for his quest.

Relief filled me. All we had to do was find a way in, knock off a hundred-headed dragon-snake, and steal some apples and an invisibility helmet, and we'd be on our way to finding Perseus.

We stopped at the base of the wall and looked up. Herk was tall, but even if I stood on his shoulders, I wouldn't be able to see over the top.

I turned to Damian. "So, what's the plan?"

"Hercules just needs to shoot his arrow over the wall, and it will strike the serpent and kill it," he said.

There was silence, and then Angie snorted. "That's the dumbest thing I've ever heard. How is he supposed to aim?"

Damian flushed. "Look, mythology skips over a lot of parts, and there are dozens of different versions of the same story. Obviously, to shoot over the wall, he must have been able to see Ladon. So there has to be an opening."

"Right," I said. "All we have to do is find it. Let's split up. Herk, you're with me. Angie, Damian, scout that direction. Whistle if you find the gate."

Truth be told, I wanted a little alone time with this half-brother of mine. Herk had already stridden off, and I hurried to catch up.

I fell into step next to him. "So, Herk, what do you think of Pops?"

He glanced sideways at me. "Pops?"

"Zeus."

"Oh, I really haven't spent any time with him. Hera doesn't like me much."

"Hera's the queen of the gods."

"They fight a lot. She's very jealous."

We walked a few more paces, and then I asked the hard question. "What made you . . . you know . . ."

"You mean why did I destroy my entire family?" He stopped, and his head hung low.

"I'm sorry." I put a hand on his arm. "I shouldn't have brought it up."

"No, it's okay. I was traveling in Argos when I received news my wife's father, the king of Thebes, was killed by a man named Lycus. Lycus claimed his crown and was going to have my wife and children executed, so I rushed back and did to him what he had done to my father-in-law."

"So you saved your family."

His face darkened. "Yes. And then in the midst of rejoicing, I took my bow and . . ." He shook his head. "It doesn't matter. If Athena hadn't arrived and knocked me out, I'd have probably destroyed the entire city, such was my madness."

"Athena has a habit of arriving at just the right moment." We started walking again. The wall ran in an endless line with no break in sight. I was beginning to think there was no gate when a whistle trickled in the air.

"That's Angie," I said. "Come on, they must have found something."

We jogged back along the wall until Angie and Damian came into sight.

They stood in front of a wrought-iron gate made of aged bronze inset into the wall in an arch shape. The metal was intricately carved with leaves twined around the bars. I pressed in next to them and peered in. Dappled light filtered through the trees onto a lush green lawn with scattered flower beds.

The apple tree was impossible to miss. It rose three stories tall in the center of the garden, with thick leafy branches fanning out. Glints of golden fruit caught the sunlight. The trunk appeared to be a living thing, all diamond patterns sliding in different directions. No, that wasn't right. The trunk wasn't alive. It was a snake coiled around it several times. Dark shapes moved in and out of the branches above, briefly visible.

Two women with white-blond hair tended to some flowers across the clearing. Another appeared, and all three laughed at something. The last nymph I'd met had been on the unfriendly side, so I wasn't expecting these to be helpful or welcoming. The good news was there was a clear line of sight between the gate and the trunk where that squirming snake body was completely exposed.

I yanked Herk closer. "There's your target." I pointed at the trunk. "All you have to do is shoot your arrow into it. One shot and the first deed is done."

Herk took his bow and notched an arrow to it. "These arrows have been tipped in poison I milked from the hydra's rotting carcass." He put two fingers to the bow-string and tried to draw it back, then grunted in pain, lowering the bow.

"What's wrong?" I asked.

"My arm is weak from the manticore sting. Let me try again." He held up the bow, pulling back until his arm quivered with the effort, but the string was too taut, and he lowered it again. "I am ashamed. I am too weak. I will throw myself into the fiery pits of Tartarus as punishment."

"Stop with the fiery pits," I said. "I've been to the underworld—it's not a fun experience, and you'll lose that tan of yours. We'll find another way to kill Ladon and get you those apples."

Herk's shoulders sagged. "I can't receive any help or else my trial will be null, and I'll be back to where I started."

"We won't help you. We'll just strategize, like this: Damian, any ideas?"

Genius boy studied the gate, pulling on it with both hands. "I've tried opening it, but there's no latch."

Angie sighed. "You guys think too much." She put her fingers to her lips and whistled shrilly. "Hey there, girls! I've got a handsome man for you."

"Angie, are you crazy?" I hissed, but it was too late. The three nymphs stopped what they were doing, looks of surprise on their faces at the sight of our group behind the gate.

Angie waved. "Ladies, over here. This guy is single and ready to mingle." She elbowed Hercules. "Flex." She demonstrated when he looked confused.

"Oh, like this?" He raised his arms, clenching his fists, and his biceps rose up like mountains.

The three nymphs whispered to each other, then drifted closer.

"What brings you to the Garden of the Hesperides?" the closest one asked. "It is forbidden to enter here." Her eyes were oversized and a bright cornflower blue. She reminded me of a porcelain doll with her flawless pale skin and tiny nose.

"Hermes sent us," I said.

At the mention of Hermes, she stepped closer, her eyes lighting with excitement. "You have spoken to Hermes? Did he mention me?"

"Er, maybe, what was your name?" I asked.

"I am Hesper. These are my sisters, Aegle and Erythea." Hesper looked to be the oldest of the three and the spokes-nymph of the group.

"Hesper, yes! He said you were his favorite, right, Angie?"

Angie nodded quickly. "He went on and on about how beautiful you were. Couldn't get him to shut up."

"I thought I was his favorite," Aegle pouted, folding her arms. She had braided flowers in a crown around her head.

"No, I was. He told me so right there under the apple tree." Erythea's face softened at the memory. Her eyes were the same blue as her sister's, but she'd painted her lids with blue shadow to make them look even bigger.

"Hush," Hesper scolded, then fixed her gaze on me. "Tell us what it is you want."

"We need Hades's helmet—the one that makes you invisible. Hermes said you might have it here."

Hesper's face grew wary. "For what purpose do you need it?"

"It's not for us. It's for my brother. He's been tasked with slaying Medusa. We need the helmet so she can't see him and turn him into a rock."

Hesper drew nearer. "Being invisible won't save you from the claws and fangs of her two sisters. They'll tear you to pieces, and then we will have lost our most precious item."

"The helmet belongs to Hades," I reminded her.

"And he entrusts us with it," she said coolly.

"Who is this with you?" the one named Aegle asked, idling closer and slyly eyeing Herk.

"He's handsome," the one named Erythea cooed, eyeing him up and down.

"This hunk is Hercules," I said. "Herk, say hello."

"Hello," he mumbled, sounding glum as could be. Not much of a ladies' man, my brother.

"Look, if we could just come in and talk about it," I began, but Hesper shook her head.

"No, it is not allowed." But the gate popped open by some invisible force. She whirled on her sisters. "Aegle, Erythea, no!"

Aegle elbowed her aside. "You're not the boss around here. We're bored." She grabbed Herk by the hand and dragged him inside the gardens.

We hurriedly followed as the gate started to swing shut. Angie subtly tipped a small rock over with her boot, wedging it in the opening so the gate didn't close all the way.

"Fine, we will share a meal, and then you will go." Hesper's eyes were like ice. She didn't want us here, which was too bad. Things were going to get a lot worse when she realized what we were really after.

Aegle fell into step with Herk, hooking her arm in his and eyeing him with adoring eyes. Erythea hooked hers in his other arm, and both chattered away, not minding at all that Herk didn't say anything. He was kind of a stick in the mud—but given what he'd done to his family, I guess I could understand.

Insects hummed, and the air was heavily scented with a fruity smell. There weren't just apples growing but fruit trees of all kinds. We passed apricot trees, peach trees, pear trees—their branches all groaning with fruit. A stand of olive trees held fruit the size of large plums. Goats wandered about, chewing idly on the grass. Pebble-lined paths led deeper into the gardens. We entered into the shade under the boughs of the apple tree. Up close, the diamond pattern of the snake was green and brown, making it blend well with the tree. Its body wasn't as big as Python, who had been the size of a subway train, but it was still too big to wrap my arms around it.

The body never stopped rotating around that trunk, like a barber pole that spun endlessly, splitting into dozens of smaller necks when it reached the branches and twining into them. The base of the tree was encircled by shrubs, so it was impossible to see where Ladon's body ended. I'd expected a dragon to have a squatty body and wings. Maybe this thing was harmless—Herk had supposedly killed it with a single arrow. I relaxed, and then one green serpent head suddenly struck up at the sky, snapping its jaws around a passing bird before sinking back into the tree again.

Not so harmless.

"If Herk can't draw his bow, how is he going to kill that thing?" I whispered to Damian.

"I don't know."

"I can always send some lightning at it."

"That would defeat the purpose. Hercules has to do it unassisted."

"Then you better think of something fast."

CHAPTER 14

Hesper led us to a wooden table under the boughs of the giant apple tree. The nymphs didn't seem bothered by the presence of hungry snakes hovering directly over our heads. A constant slithering noise and the rustling of leaves kept us eyeing the branches warily. A large mound rose up behind the tree, but thick shrubbery and a small cottage built of stone masked whatever it was. The two love-struck nymphs fought over who was going to sit next to Herk and ended up taking a seat on either side of him. Damian, Angie, and I sat opposite them. Hesper disappeared into the cottage.

Could they be keeping Hades's helmet in there? I turned my head, trying to sense it the way I'd felt Hermes's lyre in Julia's locker. Surely an item that belonged to the lord of the underworld would give off huge power vibes, but I felt nothing.

The nymph emerged a few minutes later holding two platters of food and a basket of bread. "Aegle, plates for our guests, please." Aegle swiftly ducked inside. A cupboard creaked open, and a sudden wave of power washed over me.

Bingo.

Crockery rattled as she grabbed plates, and then the throb of power was cut off.

The helmet was in the cupboard where they kept the dishes. All we had to do was distract the nymphs long enough to find it. I nudged Angie with my foot, jerking my chin at the cottage and casually running a hand over the top of my head.

Angie nodded her understanding as Aegle returned with the plates and doled them out. Hesper set the platters down in the center of the table. The first was piled with fruit from the garden. The second held sliced cheese and dried meat. The bread basket was filled with thick slices of brown bread still warm from the oven.

"Come, let us eat," Hesper said. "And then you can be on your way."

Aegle giggled at us as we attacked the platters of food. Herk speared half the dried meat with one stab of his fork. We made makeshift sandwiches with the thick bread. Herk finished his second sandwich and started a third before I'd gotten halfway through my first. As we ate, the leaves continued to rustle overhead as the snake endlessly wound around the trunk. Strangely, I thought I heard whispers in the trees, as if the snake heads were having a conversation.

"Eat them."

"No, we mustn't."

"Sssso hungry."

I shifted in my seat, eyeing the branches. "Does it bother you being this close to all those snakes?"

Hesper raised an eyebrow. "Bother us? Ladon is a wonderful pet and amusing company."

"He tells the best jokes." Aegle batted her eyes at Herk, but the guy was too busy eating to notice.

"What's so special about an apple tree?" Angie asked Hesper, taking a bite out of a giant apricot. Orange-colored juice dribbled down her chin.

"It was a gift from Mother Earth herself, Gaia, to Hera on her wedding day. The apples it produces are sacred."

"Sacred how?" Angie wiped the juice away with the back of her hand. "I mean, an apple a day keeps the doctor away, but it doesn't make you immortal."

The nymphs went still, even the two simpering sisters.

I straightened in my seat, suddenly curious. "Damian, what is it that they do?"

He put his sandwich down, brow furrowed. "I'm not really sure. There's not much written about the golden apples beyond the fact they belonged to Hera and she refused to share them with anybody."

"But it's possible they grant you immortality?" I asked.

"Possibly, though you'd probably have to eat more than one."

"Immortality? For real? I need me one of those." Angie stood, eying the branches for low-hanging fruit, but I yanked her back into her seat at the malevolent look in Hesper's eyes.

"No one can take of the fruit except Hera, or they will face certain death," the nymph said coldly, then switched subjects. "Tell me why it is you wish to face the gorgons."

"I don't." I reached for the last slice of cheese, but Angie snapped it up before I could grab it. "It's my brother. He's been challenged to bring back the head of Medusa."

The nymphs looked shocked. "Is he a child, like you?" Erythea asked.

"Yes—my twin, actually."

"Then you are both as good as dead," Hesper said waspishly. "Being invisible will not protect you from the lethal claws of her sisters, Euryale and Stheno, both of whom are immortal. Medusa is the least powerful of the three, and even she can turn you to stone with a single glance."

"Not if she can't see me. Please, we have to try."

"And how will you remove her head?" Hesper challenged. "She is like stone herself. There is only one blade in this world strong enough to remove it."

"Yeah, so we heard." I popped a fat grape in my mouth, savoring the burst of flavor. "The Argus Slayer is on our list. Hermes said he lost it in a card game."

"Did he say to whom?" Hesper asked.

I shook my head. "Only that the guy had a head for cards."

"Three, to be exact. Geryon is a three-headed monstrosity who lives on an island of red earth in the far west. He uses the Argus Slayer to guard his flocks of cattle, along with a two-headed dog named Orthus."

"We'll just have to make him see reason," I said. "We can be very persuasive." *Or we could steal it*, I added silently, *once we have, say, an invisibility helmet.*

Hesper leaned forward, speaking quickly. "Even if you were to gain the Argus Slayer, you would still have to find the lair of the gorgons and get past Stheno and Euryale, who will protect Medusa with everything they have, so no." She sat back, folding her arms. "We have earned Hades's trust these many years by keeping his helmet safe. Just like Hera trusts us to guard her apples. We have never let her down, nor will we ever."

"Er, that's not exactly true," Damian said, holding up a finger.

She swiveled her head to glare at him. "What do you mean?"

He shrugged. "As I recall, the whole reason Ladon is

here is because you were caught helping yourself to some of the fruit."

Her face turned a shade of scarlet. "That is a lie. Hera gave us Ladon as a pet to keep us company."

Aegle and Erythea remained silent, staring down at their plates, but I could feel their guilt hanging like a cloud over them.

"A talking snake with a hundred heads sounds like the perfect mole," I said. "You guard the tree from outsiders, and it guards the tree from you. You could silence one snake head, but ninety-nine of them?"

Hesper's voice trembled with fury. "Hera knows we would never steal from her."

This was fun, getting under her skin. I figured if I annoyed her enough, she'd give us the helmet just to get rid of us. "Admit it, she doesn't trust you. How can she ever be sure? There are thousands of apples on that tree. I could pocket one right now, and you would never even know it."

Hesper rose from her seat, twin spots of color on her cheeks as she placed her hands on the table and leaned down so her face was inches from mine. "Do not consider taking one—not a leaf off the tree, not a twig—or we will know, and you will face the consequences."

A whisper of noise brushed against my skin, as if something was moving above me. I looked up in time to see the diamond-shaped head of a snake lowering itself over my head. Others hovered over Angie, Damian, and Herk. It opened its jaws, revealing twin sets of fangs. I shoved my chair back, calling up a lightning bolt in my hand, while Herk swiftly wrapped one around his arm like a coil of rope, ready to strangle it.

"Stop!" Hesper called.

I kept the bolt ready but didn't use it.

"You are a daughter of Zeus," Hesper said, eyeing my lightning.

"Yes, and Herk here is my brother. Zeus will be angry if your pet eats two of his children."

She hesitated and then jerked her head. "Ladon, retreat."

"But misssstress," the snake in front of me whispered in an oily voice, its tongue darting out as it eyed me hungrily. "Ladon is hungry."

"Sssso hungry," the other heads sang in unison.

She snapped her fingers at it, and the snakes sighed, and then their sinuous bodies drew back up into the tree.

"I suggest you leave now," Hesper said, "or next time I will let Ladon feast until there is nothing left but a pile of bones."

"We're not leaving until we get what we came for. Give us Hades's helmet, and we'll be on our way."

"Sister, when do I slay this Ladon and steal the apples?" Herk the Jerk whispered loudly.

There was stunned silence, and then Hesper's face twisted into a mask of rage.

"Ladon, kill!" she screeched.

Dozens of snakes dropped out of the trees. My first swing severed eight heads, dropping them down on the table in big squelching splats as the heads continue to snap.

Hesper screamed at my attack as Aegle and Erythea dove under the table.

"Angie, Damian, find the helmet. Kitchen cupboard near the plates." They ducked low, running for the door of the stone cottage while I swung my lightning bolt at the snakes.

"Hercules, some help here!" I swung harder as more and more heads appeared. Herk grabbed five snakes around the necks, swiftly tying them in a knot, and then did it again, but they were quickly surrounding us.

"Herk, you need to kill this thing, not tie it in bows."

He drew his golden sword and joined me in slicing at them. "But how? I can't draw my bow."

"Then I guess you'll have to cut off all hundred heads."

"Fine. My blade is strong and my arm steady. Step aside, sister. I can't have any help."

At that moment, the snake heads whipped back up into the tree, leaving us alone.

"What just happened?" I asked.

"It must be scared of me. Ladon, you coward, come face me!" Herk crouched, his sword held in front of him.

Where is Hesper? My eyes darted about the clearing. Her two sisters continued to cower under the table, but the head nymph had disappeared. I spotted a flash of white in the shrubbery by the large mound. She held a brass skeleton key. The bushes parted, and I could see a chain with a padlock around a thick scaly leg.

"Herk, we have to go."

"No. Not until I kill this beast."

I dragged him backward by his leather chest straps. As we got out from under the tree, we stopped in our tracks at the most amazing sight. The snake heads were all thrust high into the sky, and then they began to twist, braiding themselves together like a giant Twizzler.

When all the necks were entwined, Ladon began unwinding its body from the tree trunk. As it uncoiled, the mound behind the tree grew, like the neck was disappearing inside it. The many heads fused together to form one big head, which flattened and widened, its eyes hooded under fearsome scaly brows. Twin nostrils snorted as it opened jaws lined with needlelike teeth.

And then the mound moved.

Holy guacamole. Ladon had transformed from a hundred-headed snake to a Sherman tank. It was low to the ground and squatty, with well-muscled thighs, taloned toes, and a thick scaly chest.

It bellowed loud as a foghorn and stomped forward, running straight at me. For a squatty lizard tank, it moved fast. Herk stood staring at it, his jaw hanging slightly open.

"Herk, we gotta move it." I grabbed his arm, but he shook me off.

"No, it is time I kill him." He held his sword in his hand. "Ladon, come face your destiny, you beast."

The dragon shook his head out, snapping his jaws, and laughed in a hissing voice. "A demigod. *Yummmm.* I hear the flesh is *delicioussss.*" Ladon warily circled my brother, snapping at him as Herk swung with his sword. The beast feinted with its head, then swung its tail around, knocking Herk flat on his back.

"Herk! Watch out!"

Ladon's head came down, jaws open, ready to swallow my brother, but Herk jammed the sword in its mouth, forcing the jaws apart.

I darted in, dragging Herk backward as Ladon swung his head, trying to spit out his sword.

"Come on."

We took the nearest path into the gardens as Ladon let out a roar, stomping after us.

"Kill it already," I said as we ran.

"How? I can't draw my bow, and I've lost my sword."

"What if you stab it with a manticore stinger?"

His eyes lit up. "If it reached its heart, that might work, but I don't have any."

We ducked behind a tall cypress tree. I quickly dug into Calypso's bag, almost jabbing the deadly stinger into my palm before carefully pulling it out.

"Here. Don't drop it. I'm going to distract it while you get close enough to drive it into its heart."

He stared down at the stinger in his hands. "What if I fail?"

I gripped his arm. "Then we'll probably both be dead. Just don't, okay? Up in the tree, now."

He grinned, flexing his shoulders. "Okay. I like you, sister." He scrambled hand over hand up the trunk of the tree, disappearing into the branches.

I stepped out from behind the trunk. Ladon sat waiting, steam coming out of his fat nostrils.

So this is what it feels like being the bait.

"Another tasty demigod to pick my teeth with," he snorted, advancing on me.

I drew twin lightning bolts to my hands. "Okay, Ladon. Let me introduce you to my little friends."

He shuffled back a step at the sight of my lightning.

Two quick jabs with them and this dragon would be toast. But then Herk's labor wouldn't count—but this dumb dragon didn't know that. "I'm going to drive this one"—I twirled one bolt—"into your left eye. And this one"—I twirled the other—"into your right."

Ladon bellowed in rage and clawed forward.

"Now, Herk!"

I held the lightning, prepared to use it. Ladon opened his jaws, anticipating biting my head off, but Herk jumped out of the tree, soaring through the air like Tarzan, the manticore stinger held high. At the last second, Ladon spied him, swinging his head around to snap at him. Herk punched him in the jaw, knocking the dragon back a step, before tumbling to the ground. He was back on his feet in an instant, reaching up to drive the manticore stinger into the soft part of Ladon's chest. The dragon roared in pain, batting Herk with his head and sending him flying. It tried to claw at the stinger with its front paws but just pushed it in deeper.

It lifted its head, letting out a mournful wail, and then the head began to come apart as the neck untwined until all hundred heads were screaming in the air like banshees.

Then they dropped dead, flopping down onto the grass.

"Ladon!" Hesper screamed, flinging herself at him and gathering an armful of heads on her lap. She raised enraged eyes to glare me. "You killed our beautiful pet, and now we will kill those closest to you."

Aegle and Erythea dragged Angie and Damian forward, holding sharp blades to their necks.

"Sorry, Phoebes," Angie said. "They snuck in a back door while we were searching."

"It's okay. I got this." I still had my lightning bolts. I twirled them faster and faster until they were a blazing blur, and then I released them. They spun in a high arc across the clearing, right into the branches of the apple tree.

The nymphs all gasped in horror as the branches smoked and flames spread quickly. Hesper's features were etched with fear as she whirled on me. "You cannot burn Hera's sacred tree. Stop it now or you will suffer for eternity."

"Yeah, pretty sure that's already in the cards. I want that Helmet of Invisibility. Give it to me now or the tree burns to the ground."

"Fine." She snapped her fingers, and Erythea went running.

I looked around for Herk, but my half-brother had disappeared. Hesper was too busy alternating between wailing over her dead pet and crying over the burning tree to notice.

Erythea reappeared, hurrying across the grass and carrying a helmet in her hands.

I'm not sure what I expected, probably something bronzed and flashy like Athena's, but this was made of a dull metal like tin. A long nosepiece covered the face, but otherwise it was an ordinary-looking old helmet.

"Put the flames out now," Hesper said.

"How do I know it's not a trick?"

She took the helmet from Erythea and put it over her head, instantly vanishing from sight. The next moment I felt a whisper of air next to me, then the prick of a sharp blade at my throat.

"Put it out now or die." Hot breath fanned my face.

"Fine. Take off the helmet and let my friends go."

She pulled it off, shimmering back into view, set it on the grass, and took a step back. Angie and Damian hurried over and stood behind me.

I clapped my hands, bringing them together over my head as I shouted, *Megalo Fortuna!*"

A moment later, a rolling black cloud blotted out the sun, and a blast of thunder shook the ground. And then rain began to fall. Sprinkles at first, and then it quickly grew in intensity, pounding the ground around us with fat drops. The flames quickly died out, but not before a large branch broke free, crashing to the ground.

Hesper was busy mourning and wailing over Ladon while the other two were trying to put out the remaining flames as the rainstorm passed.

"We should hit the road," Angie said.

"Yeah, second that." We ran for the gate. Damian held it open as Herk came running from the direction of the apple tree, chased by the other two nymphs.

"Give us back those apples!" Aegle screamed.

Hesper leaped to her feet, leaving Ladon's side to give chase. Herk made it through the gate, dumping the apples in the bag I held open, and Angie slammed it shut. I jammed a lightning bolt into the lock to stop them from opening it. We took off for the opening in the vines, retracing our path. We didn't stop running until we reached the edge of the water.

Damian hesitated.

I took his hand. "Come on. I got you."

We jumped in feetfirst. He flailed his arms, sputtering, and then we set off for the other shore. We made quick work of it, spurred on by the thought of those nymphs coming after us. My feet finally touched bottom, and we climbed out of the water, wringing our clothes out as we turned to stare at the island.

Hesper stood on the shore, her fists clenched at her sides as she glared at us. A dark ring of smoke hovered over the center of the island, and we could hear the faint sound of wailing.

"That was amazing."

We turned. Herk was pacing back and forth on shore.

"I mean, that was . . . sister, how can I ever thank you?" He swept me into a bone-crushing hug before holding me at arm's length to gaze excitedly into my eyes. "You know what this means, right?"

"No."

"You have to come with me on all my labors. You're my good luck charm."

"I can't."

His face fell. "You mean won't." He released me, taking a step back.

I stepped closer, reaching for him. "No, you don't understand."

He held a hand up. "No, I do. You have a real brother, one who's not me. Never mind. I'm sorry I asked."

He picked up his bow, slinging it over his shoulders, and started to walk away, but I jumped in front of him.

"No, you do not get to walk away from me. Family means—I don't know—I'm new at this, but I think it means forgiving people even when they disappoint you. I'm sorry I can't go with you, but you got this. History doesn't lie. You're an amazing hero, Herk, so don't you forget it or me."

He wavered, and then his face broke into a smile. "Family. I like the sound of it." He swept me into another hug and then slapped Damian on the back. "You're one of the smartest people I've ever met." Damian glowed. Herk stuck his pinkie out at Angie. "Pinkie swear you won't forget me."

"Like I could," she said with a grin, gripping his pinkie with her own.

He turned back to me. "Sister, if I could have my three apples, I'll be on my way."

I reached into the bag and rummaged around until I found the globes. They were average sized and hard as a lump of gold. I held one up in the sunlight. "They're really beautiful, but what good is an apple you can't eat?"

Herk shrugged, tucking them into a pocket in his loincloth. "It wouldn't matter if they were made of manticore dung. What matters is I complete the labor, and I did, with no help from anyone."

Impulsively Phoebe threw her arms around him. "I'm sorry I called you a not-real brother. You're the best big brother I could ask for."

He hugged her back and then stepped away, his eyes suspiciously bright before turning to walk jauntily off.

"You okay, Katzy?" Angie asked at my side.

"Yeah. Remarkably so. Family is just . . . it's crazy, isn't it? You love them, hate them, are annoyed by them . . ."

"But in the end you need them."

"Yeah. I do. Let's go find Perseus."

CHAPTER 15

The pegasuses whickered happily when we returned, rubbing their noses against us. Even better, Argenta flared her wings out, preening them in the sun.

"Are you sure?" I asked.

She tossed her head, and I looked at the others. "I think they're ready to fly."

"Then what are we waiting for?" Angie hopped up on Nero's back.

Damian looked troubled, gnawing on his thumb.

"What is it, D?"

He dropped his hand. "Look, I don't want you to think I'm blaming you for what happened, so don't go ballistic on me, but burning Hera's tree was a really bad idea."

I reined in my impatience. He had told me not to get mad, so I tried. "You know I had no choice."

He sighed. "Says Phoebe Katz every single time."

"Angie, back me up here."

"The nymphoids did want to kill us," she said.

"Yes, I know that," Damian agreed. "It's just . . . Hera is really powerful, second only to Zeus."

"Who happens to be my dad," I reminded him. "So I've got an inside track there."

His face darkened. "No, you don't. Hera hates all of Zeus's children from other mothers."

I threw my hands up. "I don't need her to mother me. I've already got one who doesn't even know I exist."

"It's not that. Just listen. Hera is the one who enchanted Hercules, according to myth."

My head reeled. "Wait, are you saying Hera was the one who made him off his own family? Why would she do that? That's—"

"Twisted."

"Yeah."

"This is Greek mythology, Phoebes. The stories are not pretty. Hera was jealous."

"Okay, well, bad news for Herk, but what does that have to do with us?"

He shook his head. "I can't believe you're that dense."

"Spell it out for me."

"Y-o-u-b-u-r-n-e-d-h-e-r-s-a-c-r-e-d-t-r-e-e."

"I what?"

"You burned her tree, Katzy," Angie said. "Damian, we know that. What's your point?"

"It's her sacred tree—something she holds above almost everything besides her son."

"So who's her son?" I asked.

He sighed. "You really don't know your Greek heritage, do you?"

"Damian!"

"Ares."

Shock floored me. "Ares is her son? Why didn't you tell me? We had him sent to—"

"Tartarus."

"So she's probably not happy about that."

"You don't want a powerful goddess like Hera mad at you, Phoebes. You really don't."

"Well, too late." I got up on Argenta's back. "If you're done killing the moment, we should be leaving before the nymphs decide to come after us."

The pegasuses took a running leap, and then we were airborne. I avoided looking down at the singed tree. No one spoke as the winged horses made their way toward the distant Atlas Mountain, where we hoped to find three old ladies that shared an eye and a tooth, and with any luck, my brother. I brooded over Damian's words. I mean, how many people in this world held grudges against me? I had done nothing wrong besides being born and gifted with a few random powers. Like it was my fault I could throw lightning to burn down Hera's tree. Even if I had meant it, it wasn't as if I had a lot of choice. No matter what Damian said, my friends were more important than some stupid tree, even if the fruit did give you immortal-level powers.

My eyes grew heavy, and I laid my head on Argenta's neck, comforted by her warmth.

When I sat up, the ground below us had changed from desert to varying shades of red earth and green shrubbery. The mountain loomed large ahead of us, completely bare of vegetation, all black shale and white granite. The wind whistled past my ears as we made a pass by the front.

Down below us, a small figure in a white tunic walked boldly toward an opening in the side of the mountain.

"Is that Perseus?" I asked.

"It has to be," Angie said, riding up next to me.

"What an idiot. He's not even trying to be subtle."

Then my heart dropped as I spotted something else. A manticore was crouched behind a pile of rocks, just waiting for my brother to come closer. He was walking right into a trap!

"Perseus!" I shouted, but the wind carried my voice away.

He couldn't see the ugly troll-faced lion with the scorpion tail waiting to tear him to pieces.

I sent Argenta into a dive, shouting his name again, but we weren't fast enough. The manticore leaped out from behind the rocks and landed on Perseus. I tried to raise my arm, to throw a lightning bolt at it, but I couldn't do anything, couldn't lift my arm, as if my limbs were mired in molasses. I struggled, fighting it, and then cold water splashed on my face.

"Wake up, Katzy."

I shouted, fighting back, and managed to land a blow on Damian's cheek before I woke up.

"What happened? Where am I?" I was lying on hard stony ground, looking up at my friends.

"We're here. At the base of the cave. You fell asleep on Argenta, and we couldn't wake you."

"I was dreaming," I said. "It was so real. Perseus was here. There was a manticore waiting to jump him. I tried, but I couldn't reach him, and the manticore attacked him."

"Perseus is fine," Damian said.

I scrambled to my feet. "How do you know that? It could have been an omen. He could be in danger. He could he dead. He could be—"

"Standing right here," a cocky voice said. A voice I had heard once before.

I spun around and saw the slight boy with a ragged sheaf of hair that fell over his forehead. He had the same chin as me, and his eyes were a paler version of my own. I stepped forward and flung my arms around him.

"Perseus, you're okay."

"I'm fine." He disentangled himself and stepped back, looking wary. "You're the one from the marketplace."

"Yes. We were chased by those boys."

"I remember it well." His eyes grew dark. "I was thrown in prison because of it. After Polydectes left my house, he sent men to arrest me for assaulting his son."

"I'm sorry."

"You should be. If you had just minded your own business, none of this would have happened. He's going to have me executed unless I bring him back the head of the gorgon Medusa."

"We know. That's why we're here. To help you."

"Help me?" Anger flashed in his eyes. "Thanks to you there's no one to protect my mother."

"Hey, she's my mother too," I said, matching his anger.

His eyes grew wide. "What lie is this?"

"You're my brother. My twin brother."

"You lie." He took a step back, his eyes moving between us. "You're the ones Athena warned me about."

"Athena? You spoke to her?"

"She told me strangers would spin a story to distract me from my purpose and not to listen."

"She did not," I said hotly.

"She said you were reckless."

Well, that part is probably true.

"And that if I wanted to live I should stay far away from you."

"Athena would never say that."

Damian cleared his throat. "Just what else did Athena tell you?"

Perseus's eyes were suspicious. "I'm not going to tell you."

"Did she tell you not to look at Medusa or you would be turned to stone?"

"No."

"Did she give you her shield to reflect Medusa's gaze?"

"No. She gave me a sword to cut her head off, not that it's any of your business. That's all I need." He patted the small sword that hung from a makeshift rope belt at his side.

"Let me see it," I said.

He put a hand over it defensively. "No, I'm not giving it to you."

"Yes, you are." I grabbed for it, but he stepped back.

"No, it's mine. Athena gave it to me."

"Damian, please tell my idiotic brother to let me have the blade."

"I'm not your brother," he said.

"Would you two please stop fighting!" Angie said. "You're giving me a headache."

"Can I please see it?" Damian asked.

Perseus hesitated and then drew it out and handed it to Damian.

He studied it, running his finger along the edge. "I'm not an expert on metals, but this blade doesn't seem very sharp. And the handle is loose." He jiggled the hilt. "If Athena gave this to you, it's not what I would expect."

Perseus snatched it back and put it away. "I don't need your help. So leave me to it, and you can be on your way."

"When did Athena give it to you?" I asked.

"I was leaving Seriphos when she appeared."

"Have you ever met her before?" I challenged.

"No."

"Then how do you know it was her?"

"Because she said, 'Hi, I'm Athena.'"

Was my brother a log?

"It could have been anyone," I snapped in annoyance. "Did she have her helmet or shield? Was she all bossy?"

"No, she was very friendly and helpful. She gave me this blade to cut off the gorgon's head. Maybe she didn't like you."

"Maybe I know what I'm talking about."

"Maybe you don't," he said

"Oy!" Angie said. "Can we get back on the subject?"

"Fine. How are you going to do this without Athena's shield and Hades's Helmet of Invisibility? Not to mention you need a magic bag to put the head in, unless you want to turn into a rock after you kill her."

"I'm going to find the nymphs of Hesperides after I find out where the gorgons' lair is. Athena told me what to do. I'll get the helmet from them."

"We just came from there, dum-dum." I reached into the magic bag and pulled out the helmet. "Two steps ahead of you, bro."

He stuck his hand out. "Hand it over."

I put it away. "I'm not giving you this. Or the magic bag. You can't do this without us, so face it."

His fists clenched at his sides. "If I don't return with the head of the gorgon, my mother—"

"Our mother," I corrected.

"My mother will have no one to protect her. If I had a twin, she would have told me."

"Yeah? Well, did she mention who our father is?"

"My father was a fisherman who was swept out to sea in a storm," he said. "The same one that carried us to the island of Seriphos."

"Wrong! Your father is Zeus, and your grandfather sent you and our mother away because of some stupid prophecy that predicts you're going to kill him someday."

He chewed on his lip. "How do I know you speak the truth?"

"Trust me," Angie said, "I've never met two people more annoying. You gotta be related."

Ignoring her, I took his hand and put it over my heart. "Feel that? Before we were born, we could hear each other's heartbeats. I still hear yours sometimes when I'm about to fall asleep. Has that ever happened to you?"

A strange look came over his face, and then he slowly nodded. "I always thought it was just my imagination."

"I am your sister, Perseus. Like it or not."

His eyes grew clouded. "Then where have you been?"

"That's a long story. Right now we need to focus on helping you with this gorgon."

"Fine. You can come along, but it is I who will slay the gorgon, understood?"

I shrugged. "I don't care who lops her head off as long as she doesn't turn you into stone." We turned to study the entrance. "So what's the plan?"

"I say we just walk in," Perseus said.

Angie rolled her eyes. "Is he exactly like you, or what?"

I grinned. "Perseus, Angie and Damian think it's a bad idea to just walk in. Did father grant you any special powers?"

"None that I know of. You?"

"One or two."

"Not fair."

"Hey, you got to know our mother. I was left on a bus stop."

"What's a bus stop?"

We burst into laughter.

CHAPTER 16

Inside the entrance the air was cool and dank. Water dripped from the ceiling and puddled underfoot. I carried a small lightning bolt to light our way, which Perseus was in awe of. The tunnel was tall and wide; whoever or whatever had carved it had made it large enough to drive a truck through.

"There aren't any snakes or monsters I need to be aware of, are there, Damian?" I asked as we quietly walked deeper into the mountain.

"No. At least, I don't think so."

"The Graeae only have one eye they pass between them," Perseus said. "I think if I sneak my hand in when they're blind, I can get them to pass it to me."

"That's stupid," I said. "No one would be dumb enough to hand away their only eye."

"Phoebe, that's literally what happened in the story," Damian said.

The distant sound of voices arguing made us pause.

We crept forward until the tunnel ended in a vast cavern with a large pool of water in the center.

Three gray-haired crones sat on thrones carved into the stone walls. The arms were carved in the shape of lobster claws. The crones wore shapeless gowns that hid their figures, which appeared plump and round. Their bare feet stuck out of their gowns with the gnarliest toes I'd ever seen. Long yellowed nails curved around the ends of their toes. Their feet were as shriveled and wrinkled as their faces, like pruny apples gone bad.

Two of them had their eyes shut, flapping their lips over empty gums as they argued, each of them tugging on the arm of the one in the center, who was the only one with an eye open and a tooth poking over her top lip.

"It's my turn," one said, yanking on her arm.

"No, it's mine," the other argued, yanking her back. "Give it to me."

The middle one shrugged them off, suddenly leaning forward. "Sisters, I smell something."

They stopped their arguing and sniffed the air.

"Children," the one on the left crowed. "We smell sweet children. Mother will be pleased."

"Yes, I see them," the one with the eye said, beckoning. "Come closer."

"I want to see them," the one on the left said, reaching up quickly to snatch the eyeball out of the other one's socket; with a *pop*, she pushed it into hers. She clapped her hands in delight. "How precious! Step out of the shadows, children, so that we might see you better."

"My turn," the third one said. She held her hand out, and the first one sighed, passing her the eyeball.

So Perseus was right; they did lob it around like a hot potato.

"Wait," I said as Perseus was about to step forward. "Put this on." I opened Calypso's bag and pulled out the invisibility helmet, fitting it on his head. He shimmered briefly, then disappeared.

"By Zeus, that is amazing," he whispered.

"We'll distract them while you wait your chance to get the eye, then we'll get them to tell us where Medusa's lair is."

We stepped carefully into the cavern, keeping a safe distance from the crones.

"We were passing by and thought to take shelter in the cave," I said.

"Yes, shelter. Perfectly safe to visit," the one with the eye said. "Come closer. We're quite thirsty. Perhaps you'd help these old ladies out and refill our cups for us." They rapped tin cups against their stone armrests with loud clanks.

We looked at Damian, and he shrugged. "I don't think they're dangerous."

"Stay here and keep an eye out." I nodded at Angie to follow me. I sensed Perseus at my side but couldn't see any sign of him.

We approached the thrones. The crones' hair was frizzy and gray. They were muttering among themselves and passing the eyeball back and forth as if it were a game of hot potato, each wanting to see and impatient when they didn't get it back right away. If we timed it right, we just might snag it.

"Angie and I will refill their glasses. Perseus, wait for them to pass the eye, and then grab it," I whispered.

We took the metal tumblers from them. The one in the middle had the eye. It was a strange color, cloudy gray with shades of purple. Her tooth worked her lip. "Thank you, daughter of Zeus. Your kindness will be remembered."

I froze in the act of turning away. "How did you know I was a daughter of Zeus?"

"The lightning, dear. Only children of Zeus carry lightning."

Duh, I still held the small bolt that had lit our way. Reassured, we approached the cistern. "Damian, anything else you can remember about them?"

"They were children of sea gods, I think."

I scooped the water in the cup and then hesitated, swirling it around. I took a tiny sip and spit it out. "Saltwater."

"It can't be. We're miles from the sea." Damian frowned, biting his thumb. "Unless there's an underwater channel."

I thought back on their words. "Who was their mother, Damian?"

"Why?"

"Because they said, 'Mother will be pleased.'"

His eyes widened. "Oh, that's bad."

"Why?" Angie asked. "Don't tell me she's got lots of heads."

"No . . . er . . . their mother was a sea monster. Her name was Ceto. She also had Ladon, the gorgons, and Echidna."

"Echidna? Wasn't she the mother of all those monsters we faced last time?"

He nodded.

"So she's, like, the mother of the mother of all monsters. Brilliant." I cast a glance over my shoulder. The three sisters were muttering among themselves, waiting for us to return with their cups. "Come on, grab it already," I muttered, wishing Perseus would hurry up. But the crones' hands were fast, and it wouldn't be easy to snatch.

"Come on, Angie, my brother needs our help. Damian, wait here. Keep an eye out."

We started to walk back toward the thrones when a gurgling sound made us stop and turn. Bubbles rose in the center of the cistern, and the water churned as though someone had turned on a jacuzzi. The water level rose, sloshing over the sides.

Red spikes appeared, then a scaly crustacean head with two large beady eyes on the end of thick stalks. A pair of large pincers snapped in the air as the creature's mandibles worked up and down.

The grandmother of all monsters was a giant lobster.

"Mother's here!" the crones sang, clapping with glee, swinging their feet on their stone thrones as the freakishly large lobster crawled onto the ledge. Its torso was the size of a city bus, carried along by spiny legs.

Damian stood staring up at the lobster as it snapped its pincers in the air, its stalk eyes waving from side to side as it crawled right toward him.

"Damian, move it!" I shouted.

But he was frozen in place, probably from shock. Before I could react, Angie tackled him as a deadly claw snapped the air where he'd been standing.

Angie pivoted and drove her knife into the meaty part of its pincer. It squealed in pain, waving the claw in the air.

I helped them to their feet. "Damian, what do you know about lobsters?"

"They're from the family *Nephropidae*. They have two claws—one for pinching and one for crushing."

"Something useful so I can kill it," I said.

"Um, they live at the bottom of the ocean, but, Phoebes—you can't kill it."

I groaned. "Let me guess—it's one of Herk's labors."

"No, Perseus has to face it in a few years to save the love of his life, Andromeda."

Great. "So we can't kill it. We have to scare it off."

"Use your lightning," Angie said.

"Yeah, I would, but Damian just said not to kill it."

"Not to hurt it. To scare it. It likes the dark."

Angie was right. If it lived at the bottom of the ocean, it was used to darkness. I twirled the lightning bolt, adding power to it, letting it grow in intensity until my hand tingled so badly I almost dropped it. White light filled the cavern, and the lobster screeched, its stalk eyes waving back and forth as it backed away. Blue blood dripped down onto the floor where Angie's knife stuck out of its claw.

The Graeae were cackling and shouting at each other, fighting over the eye, each wanting to see what happened.

Ceto reached the edge of the water but didn't back down, swinging her tail around in a sudden sweep that sent Damian and Angie flying. At the last second, I ducked, but I'd had enough of this crustacean. I heaved the lightning at the ceiling. Rocks tumbled down, pelting the hard shell of the lobster and finally driving it back into the water, where it slowly sank, taking Angie's knife with it.

Damian and Angie limped over. "My dad's gonna kill me," she said as the last trace of the lobster behemoth sank out of sight. "That was his favorite fishing knife."

Behind us the Graeae sisters started wailing.

"Where's the eye? Give it to me!"

"I don't have it!"

"It's gone!"

Perseus whipped the helmet off, holding the eye triumphantly in his hand. "Got it!"

They swarmed him, grabbing at his clothes and searching him. He tossed the eye to me.

"Tell us where your sisters the gorgons live," I said, "or this eye gets tossed into the water for fish food."

Their heads turned toward my voice.

"We can't tell you that," the center one whined. "They depend on us to protect them."

"Fine, fish food it is."

"No," they chorused, hands out, imploring. "Please, we can't see a thing without it." They whispered among each other and then nodded.

The one with the snaggletooth spoke. "Our sisters live at the edge of the world. Head west as far as you can, until there is nothingness, and then go even farther. There you will find an island with a black spire that rises from the endless ocean. It is there those monstrous sisters of ours dwell. Now the eye, give it back."

"How can you know it so well? Have you ever been there?" I asked.

"No. The eye shows us."

As she said it, she realized her mistake.

I grinned. "If the eye can show you, then perhaps it can show us the way."

"No, give it back. You promised." They reached their hands out, rushing at me. I tossed it in the air to Angie, who stood by the edge of the cistern.

"Over here," she said.

The crones turned to rush her, not realizing how close they were to the edge. They tripped on the rim of rock around the cistern and went flying into the water, bobbing around like gray seals as they flailed and splashed.

Outside the cave, Perseus flopped on the ground and stretched his arms out. "What an adventure! Is it like this all the time for you?"

I scooped the helmet up and stored it safely in the bag. "Pretty much. Damian, are you all right?"

He nodded.

"Angie?"

"Still got ten fingers and ten toes." She wiggled her hands in the air. "And this disgusting eyeball." She held up the grayish blob with the black pupil. It shrank in the sunlight. "How does it work?"

"Let me try." Damian put it up to his eye, looking through it. "I want to see the gorgons' lair."

We waited, holding our breath.

"I see something. It's dark and raining. It's just an empty sea." He turned slowly in a circle, then stopped. "Wait . . . there's a rocky spire." He turned left, then back. "It appears when I'm looking directly west." He lowered it. "This can guide us straight to it."

"Great, let's go now," Perseus said as Angie whistled for our rides.

"We can't," I said. "We don't have everything we need."

"We have enough," Perseus argued. "That helmet will make me invisible, and my sword will do the rest."

I sighed. "How many times do I have to tell you that sword won't cut grass? Damian, tell him."

"She's right," Damian said. "We still need Hermes to give us his winged shoes. And we have to find this Geryon and get him to give us the scimitar."

"But we don't have time," Perseus said, his face pinched.

"What do you mean?" I asked.

"Polydectes intends to marry our mother in a fortnight if I don't return with the head of the gorgon."

"A fortnight." My brain stopped working. We could never complete everything. "That's not enough time."

Angie clasped us on the back. "It is if we stop wasting time talking."

CHAPTER 17

Argenta and the other pegasuses landed in front of the cave. Argenta seemed troubled. Her eyes flared, showing the whites, and she stomped her feet nervously.

"What's up, girl?"

An unmistakable flaming missile hit the ground next to us, spraying gravel every which way.

The Erinyes, the sworn avengers of Olympus. *Not again.*

"You have defiled the sacred tree of Hera." Alekto, the head of the winged avengers, floated down to the ground, her flaming arrow nocked and aimed at me. Her two sisters landed on either side. "You will stand trial in front of the council of gods and receive your punishment."

"Alekto, come on, give us a break," I said. "I'm trying to fix things."

"By defiling a sacred tree belonging to the most powerful goddess in this world?" She pulled the arrow back farther. "Believe me when I say I hope you will resist so that I can rid this world of you once and for all."

"Look, I'm sorry about the tree. It was an accident. We were trying to help Hercules get back on track. Thanks to my last visit, he lost his first two labors, and according to an oracle we know, he was losing hope."

"One less demigod in the world is no great loss," she said.

I sighed. "I would agree, but he happens to be an important one. He becomes an immortal hero. Or at least he's supposed to, but after my visit, things changed. I know you probably don't believe me, but burning that tree was way better than what was going to happen if I'd let Ladon eat him and me."

She slowly lowered her bow. "Who is this oracle?"

"The same one who took me from this place to the human world. Look, I'm happy to face trial and all, but there's one more thing I have to fix. This is my brother Perseus." I jerked a thumb at him. "He's supposed to face Medusa in a couple years and lop her head off, but thanks to my visit, King Polydectes threw him in jail and forced him to go now, making him turn into stone."

"What?" Perseus spun me around. "I'm turned into stone?"

"No . . . I mean yes . . . that's why we came back . . . to stop that from happening."

"I'm sorry, but you must come with us," Alekto said. "The gods will sort out your fate."

"I'm not going to let my brother turn into a rock." I twitched my fingers and held up a lightning bolt.

Her eyes narrowed, and her two sisters raised their flaming arrows to aim them directly at my friends. "Put that down or your friends will perish before you can raise it high."

I lowered my arm. "Please. I'm begging you. He's the only brother I've got, and I've just found him after all these years. I swear on my life I'll come to Olympus and face whatever punishment the gods hand out, but I have to go with him."

"I can handle it," he said indignantly. "I'm not a child."

"You are twelve, which is literally the definition of a child," I said.

Alekto sighed. "I will agree on one condition. To guarantee your return, we must hold something you value more than your life."

"Like what?" I asked.

She nodded at Damian and Angie. "Your friends will do."

"No!" The word burst out of me. "I can't do this without them. You might as well shoot me with that arrow now. Damian keeps me from messing everything up, and Angie keeps me from getting killed. Please, something else."

Her eyes fell on my lightning bolt. "Then surrender your lightning."

My heart dropped. "What do you mean?"

"Surrender your power to call on lightning. We will hold it until you return to Olympus."

"My lightning?" I looked down at the glowing bolt in my hand. The bolt I loved so much—the feel of it, the electrifying power of it. "But I can't."

"It is your choice. Either surrender your friends or give me your lightning."

"It's fine, Katzy," Angie said. "We'll go with them, and you and Perseus take care of the gorgon."

"No. I won't let you go," I said.

"You don't have a choice," Damian said. "Isn't that what you always say?"

His words hit me like a two-ton brick. "Yes. I do. And I'm usually wrong. Which is why we're in this mess." I turned back to Alekto. "Fine. Take it." I held the bolt out, and she grasped it. Light ran up her arm. The bolt grew brighter until I had to shield my eyes. It grew warm in my hand as energy pulsed along it, flowing from me into the bolt. This must have been what sun-brain had felt when Hades took his sun power in the underworld. I could feel my battery draining, a battery I didn't even know I had. Slowly the lightning bolt grew dim until it winked out, but it remained a solid thing, like a pale stick.

I released my grip, shaken and weak. Alekto stuck the bolt in her quiver. "I will safeguard it, Phoebe of Argos, until you return to Olympus and face trial. You have my word."

She lifted off the ground, followed by her two sisters.

"Wait," I called. "We have to find a three-headed guy named Gerry."

"Geryon," she corrected.

"Can you tell us which way to go?"

She hesitated and then said, "Fly due west until the land ends, then head north until you see an island of red earth. You will find Geryon there." They quickly winged out of sight.

After they were gone, Angie turned on me. "Are you crazy?" she shouted. "You just gave away your lightning power."

"Yeah, so?" I felt too numb to yell back at her.

"So? It's like cutting off your right arm."

"No, that would have been giving you and Damian to them. You're what matter—and Perseus."

My brother's eyes were troubled. "Sister, you gave away a great power to protect your friends. What if we can't defeat the gorgons? What if we needed it?"

"We'll find a way. We always do." I took a deep breath, already missing that energy core that had burned so bright in my center. "Let's get moving before the ugly sisters come crawling out of that cave with an even worse monster."

I pulled myself up on Argenta. Perseus climbed up behind me by unspoken agreement. Damian and Angie took flight, but I hesitated.

"Having second thoughts?" Perseus asked.

"No."

"These friends of yours are special."

"They are."

"I still can't believe Zeus is my father. I wish he'd given me powers."

"Trust me, you got the better end of the deal. I would have given anything to have had a mother."

"I suppose you're right."

"Promise me you won't do anything foolish." I twisted in my seat to look him in the eyes. "You have to make it out of this alive."

"I'm not—"

"Look, you're my twin, so I know when you're lying, and I need you to promise. If anything goes wrong, you have to make it out. We'll find a way to get Medusa's head, but you can't get turned to stone."

"Why is it so important to you?"

"You're my brother, dum-dum."

"But you hardly know me," he said quietly.

"Well, we have a long ride." I urged Argenta up into the air. "Fill me in on all the details. Start with your earliest memories of Mom."

We spent the next hour trading stories about our lives. It was strange being this close to my brother. He was similar in size and coloring to me but so different. He'd been raised in a poor fishing village with nothing to speak of but love. I'd been raised with nothing to speak of and no love.

Scratch that, I thought, remembering Carl. I'd had someone. Just not a mother.

He told me about long days spent fishing with some guy named Dictys, who was brother to the king but much nicer.

"Dictys found us and helped my mother. I just wish he could marry her and protect her."

"What about that bully who beat me up? Doesn't he have a mother?"

"No. He must have, of course, but no one's ever heard her name. Polydectes brought him home from a long trip. Some say he just found a child and claimed it as his own because he has no heir."

"Well, they're like father and son when it comes to being jerks."

"Tell me about your life in New York City."

I sighed, thinking of all the wonderful things I missed. "It's busy. People are always in a rush."

"Why? It must take forever to go places."

"No. We have subways, trains, taxis, airplanes."

"Airplanes?"

"Things that fly like birds only they're giant machines. They carry hundreds of people at a time around the world."

"You lie."

"No. We even have devices we carry with us that let us talk to people miles away. We can send messages, even FaceTime them."

"FaceTime?"

"You know, talk and see people on the screen at the same time."

"I think you're making these things up. They are too fantastic."

I laughed. "You should see video games. Or taste a slice of authentic New York pizza."

Damian signaled he was landing. We had been flying westward along the edge of the coastline for some time now. I guided Argenta down onto a flat bluff above the sea. A thin creek gurgled, running over the edge of the cliff, providing much-needed water for the pegasuses.

We took a moment to stretch and snack on some dried bread and cheese Perseus had. It wasn't much, but it took the edge off our hunger.

"How much farther, D?" We had been flying for hours, and I could tell the pegasuses were tired. They nosed among the bristly grass, tugging up dried clumps.

"We're nearly to the edge of the continent of Africa. If we continue west, we'll run into Medusa's lair. If we head north, we should find this red island."

The sun was sinking low in the sky, and I made a snap decision. "It's getting dark. Let's make camp and head out in the morning."

We built a fire ring with some rocks and gathered kindling and dried grass. There was plenty of dead wood scattered around. Out of habit, I crouched down, twitching my finger to call up a spark of lightning, but my fingers were cold.

Crud. I didn't have my lightning anymore. The loss hit me all over again, and an emptiness rose up in me. What if I never got it back? What if Alekto kept it for herself?

Angie squeezed my shoulder once and then leaned in and lit the grass with a small lighter she pulled from her pocket. The crackling warmth did nothing to allay my coldness.

Perseus made himself useful, picking his way down the cliff to catch some fish. I sat on the bluff above and watched him skillfully throw a fishing line into the water and reel it back in as the sun hovered on the horizon like an orange tennis ball. It took him half an hour before he turned, holding up three nice-sized fish.

He swiftly climbed back to the plateau and deftly cleaned them with a folding knife from his pocket, then wrapped them in some strips of bark and buried them in the coals. Soon the smell of roasting fish made everyone's eyes light up. When he finally dug them out with a stick, the outside was nicely charred, and the inside was light and flaky. We picked out every morsel.

"We've been here three days," Damian said, "which means today's Friday."

"So? It's just another day here." I wiped my fingers on my tunic, wishing there was another fish or two.

Damian poked at the fire. "Not any day. I mean, technically, it's my birthday."

My head snapped up. "Oh, crud. It's Friday. Your birthday."

"Happy birthday, Big D," Angie said.

"We don't celebrate birthdays here," Perseus said. "But many happy returns."

"Do you think your parents called?" I asked.

He shrugged. "If they had a signal. On my tenth birthday, they were locked in an ice floe and couldn't get out for six weeks until the thaw came."

"And you spent the whole time with robot lady?"

His face grew sad at the mention of his beloved robot. "Hilda is . . . I mean *was* the best. She would always make me a cake and decorate it with something funny, like the opening lines of the Constitution, or one year, it was the complete table of elements."

I didn't want to be rude, but a cake with the table of elements written out sounded anything but funny.

"Don't you have any other family?" I asked.

"No. My parents were both orphans. Kind of what drew them together. They used to take me on trips with them when I was young, but then . . ." He stopped and gnawed on his thumb like he did when he was nervous or didn't want to admit to something.

"What?"

"Come on, D, you can tell us," Angie said.

"I fell off the side of the ship and into the water. It was freezing, and I was fully clothed with boots on. I panicked. My boots filled with water, dragging me down, and my clothes were so heavy. I started sinking, thrashing around instead of doing the logical thing and kicking off my boots."

"That's why you're scared of water."

"It's silly. I know how to swim, but whenever I go in, I remember how it felt to not be able to, and it's like my muscles don't work."

"I'm not afraid of anything," Perseus boasted.

We turned on him. "Excuse me?" I said. "Damian was baring his heart here. We don't need to pick on him for it."

Perseus flushed. "I didn't mean anything by it. It's just, I'm not afraid of anything."

"Well, you should be. Medusa is no laughing matter. One look at her, and like that"—I snapped my fingers in his face—"I'm an only child."

"I am sorry," he said stiffly to Damian. "I wish I had friends who stood up for me like you have." He got up from the fire, stalked to the edge of the cliff, and sat down, staring out over the sea.

"I think your bro is worried," Angie said. "You should go talk to him."

"He just said he's not scared of anything," I pointed out.

"Statistically speaking, people rarely say what they mean in the heat of the moment," Damian said.

I sighed, getting to my feet. "Fine. Family meeting time."

I walked over to where Perseus sat and dropped down next to him, letting my legs hang off the edge like his. The moon had risen, and the sea sparkled in the white light.

"So, wanna tell me what's going on?" I asked.

He scoffed. "Nothing. I was just tired of the fire."

"I think you're jealous," I said.

"Of what?"

"Of my friends. Of our bond. But you know, you're my brother. I'd do anything for you. I came back here just to help you."

His shoulders hunched. "I know. I'm sorry. I miss Mother. I'm worried I won't return in time. That he'll take her away."

I looped my arm around his shoulder. "One thing I know, the two of us are tough, right?"

He nodded.

"Which means our mother is probably pretty tough herself. So let's focus on finding that sword to replace the junky one you have, and then we'll deal with Medusa."

He blew out a long breath. "You really think we'll be able to do it? Even without your powers?"

The pain jabbed me again like a hot poker in my heart, but I put on a brave face. "Powers aren't everything, you know. We have each other. If we stick together, no one will be able to defeat us."

CHAPTER 18

At first light we were on our way, winging swiftly over the blue sea. I wasn't afraid of facing a two-headed dog. *Been there, done that, incinerated one along the way.* I was more concerned about the three-headed ogre who, according to Damian, had three torsos to go along with the three heads, and six well-muscled arms. *That* worried me.

Perseus was the first to spot the red speck in the ocean. We guided the pegasuses closer. The island was large, with rolling pastures that covered the hills and swathes of red earth. The center rose to a dark red peak with scattered trees covering it. It was hard to see much because clouds of dust had been kicked up by a large herd of cattle moving along a wide road. A small figure was driving the cattle toward a round pond with stagnant green water, but the cattle didn't seem to mind, burying their heads in.

We kept out of sight, flying low, and landed in the shade of some trees. The air was warm and smelled strongly of cows.

"So, Damian, what's the plan?" I asked.

"I say we cut the throat of this Geryon and take the scimitar by force." Perseus tapped the blade at his side.

"That blade wouldn't cut a stick of butter, dodo, and besides, he's super strong. We'll find another way to take him out."

"Hold on—we can't do anything to hurt him," Damian said.

"Why not?" I asked.

"Because Geryon is one of Hercules's labors. He has to steal the cattle away without asking for them."

"How does he do it?"

"First he fights the herdsman, then he shoots an arrow through all three bodies of Geryon at once."

I threw my hands up. "So what are we supposed to do? Ask him nicely to hand over a priceless blade of the gods?"

"We could steal it," Angie said. "One of us could put on that invisibility helmet and take it right out from under his nose."

"That would work if we knew where he kept it," I said.

"Maybe we can trade him something that he wants," Damian said.

"Like what?"

"I don't know yet."

"I think my plan is best," Perseus said. "I will face him and demand he hand it over."

"And this is why you get turned into a rock," I said with a sigh.

Angie tapped her fingers together. "What if we offer him our pegasuses for the blade."

We all looked at her in horror, even Perseus, who'd grown fond of Argenta.

"Are you nuts?" I asked.

She rolled her eyes. "I don't mean actually trade them, just, you know, pretend they're dumb animals."

Nero snorted at her, and Argenta gave her best imitation of a growl.

"Easy." Angie motioned for the winged creatures to stay calm. "I know you're all noble and way smarter than me, but Gerry the ogre doesn't know that, and we could, you know, pretend we're desperate."

"It's a good plan," I said. "I'll take Argenta while you all stay out of sight."

"Not a chance," Perseus said. "I'm not letting you have all the fun, and besides, you don't have any special powers, while I have a sword."

"A sword that looks like it could cut a piece of paper if it was already torn," I taunted.

"We all go," Angie said. "If you two keep arguing, my head is going to explode. We'll offer to trade one pegasus for the blade, maybe go as high as two. And then once we have it, we'll take off on the pegasuses."

We remounted and trotted along the dusty path toward the line of cattle we'd seen while flying overhead. The dust was thick, making it hard to breathe. We came upon the rear of the herd. The cattle were large with shaggy red hair and wide horns sticking out the sides of their heads. They glanced sideways at us, then ignored us.

We neared the front, and the herdsman came into view. He was young, in his twenties maybe, and dark haired. I had an eerie feeling I'd seen him before, the same feeling I'd had from that woman in the marketplace back when we'd rescued Athena. They could have been brother and sister, though he was quite a bit younger than her.

Using a long staff, he poked at a large cow with a bell around its neck. "Come on, you stubborn cow, time to go."

The cow didn't want to leave the water, so he kept prodding until it turned on him and headbutted him, sending him flying backward into a pile of cow dung.

He slammed his fists into the ground. "I hate this stinking place!"

We started laughing, and he looked up, scrambling to his feet and holding the staff out like a weapon. "Who are you?"

"I'm Phoebe. These are my friends, Angie, Damian, and Perseus."

At the mention of our names, a flash of excitement crossed his face and then swiftly cooled. He lowered the staff. "I'm Eurytion. What are you doing here?"

"We're looking for the owner of these cattle."

"Geryon doesn't like visitors."

"He has something we need," I said.

"Not one of his cattle? He wouldn't part with one if it cost him one of his heads."

"No. He has a curved blade we need."

"The Argus Slayer? He won that off Hermes fair and square. I don't see why he'd give it away."

"Not even for one of these?" I ran my hand along Argenta's neck.

"A winged horse?" His eyes grew thoughtful. "Tell you what, give the animal to me, and I'll take it to him and see if I can bargain on your behalf."

Angie snorted. "Do we look like fools? These are pegasuses. One of these is worth more than his entire herd of four-legged steaks."

He shrugged. "Fine. I'll take you, but don't be surprised if he feeds you to Orthus and keeps your winged pretties for himself."

He turned his back on the cattle and began striding off down the road. I stifled a laugh at the cow dung clinging to his tunic.

"So, how did you come to be here?" I asked, riding up alongside him.

"My father thought it would be good for me to learn humility."

"And have you?"

He laughed harshly. "No, I've learned I hate cattle. But soon I will earn my freedom," he added cryptically. "Very soon indeed." He started whistling to himself.

Before long, he turned off the road and led us along a hardened path that led uphill. As we neared the top, a low-slung house made of stacked stones came into view. Smoke rose from the chimney, and wash hung on the line. The drying shirts were comical—like someone had sewn three shirts together. They flapped like sails in the wind.

In front of the house, a giant of a man was bent over a pile of logs. When he straightened, my jaw dropped. I'd seen a lot of strange things in this place, but a three-headed man was the oddest. From the waist down, his body was wide and brawny, but from the waist up, he divided into three separate shirtless torsos with two arms each, giving him a total of six. In each set of hands he held a large axe he raised over his three heads. One head was bald as a cue ball, one had a thatch of red hair, and the third had a stripe of brown hair that stood up in a mohawk. He brought the axes down in a synchronized swing, and three logs split in half, flying off to a growing pile.

He turned as we stopped at the top of the hill and slid down from our pegasuses.

Baldy spoke first. "Eurytion, you worthless cur, what strangers have you let on my land?"

"They are visitors who wish to acquire that scimitar of yours," the young herdsman said.

"Geryon is not interested," Redhead said. "The blade is too valuable."

"You should leave," Mohawk added, slapping his axe in his meaty palm.

"We were hoping you might take one of our winged horses in trade." I ran my hand over Argenta's neck. "She's a fine specimen. She could help you watch over your cattle."

All three sets of eyes narrowed. "What use have you for the Argus Slayer?" Baldy asked.

"We need it to take the head off a very nasty snake-headed lady," I said. "Look, a pegasus is more valuable than a useless blade. Who would bother to come here to steal your cattle?"

"No one would dare," Mohawk said. "But it is mine, nonetheless. I have no need of a winged horse. I have Eurytion to watch my cattle." Three right hands snapped their fingers, and from the porch of the house, a massive two-headed dog rose and trotted forward to stand at his side. "And I have Orthus to take care of intruders."

Orthus looked like a mashup of a rottweiler and a dump truck. Brawny shoulders held up two growling heads. He planted four giant paws in the dirt and proceeded to growl like an outboard motor.

"Can we at least see it?" Perseus asked. "We have come a long way. It would be a sight to behold the famed Argus Slayer in person."

"Why would I show it to you?" Redhead asked. "I have work to do. Be gone, or I'll feed you to Orthus myself."

With that, Geryon turned his backs on us and lined up three more logs to split.

We stayed where we were until Orthus bared his fangs, taking a menacing step closer. We backed up and led the pegasuses back down the hill.

"What are we doing?" Perseus whispered. "We can't just give up. Let's fight him."

"Did you see how big he is?" I whispered back. "And you probably saw he has a two-headed dog that can rip your arm off. We need to make a new plan."

As we passed the pond where the cattle still milled about, a voice called from the trees.

"Psst." Eurytion beckoned us over. He had changed out of his soiled tunic and now wore a clean one. "I know how you can steal the Argus Slayer."

"How?"

"Geryon keeps it hidden in a cave not far from here. I can take you there."

"Why would you help us?" I asked.

His face darkened. "I hate this place. Take me with you, and I'll show you where to find this blade."

"I wish we could," I said, " but we're on a quest that will take us far west from here."

"I don't care where we go. I have to get away from these stinking cows. Please. Drop me anywhere, and I'll find a way home."

I looked at Damian and Angie. Damian shrugged. "We could probably take him on Albert."

"We'll do it," Perseus said quickly. "Just show us where this cave is."

"I have your word?" Eurytion asked, extending his hand.

"Sure. We'll take you." I shook his hand, still unable to place where I'd seen him before. His eyes were a glacial blue that felt so familiar. "How far is it to this cave?"

"Not far. There is a path behind the house that leads upward to the highest point on the island. We can fly on the pegasuses. It won't take long."

Damian pulled him up behind him. Albert trotted a few steps before launching into the air. We followed, soaring above the island toward the red peak we'd seen on our way in. Within minutes we were landing on a flat boulder surrounded by a small copse of trees.

"The cave is just over there." Eurytion pointed through the trees. "I can wait here with the winged ones while you fetch it."

A sudden flicker of unease ran up my spine. "How do we know you're telling the truth?"

"I'd go in with you, but someone should stay here and keep an eye out in case Geryon decides to check on his treasure." His eyes were bland, but there was a coiled tenseness in him.

He had a point. "Angie, Damian, stay here with Eurytion while Perseus and I fetch the blade. It shouldn't take long. There aren't any traps or hidden dangers?"

The herdsman shrugged. "Traps? Not that I know of."

He was lying, I was sure of it, but there wasn't time to cross-examine him. That uneasy feeling increased as we walked closer to the pile of rocks and a black opening appeared.

"Is it just me, or do you have the heebie-jeebies?" I asked.

Perseus drew his flimsy blade. "It's like there are eyes watching us."

"You think Geryon is already here?"

"I don't think he could have made it here ahead of us."

Our feet were silent on the soft pine needles. We stepped inside the entrance and waited for our eyes to adjust to the dimness. It wasn't much of a cave, more of a large space formed by tumbled boulders. A stone pedestal stood in the center. Something glinted on it.

"I think it's there," I said. "We found it."

Perseus was already hurrying over to it. "I can't believe it was this easy."

His words triggered something in me. Nothing in this place was easy.

"Perseus, watch out!" I shouted too late. He picked up the blade and turned to give me a grin when a shadow moved in the corner. There was a whooshing noise. I threw myself at him, knocking him flat. Something sliced across my shoulders. A wooden spear at least eight feet long clattered against the stone wall behind us. I was already on my feet, scooping it up and turning to find a woman dressed in black leather armor holding a sword against my brother's throat.

"Drop it." The voice was low, female, and definitely familiar.

I ignored her command, gripping the spear tightly. "You're one of Athena's acolytes."

"Drop it or I will remove his head."

The scimitar lay on the ground between us, knocked loose when I'd tackled Perseus.

"Go ahead. Dive for it," she said coolly. "Your brother will be dead by the time your fingers touch metal, and you will be dead before you can wield it."

"What's your problem?" I asked. "Why are you following us?"

"I am Enyo."

She said her name as if it was supposed to mean something, but without Damian to translate, I was lost.

"She's the goddess of war," Perseus gasped out. "She's going to kill us anyway. Take the blade and save our mother."

"I'm not leaving you. What do you want?" I asked Enyo.

"Revenge."

"Revenge? What did I ever do to you?"

"Not me, you fool. My brother."

"Do I know him?"

"You should. You sent him to Tartarus."

"Ares is your brother?" *Great. My family tree just keeps getting better and better.* "And Eurytion? Is he part of this?"

"My nephew. I promised to take him with me when I bring your head back to my mother." She tightened her grip on Perseus. "Drop the weapon, or your mother will be weeping over the loss of both her children."

If I'd had my lightning, the battle would have been fair. She was probably going to kill us both anyway. Better to go out a hero than a zero. I was about to dive for the blade when something blocked the light into the cave.

"Who dares enter Geryon's cave of treasures?"

I'd never been so happy to see a three-headed ogre.

Perseus took advantage of Enyo's distraction and stomped on her foot, then twisted out of her grasp. I dove for the scimitar and brought it up just as she swung her sword down at me, striking the blade and jarring my arm.

"Die, daughter of Zeus. I will make you pay for what you have done."

If someone was going to pay, it wasn't going to be me. I bent my knee and kicked her hard in the stomach, sending her crashing back into the waiting arms of Geryon.

He grabbed her by the back of her neck and lifted her off the ground.

"Where did this pretty thing come from?" Baldy asked, using one of his hands to tickle her under the chin.

"Put me down, you filthy beast." She tried to stab him with her blade, but he grabbed her arm with one of his six and bent it back until she dropped the weapon.

"A feisty little thing," Mohawk said. "She will make a good wife. Take the scimitar," he said to me. "It is a fair trade."

"Let's go," I said to Perseus. We scooted past them as Enyo fought Geryon like a wildcat.

"Put me down, you big oaf!"

We exited the cave as she continued to flail at him with both arms.

"Why didn't Angie and Damian warn us he was coming?" I asked as we ran back to where the pegasuses were.

The answer was soon clear. Angie and Damian were hanging by their feet, swinging from the branches of the tree.

"Phoebe, the rat set a trap. Be careful!" Angie shouted.

Eurytion was trying to climb on Albert's back, but the pegasus kept flashing his hooves at him.

"Stop it! Just let me on, you stupid animal."

"Get away from him," I said.

He whirled around, red-faced. "Where is my aunt?"

"She's got her hands full." I nodded at Argenta.

The pegasus planted both back hooves in Eurytion's backside, sending him flying off the top of the boulder.

"Get us down," Angie said, flailing at the air.

Perseus grinned at her. "Say please."

"I'll show you please." She tried to take a swing at him, but he danced out of reach. Using his folding knife, he cut the rope holding them, and they dropped to the ground with a thud.

"Thanks a lot," Angie grumbled, untangling the ropes. "You could have set us down gently."

"You shouldn't have let yourself get caught in a trap," Perseus said smugly.

"Zip it you two," I said.

We jumped on the pegasuses and took flight, quickly winging away from the red island. We turned west toward the setting sun. Damian held up the eye of the Graeae, using it to navigate. If he looked south or north, the eye was blank, but if he looked west, the black spire rose out of the waters. We just had to head in the direction the eye pointed when the spire was in view. Fortunately, there were plenty of small islands in this part of the world, and when the pegasuses tired, we set down on a rocky bluff.

"We can rest here for a while, then keep going." I quickly filled in Damian and Angie on the appearance of Enyo in the cave.

Damian gnawed on his thumb. "I haven't read anything about Enyo in any of the stories, but if she's Ares's sister . . ."

"No wonder she looked so familiar," I said. "She has the same eyes as Ares and those rotten offspring of his Phobos and Deimos. She wanted to take my head back to her mother, Hera. I bet Hera's behind all this. She blames me for sending Ares to Tartarus."

Perseus yawned. "All this adventuring has made me tired. Maybe we should stay the night. Start fresh in the morning."

I was anxious to keep moving, but the sun was already sinking low on the horizon. "Fine. It will give us time to see if Hermes comes when we call him. It's time he handed over those winged sandals of his."

"Why do we need them?" Angie said. "We've got our rides."

"We need to stick as close to the mythology as possible," I said. "And Perseus will need a way home, right, D?"

"She's right, Angie. We have to put things back the way they were as best we can." Damian unloosed the lyre from Albert's back and sat down cross-legged. Angie busied herself gathering wood for a fire.

"That is some lyre," Perseus said, eyeing it.

"It belongs to Hermes." Damian strummed a few notes.

"What makes you think he will come?" Perseus asked.

"He said he would if we got the things we needed." The notes trickled up into the air, carried away by a soft breeze.

We waited, expecting him to appear at any moment, but the only sound was the ocean surf pounding on the sand.

"Try again," I said.

Damian stroked it again, picking out notes and strumming a familiar tune. He played song after song, waiting between each one, but there was no sign of Hermes.

I stood up, stomping over to Damian. I wanted to take the lyre and throw it off the cliff, but he held it away.

"Patience, Phoebe. Maybe he's busy. He'll come."

"When?"

"Soon."

For once Damian was wrong. Perseus caught some fish for dinner, only two this time, but enough to stave off our hunger. The moon slowly rose over the water, and the stars shone brightly in the velvet sky, but their beauty did nothing to soothe my mood. King Polydectes had my mother. Even now he could be forcing her to marry him.

"I don't understand how you know so much," Perseus asked.

"Everything that happens here is written down and retold in stories," Damian explained. "When Phoebe was born, she was sent away to our world, where all of these things have already happened. That's why when we came the first time, we messed things up by changing them."

"And I am one of these stories?" he asked.

"One of the best," Damian said. "They even named a constellation after you." He pointed up at a patch of stars.

It looked like a one-legged man with a pointed head to me, but Perseus seemed impressed.

"And over there, that next batch of stars is named for Andromeda. She's the woman you marry one day—after you save her from Ceto."

My brother's eyebrows shot up. "Wait, I have to fight that sea lobster again? I hope she is worth it."

Damian gave him a thumbs-up. "Andromeda was not only beautiful but the daughter of a king. Did you know we are all made of stardust? Everything in the universe is made from the remnants of stars that exploded billions of years ago. These supernovas spread carbon matter throughout the universe . . ."

Damian droned on as the fire died down, and one by one we drifted off to sleep. Perseus was the first to crash, curled up on his side, his face to the fire.

I watched him as he slept. It was still hard to believe I had a brother. We had shared the same womb. And even though I hardly knew him, I would tear apart anyone who tried to hurt him.

CHAPTER 19

The sun was fully risen when I sat up, rubbing sleep from my eyes. The fire was long dead, mere ashes. Angie lay facedown on her bag, arm slung over her eyes. Damian had curled up by Albert. The spot where Perseus had slept was empty. He was probably down by the water catching more fish. I wouldn't mind another fillet for breakfast.

I stood, stretching my arms. Nero and Albert were nibbling on dry grass. Argenta had to be around somewhere. I turned in a circle, searching for the silver pegasus. There was no sign of her. Alarm bells rang in my head. I hurried to the edge of the cliff, searching the beach below.

"Aarrgh! You stupid, stupid jerk."

"What's wrong?" Angie came running, still half-asleep, her hair standing up in a wild mess.

"Perseus is gone. He took Argenta."

"No, no, no! He took the lyre." Damian clapped his hands to his head.

"What about the Argus Slayer?" Angie asked. I had wrapped it in a thin blanket and left it by the fire. I dove

193

for it, unravelling the cloth, and found Perseus's cheap sword in its place.

I threw the blanket aside in disgust. "What about Calypso's bag?" Then I groaned, remembering I'd left it tied off on Argenta. "The little jerk took everything. Is he a lunatic?"

"No, he's your brother," Angie said with a sigh. "Reminds me a lot of you."

"Not now, Angie. We have to go after him before he does something really stupid."

"Not so fast," a voice said from behind us.

Hermes floated in the air, looking anything but pleased. His gilded sandals sported feathery wings that fluttered faster than hummingbirds. "Where is my lyre?" he demanded.

"It's not here," I said.

"I see that." He arrowed forward, angrily grabbing me by my tunic. "Do you have any idea what you've done?" His eyes blazed with a mixture of anger and fear.

"You mean almost burning down Hera's precious tree? Yes. I already had a visit from the Erinyes."

"You're going to be sent to Tartarus. You know that, right? Hera will devise a torture for you worse than anything you can imagine. Your flesh burning from your body every day only for you to wake up the next day and have the fires consume you all over again for eternity."

I pushed his hand away. "Sorry. I'm not an expert on all things Olympus. I didn't know the tree was so important. We still need those winged sandals of yours."

He flew back a step. "I can't help you, I'm afraid."

"You promised. We got everything on the list. Hades's helmet, the magic bag, and the Argus Slayer."

"I don't see them with you."

"That's because Perseus took them with him. Look, Hera isn't blameless in this."

"What do you mean?"

"Someone pretending to be Athena gave Perseus this sword, swearing it would take off Medusa's head."

Hermes eyed it. "That sword wouldn't cut a loaf of bread."

"Exactly. And someone spiked Athena's nectar and made her throw away her weapons, including the shield Perseus needs to defeat Medusa."

"That doesn't prove anything."

"Fine. One of Athena's acolytes was actually Enyo, the daughter of Hera. She tried to stop us from getting the Argus Slayer."

Hermes's brow went up. "You ran across Enyo and survived? Impressive. Look, if the queen of the gods wanted him dead, she would simply order it so. This seems like a lot of coincidences wrapped together."

"What if she doesn't want anyone to know she's involved? I met a water nymph in the middle of the desert who had the power to show me anything I wanted to see. She had a peacock with her with creepy eyes on its tail."

His eyes narrowed further. "That would be Argus, Hera's loyal bodyguard. He had a hundred pairs of eyes that kept constant watch over her until he was killed. She placed his eyes in the tail of her peacock."

"Wait, it was you that killed him," Damian said with a snap of his fingers. "I remember now."

Hermes shrugged. "I had my reasons. Hera forgave me eventually."

"If she forgave that, she might forgive me burning her tree down," I said hopefully.

"I don't think you understand how much that tree means to her. Mother Gaia gave it to her herself."

"So I keep hearing. I'll deal with that later. Right now we need to get to Perseus. He's going to try facing Medusa on his own."

Hermes's brows drew together. "Then he's a fool. He can't do it alone. Especially if what you're saying is true and Hera is working to stop him."

"Then please, help us. Give us your winged shoes, and we'll fix things."

He folded his arms, then shook his head. "I'm sorry. I wish I could help you, but I cannot cross a goddess as powerful as Hera."

It was at that moment that Damian came up behind him and conked Hermes over the head with a rock.

The god dropped to the ground.

"Quick. He won't be out long," Damian said.

"D, was this your idea?" I asked, kneeling down.

"I had to do something. It was obvious he wasn't going to help." He started wrestling one sandal off while I took the other.

"You don't think he's . . . dead, do you?" I asked.

"He's immortal. He'll be fine. Just really, really angry." Damian handed me the sandal. "Come on."

Angie jumped up onto Nero and reached a hand out to pull me up. We headed due west. As we left the smattering of islands behind us, the sky turned gray and lost its color. Even the sun dimmed, as if it were hidden behind a filter. The air cooled, dropping several degrees.

There were no more islands in sight, no land of any sort, just endless dark waves rolling below us. A long purple tentacle shot up out of the water and then slapped down. We didn't venture any closer.

"How do we know we're going in the right direction?" I shouted to Damian.

He had the eye up to his face. "It's gone dark, no matter what direction I look." His face was set, his jaw locked, which meant he was worried.

So was I. My stomach was in knots thinking about Perseus. How could he be so reckless?

Because he's exactly like me.

Wind buffeted us, tossing us around in the sky. Then icy rain splatted us, soaking my clothes and turning my fingers blue. Nero was a steady pegasus and didn't complain, but his chest was heaving with the effort to carry both of us.

"We have to turn back," I said finally. "If we don't find land soon, Nero's going to drop into the water."

"It's too far to go back," Damian said from atop Albert. "We'll never make it."

Angie leaned forward, wrapping her arms around Nero's neck and whispering in his ear. I missed Argenta so much. I couldn't believe she'd left with Perseus, but he'd probably tricked her somehow.

A bolt of lightning lit up the sky, and rain fell harder, nearly washing us off the back of the pegasus. Nero trembled beneath me. He was drifting lower and lower. The spray of salty seawater mixed with the rain.

An idea hit me. Hermes's sandals were wedged between me and Angie. I tugged off my own boots, letting them drop into the ocean, and slipped on Hermes's winged shoes. The wings hung limply at the backs of my ankles.

"What are you doing?" Angie asked, looking over her shoulder.

"Nero can't carry us both." I swung my legs over the side and held my feet out. The wings still didn't move or flutter.

"How do they work?" I shouted to Damian.

"I have no idea. You can't risk it."

Too late. I pushed myself off the back of Nero and dropped toward the water. I flapped my arms, trying to slow my fall. The sandals did nothing.

"Fly, you stupid things!" I swung my legs back and forth. The water was fast approaching. I kicked my heels together, and miraculously, the wings started moving. I careened forward, somersaulting twice before righting myself, then thrust my arms out for balance and lifted slightly.

I leaned forward and zinged along the surface of the water. I leaned more, and my speed increased. Angling my body upward, I shot up from the surface and zoomed past Angie and Damian.

"This is fantastic!" I felt like something out of a super-hero movie. Without my extra weight, Nero picked up the pace. I led the way, ignoring the stinging rain and numb-ness in my hands. My brother was out here somewhere. I just had to find him.

Lightning struck again, only this time it revealed a dark mass in the water

"I think I saw something," I shouted. "Over there."

We turned the pegasuses toward the twisted spire of rock. It was like a spray of lava that had shot up out of the sea and hardened in the air, all rivulets and gullies and no trace of vegetation. A flat landing spot near the water was our only option to set down. We guided the pegasuses there. Their hooves skidded several feet before stopping, sides heaving.

I set down hard, nearly falling on my face. The others quickly dismounted.

"Any sign of Perseus?" I put two fingers to my mouth, whistling for Argenta, but the wind and the rain swept the sound away. "Do you think they made it here?" They could be lost in that endless sea. Argenta's wings would give out. They would both drown.

Angie gripped my shoulder. Her hair was plastered to her face. "They're here somewhere. Argenta wouldn't steer him wrong."

"But where, Angie? There's no other place to land."

"Medusa's lair is in a cave. So maybe they're inside," Damian said.

If that was supposed to make me feel better, it failed. I could imagine my brother already a statue.

"Did you see an opening?" I asked.

He shook his head. "We don't even know if this is the right place. It looks like the one the eye showed me, but . . ."

My knees wobbled, and I sat down on a lump of rock, forcing words out through numb lips. "It has to be. The pegasuses can't fly any farther."

"Er, I think we're in the right place." Angie bent down to stare at the rock under me.

"Why?"

"Because you're sitting on someone."

Horrified, I leaped up, turning around to look. The rock was weathered and old, but it was definitely the shape of a man crouched on his knees, arms wrapped around his head, which was turned to the side. His eyes stared forward, forever open, and his mouth was agape, as if the last thing that had come out was a scream.

"It's not . . . my brother, is it?"

"No. It's not Perseus." Damian knelt, running his hands over it. "It's old. It's been here for years. We better hurry."

We led the pegasuses over the slippery rock. It was smooth in parts and twisted in others. There were weathered stone figures everywhere. Some were huddled in a ball with their heads down. Others were standing with their hands over their faces, but their fingers were always slightly splayed, as if something had made them look. They increased in number as we continued on.

"We must be getting close," I said, picking up the pace.

"Phoebe, we still don't have Athena's shield," Damian said.

"So?"

"So we have nothing to defend ourselves with. To not look at her when we, you know, try to lop her head off."

"We'll figure something out. Look, there's the entrance." My heart skipped a beat at the looming black gash in the side of the spire of stone. I hurried forward, then stopped.

"What's wrong?" Angie said.

"Damian's right. We don't even know if Perseus is here. You guys wait here with our rides while I have a look inside."

"Katzy, you're not going alone," Angie said.

"Look—I've got Hermes's winged shoes." I clicked my heels, and the wings sprouted out. "Give me my brother's sword." Angie passed it over. "I'm just going to have a look around and see if my dumb brother's inside. If he is, then I'll drag him out. If he isn't, I won't stay. I promise. Just wait here."

I floated away from them and entered the cave.

Water dripped from the ceiling. It was dark. Even when my eyes adjusted, it was difficult to make much out. I bumped into a rock and ran my fingers over it, shuddering when I felt the stone features of another of Medusa's victims. How many sailors had washed up here looking for help and been turned to stone?

I listened, hoping to hear some sign of life, but there was nothing but the muted wind outside and my own breathing. I gripped the flimsy blade tightly and floated forward.

The tunnel widened, and light filtered in. The air was musty and smelled of rotting kelp, like a fish market.

I slowed, keeping to the side of the tunnel. It appeared to open up ahead, where the light was coming from. I peered around the edge of the opening and saw a round cavern with a domed ceiling. Torches were spaced apart, sending flickering light up. Two other openings were on the other side of the room. There were statues scattered everywhere. Some of them looked posed, arms stretched out. All of them look terrified, as if the last thing they'd seen was a monster.

Where is Argenta? I could see no sign of my pegasus or my halfwit brother.

I crept into the room, moving from statue to statue. At first I thought it was empty, but then I heard a scraping noise, like talons on stone, and loud breathing from the far side of the room. Sweat beaded down my back. I clenched the hilt of the sword so tightly my fingers ached as I quietly moved closer.

The scraping noise came again, along with a garbled growl, and I ducked behind a portly statue. Holding my breath, I leaned out and caught my first glimpse of a gorgon.

It was like something out of a horror movie, starting with the gnarly taloned feet that could use a pedicure. Green scaly skin extended up a thick muscled leg. Her hands were tipped with curled claws that I was pretty sure could peel my skin off. Her arms were green and scaly, like the legs. Pointed wings arched up from her back, thin green skin stretching between the spines. Ignoring the obvious fact that her hair was made of snakes that hung down her back and curled in the air, all of them hungrily searching for something, it was the face that was the most hideous, like a cross between Godzilla and the swamp monster.

Tusks poked up from her bottom jaw, and her nose was squashed and flat. Her eyes were a hideous shade of yellow with red centers that glowed like embers. Was this Medusa or one of her gorgon sisters? And what was she doing?

She held something in her hand, bringing it to her face and smelling it.

I stifled a gasp. It was one of Hera's golden apples. Calypso's bag was at her feet. Hercules must have left one behind. She tossed it aside, and it rolled across the floor toward me.

The good news was Perseus was here. The bad news was I was going to murderize him when I got him out of here.

A rock scraped from behind the gorgon, and she spun, her forked tongue flickering out.

"Show yourself. Don't be frightened by my appearance." She stalked forward. "We love welcoming visitors to our home." She sniffed the air, and her serpents hissed, all focused on something in front of her.

Perseus. Of course. He was wearing Hades's helmet. If this *was* Medusa and he looked her in the eyes, his invisibility wouldn't protect him. It was up to me to save his stupid butt.

I stepped out from behind the statue. "Hey, ugly face, you looking for me?" I ran at her, holding the blade in front of me, eyes firmly cast to the ground so I didn't get turned into a lump of rock. I rammed the blade forward into her torso, but the blade shattered as it made contact, leaving me with only the hilt and a sore wrist. She grabbed me by the nape and lifted me up. I squinted my eyes shut.

"Run, Perseus!"

But of course, my brother didn't listen. Footsteps slapped on the stone, and the gorgon started to turn away from me, but I grabbed her chin. "Look at me." I braced myself to look into those glowing eyes. The red pupils widened as she stared at me, and I tensed, hoping being turned to stone wasn't as painful as I imagined it to be, but nothing happened. Then she released me as she staggered backward, screeching loud enough to bring down the entire ceiling.

Reaching behind her back, she pulled out Hermes's scimitar and let it clatter to the ground. "Who attacked me? Show yourself and die!"

She swung her arms out, swiping them in the air. She must have knocked my brother down because two things happened. The sound of metal clanked on stone as Hades's helmet rolled to a stop, and my brother appeared, sprawled on the ground.

The gorgon loomed over him, that tongue flicking out as her claws lengthened. Green blood oozed down her shoulder from where he'd stabbed her. "Die, human. Die a painful death while I tear you to pieces."

CHAPTER 20

"Perseus!"

I scooped up the Argus Slayer, raised the diamond blade over my head, and flew full speed at the gorgon, bringing the blade around like a baseball player driving in a home run. The blade cut through the head and lopped it clean off. It bounced on the ground as green blood sprayed from the severed neck. The body continued to stagger around, as if its nerves continued firing after its head was separated.

I landed and raced to Perseus's side. He lay on the ground not moving.

"Perseus, are you okay?"

His eyes were shut tight. "Is it safe to look?"

"That wasn't Medusa. It was one of her sisters."

"How do you know?"

"Because I'm not a rock at the moment." I stuck my hand out and pulled him to his feet. "Why didn't you cut off her head?"

"Because your head was in the way, and I'm getting used to having a sister." He looked past me. The gorgon was still staggering around. "Is that normal?"

"Is what normal?"

"Shouldn't she be dead?"

I watched the gorgon stagger into statues, knocking them over as she searched for something. "I'm not sure how it works, but according to Damian, Medusa's sisters were immortal."

He paled. "Then we have to get out of here. Now."

He snatched up Hades's helmet while I grabbed the golden apple and Calypso's bag. We raced for the entrance I'd come in, dodging among the statues. Suddenly iron grates above the entrance crashed down, blocking our escape.

Statues exploded, pulverized into dust as the gorgon made her way toward us. She seemed to have found her head, because it was reattached to her body, and boy, was she pissed. The snakes were standing up at attention, all pointed toward us. Her forked tongue darted in and out as she swung her fists from side to side, shattering statues and clearing the room of any place to hide.

"Move it," I said. We raced along the edge of the room, trying to stay out of sight and find an exit.

"Show yourself so I can rip you limb from limb," she screamed. "Euryale does not like being messed with!"

Euryale. Now we knew which one it was.

"Here." I shoved the helmet into Perseus's hands. "Put this back on."

"No." He shoved it back. "You wear it."

"No." I forced it into his hands. "I'm not the one who gets turned to stone."

"And I'm not going to save myself if it means you do."

"Why are you so stubborn?"

He grinned. "I take after you?"

"Don't." But I smiled slightly. The smashing of statues continued. "We need to find a way out of here before Eury the Fury gets any closer. I think I have an idea. I'll take that helmet after all."

Perseus passed it over, and I placed it over my head. It fit a bit loose, then clamped down around my ears as if it was fitting itself to me. A cold wave passed over me, and then my hand vanished. I waved it in front of my face, but I couldn't see it.

"Now climb on my back."

"Why?"

"Just do it."

Perseus felt for my shoulders and then jumped up, wrapping his knees around my waist. I gripped his thighs with my hands, and they disappeared from sight. *Sweet.* Whatever I touched became invisible. I ran forward and jumped into the air, kicking my heels together. The winged shoes stuttered, then lifted us up just as Eury the Fury smashed the statues where we had been standing.

We flew higher in the cavern, searching for a way out. We could see the gorgon smashing statues, searching everywhere. She must have realized we'd taken flight, because she spread her wings out and began flapping them, but she didn't leave the ground. Hope sparked in my chest. Maybe she couldn't fly, and the wings were for show, and then I realized what she was up to.

Dust begin to swirl in the air from all the broken statues. She flapped them harder, turning in a circle as the dust cloud grew.

"There's no escape," she screeched. "When I am finished with you, my sister will turn you into one of her pretty statues."

She stalked around the room, raising a larger and larger cloud. I shielded my eyes, avoiding the grit, and then Perseus sneezed, and she shot into the air straight toward us.

So she could fly.

I ducked down, but too late, I realized we were coated in dust and now partially visible. She changed direction, coming straight for us. I was having a hard time holding on to Perseus. My hands were sweating, and my grip kept slipping. The gorgon pursued us relentlessly, gaining with every second. I glanced over my shoulder to see those snake heads snapping in the air just inches away from us.

If only I had a lightning bolt. Anything I could use to stop her.

"Katzy! Over here."

Angie and Damian beckoned from one of the tunnel openings. They had managed to raise the bars up a few inches. It would be tight, but if we lay flat, we might make it under. I just had to shake this gorgon.

Perseus yelped. "Let go of me, you witch." Wielding the Argus Slayer, he hacked at Euryale's wrist, and she screamed as her severed hand fell to the ground. She peeled away from us, going after her lost limb.

I arrowed straight toward the grate. We hit the ground, and Perseus slipped off my back. My arms ached from holding him.

"You first," I said.

"No, you."

"Knock it off!" Angie said. "Both of you, now."

We dropped to the ground, shoved the bag, helmet, and sword through, and shimmied forward using our elbows. The bars scraped my back, but we just fit. Perseus made it in, and then claws clamped down on my leg.

"Not so fast," Euryale shrieked, raking her talons down my calf as I tried to wiggle free. I screamed, feeling the blood pour out, and then Perseus rammed the sword through the grate into her chest, piercing her heart.

She released me, staggering back to stare at him in shock.

The snakes around her head dropped one by one, like puppets whose strings had been cut. And then Eury the Fury fell flat on her back with the sword sticking straight up out of her chest.

Angie tried to drag me forward by my wrists, but I resisted, sliding back. "No. We still need that blade."

"What if she's still alive?" Perseus gripped the bars, looking worried.

"She's not," I said, limping over to her. My leg throbbed, and blood ran down freely. "Look, even the snakes are dead."

She lay staring up at the ceiling, her tongue lolling out of her mouth. I nudged her with my toe. Nothing. Gripping the sword with both hands, I pulled it out.

"See? She's dead."

I started to walk away, but something cold gripped my ankle.

Why did I not understand immortality meant *unable to be killed*?

I stomped on her wrist with my other foot and raced for the grate, then slid under as the snakes on her head roused themselves, and she groaned.

Damian shoved the grate down. I put one arm around Angie's shoulders and limped down the tunnel.

"Is this the tunnel we came in?" I asked.

"No. We did some exploring," Angie said.

"Any sign of Medusa or the other gorgon?"

"None. But wait till you see what we found."

CHAPTER 21

T he tunnel split off in different directions, but Angie and Damian continued straight on until we reached a pile of rubble. Rocks had been pushed aside, creating a small opening. We clambered over them, and then Damian and Angie pushed the rocks back into place, sealing us in. The tunnel angled upward. My leg burned from the gouges Eury the Fury had inflicted, but I'd felt worse. I still had a scar in my side from where Ares had stabbed me with the lightning scepter that belonged to my father.

The tunnel opened up to a grassy meadow. Trees and shrubs clustered around a pool of water. It was surrounded on all sides by sheer rock walls. Nero and Albert were busy grazing on the grass

"What is this place?" I asked.

Angie shrugged. "A little bit of paradise."

I limped over to the side of the pool and sat down, grateful for the rest.

Damian tore off the hem of his tunic and used it to wash the gashes on my leg. "They don't appear to have venom, so that's good," he said. "They're deep, but they'll heal up if they don't get infected."

Perseus tore a strip off his own tunic, and Damian used it to bind the wounds. I scooped up a handful of water and let the cool liquid soothe my parched throat before I unleashed on my brother.

Grabbing his tunic, I hauled him close. "What were you thinking taking off without us? Where is Argenta?"

He flushed. "I was thinking I could do this by myself. And your pegasus did not want to take me, but I whispered in her ear how much I loved our mother, and she finally let me on her back. She left as soon as we arrived."

I let him go, my anger fading. "What do you mean, left?"

He shrugged. "I thought she meant to return to you."

I looked around the grotto. "Is it me, or is it weird having this little bit of paradise on this barren island?"

"No one seems to come here," Damian said. "We saw it from above and came down. The entrance was grown over with brush. Check out the markings on the walls."

Wherever the stone was smooth, someone had carved images of sea creatures and tridents.

"Who do you suppose made those?" I asked.

"The gorgons have claws," Damian said. "They could have scratched them in. The trident might represent Poseidon."

"Isn't he one of the big three?" I asked.

"Yes. Zeus's brother, and god of the seas."

"Why would the gorgons have a shrine to him?"

"He was in love with Medusa, according to the old stories. She's pregnant with his children when Perseus cuts her head off. Two creatures spring from her neck— the famed Pegasus and a warrior named Chrysaor, who carries a golden sword."

I made a gagging noise. "Seriously? My uncle has bad taste."

"Some say he's the reason they're so ugly. Him and Athena."

My eyebrow went up. "What did my sister do now?"

"Some stories suggest the gorgons were beautiful at one time, so beautiful Medusa boasted she was prettier than Athena."

"So, what—my sister turned them all into serpent-heads?"

He shrugged. "The stories vary depending on who tells them."

"Well, that's messed up. Athena wouldn't do that. We should be moving. Eury the Fury will go after her sisters and follow us."

"We need to head back to land," Damian agreed. "Wait for Athena to find us."

"No. I'm not leaving until I've done my job," Perseus said.

"Perseus, you saw what happened with just one gorgon. We can't kill it, and we have nothing to protect us from Medusa's look of death."

"But our mother . . . she needs me to save her."

"And we will. As soon as we have what we need."

"No. I'm not going." He stood, folding his arms. "You can run away, but I will face this Medusa and bring her head back to Polydectes as promised. Just leave me what I need."

"I'm not leaving you here."

"Then I guess you're staying."

"Oh, the two of you give me a headache," Angie said. "One of you is bad enough. If Perseus is staying, then you're staying, which means we're all staying, okay? Enough arguing. Even if Damian is right, it doesn't matter, so can we get to the part where we figure out how we're going to do this?"

I couldn't help it; I started laughing, and soon the others joined in. I flopped back on the moss and stared up at the slice of sky. "The only thing we're really missing is the shield—a way to see Medusa but not look directly at her."

"So if we had another way . . ." Perseus said.

"We could do this without her."

"Like what?" Angie asked.

I rolled to my side and looked down at the water, seeing my face stare back, and I nearly choked. "It's right here in front of us."

"What?" Perseus demanded.

"The water." They leaned over, and our faces looked back at us. One by one they grinned.

"Good idea," Damian said. "All we need is a way to get her out here and lure her close to the edge."

"If only we had someone who could act as bait." I pretended to think it over. When Damian blinked, I slapped him on the back. "Come on, D. We've been here for ages, and I haven't asked you even once."

"Why can't Angie do it?"

"Because I think Angie's going to be busy fetching the gorgons."

The plan was simple. Angie would head back down the tunnel until she found the gorgons. I had to assume Eury the Fury wouldn't come after us alone. She'd find her sisters and make sure we were all mincemeat. So we'd have three gorgons to deal with—two of them impossible to kill. We also had no idea which one was Medusa. Eury would be easy to identify because we'd already cut her head off—I'd never forget that face—and she had a scar around her neck. She'd also be the one trying to murderize me first.

Once the gorgons were in the outdoor area, Angie would take off on the pegasuses and try to lead two of them away while Perseus and I dealt with Medusa. The tricky part was getting her close to the water, but I had an idea.

"We just have to make it seem like Poseidon is here," I said. "That will get her to go toward the edge."

Damian's eyes shadowed as he caught my plan. "You want me to be Poseidon. Phoebe, you know I don't like water."

"And I don't like the idea of my brother being a rock. You're the biggest one of us—and one look at Angie's pigtails and they'll know it's a fake."

He sighed, trying to look brave. "I'll need a trident, something to get her to draw nearer."

"Perseus and I will hide in the bushes next to the water and wait for her to come close enough."

"Then I jump out and cut her head off," Perseus said.

"No. I'll do it," I said.

"You do not get to steal my honor, sister. What would the stories say about me? That I was so brave I let my sister face danger? I won't be remembered at all. Is that what you want?"

"No."

"Then give me the sword. You take the bag and get ready to scoop the head up when the deed is done."

I looked around our little group. Of them all, Perseus was the only one who didn't look the slightest bit scared. Angie was biting her lip, and Damian was gnawing on his thumb.

"Look, we don't have to do this," I said.

Angie snorted. "Shove it. We're scared, which we should be. Doesn't mean we're not gonna to do it."

"I can make a trident out of these sticks." Damian broke some off a tree. Perseus used the sword to carve the ends into points and lashed them onto a longer stick. It wasn't perfect by any means, but we were hoping Medusa would be too excited to look closely. Taking a strip of cloth, I wrapped it around Damian's head, blindfolding him.

"Are you sure this is necessary?" he said. "I won't open my eyes."

"Yeah, can't have you turning into a rock. You'd sink right to the bottom. Are you sure you can handle this?"

"I'm sure. I think my fear of Medusa is outweighing my fear of deep water." He smiled and then slipped into the pool. I placed a crown of leaves on his head. He sank down, holding the stick up.

"How's this?" He looked fairly regal with the crown of leaves.

"Perfect. When I give the signal, you go under and swim toward us, slowly raising the trident. Medusa will think it's Poseidon rising out of the water and come closer. Wait for my signal, and whatever you do—"

"Don't take off my blindfold," he said. "Got it."

I tugged off Hermes's sandals and swapped shoes with Perseus. He practiced flying around the grotto until he had the hang of it. "I hope I can keep these when this is over," he said with a grin.

"Fat chance. Hermes is going to skin us alive when he finds us." I put Hades's magic helmet on his head. Perseus shimmered and then disappeared from sight. "Remember, those snakes of theirs can sense you. Try not to move much."

"I'll be fine." It was weird hearing his voice and not seeing him.

"I'll be right here."

"You worry too much."

"And you don't worry enough." I hugged him then, holding him close, and whispered in his ear. "Don't turn into a rock."

Pounding feet sounded in the tunnel, and Angie's voice rang out. "They're coming!"

"Go time." The bush we were hiding in rustled as Perseus moved back to blend in.

I crouched next to him, clutching the bag. For the hundredth time, I wished I had lightning to protect me. I had no weapon, not even a club.

Angie burst out of the tunnel and headed straight for Nero, who waited next to Albert. She leaped onto his back, and the pegasuses took flight as the first gorgon appeared out of the tunnel. I couldn't risk looking at the face, but I did peek at the chest. No sign of a wound. So not Eury. Which one though? Was it Medusa or the other sister Hesper had called Stheno?

Behind them, another gorgon appeared. Definitely Eury. A jagged wound still oozed green blood in the center of her chest.

Then the third one emerged, and I blinked. The legs were not like the others. They were human, or appeared to be, under the long gown she wore.

"After them," Eury screamed, pointing at the sky. Stheno started to take off, but Medusa put a hand on her arm. "No. It is a ruse to draw us away. Let it go. I smell humans close by." She drifted forward a few steps. "Children, come out. I just want to talk."

Her voice was soft and sweet, nothing like her sisters.

"You possess powerful weapons," she added while the other two gorgons prowled, searching the bushes. "A helmet that gives you cloaking. What a lovely gift that would be. Don't you want to give it to me?"

I did. Suddenly I had an urge to rip it off Perseus's head and hand it over to her. I pressed my hands over my ears, but I could still hear her voice.

"And a sword of such beauty it reflects the stars themselves."

Reflect the stars! Feeling for Perseus, I whispered in his ear. He pressed the sword into my hands.

Sliding it an inch through the leaves, I moved my blindfold up and caught a reflection of the clearing, and then Medusa moved into sight. It was a quick glance but enough to know she was nothing like her sisters.

The skin on her arms was fair and smooth except near the shoulders, where serpentine scales marked her skin. Her face was beautiful in an eerie way, with jutting high cheekbones and full lips. Her eyes were deep set, hard to see much. There were no fangs or talons or green scales.

But there were snakes. Lots and lots of snakes. Albino white with red eyes. They were like a cloud around her head, sifting the air with their tongues flicking out, searching for our scent.

"If you show me this sword, I'll let you pet my snakes," she said. "Wouldn't that be nice?"

It would. Those snakes were cool. Like, the prettiest snakes I'd ever seen. I wanted to rip off my blindfold and look to my heart's content. Pretty soon I was going to be like one of those statues, with my eyes peeking through my fingers forever. I pinched myself hard, trying to focus on the pain.

"You have nothing to be afraid of," she crooned, moving around the clearing. "I won't let my sisters harm you. You surprised Euryale, that's all. We're not used to guests. Come out this instant and let me greet you properly."

Her words had a bite to them, a command I could barely ignore. Perseus shifted next to me, and I stomped on his foot. He muffled a grunt but stopped.

She must have heard us though, because the sound of hissing snakes grew louder. Bushes were shaking next to us. One of the gorgons was close by. "Why do you hide yourselves? Medusa is your friend. You came all this way, and I want to greet you properly."

Something grabbed me by the collar and yanked me upward. I had no chance to escape or fight back.

"There you are." Medusa clapped her hands like a small child. "Bring her to me."

I struggled to free myself, but whoever held me—Eury the Fury or Stheno—was too strong. I kicked out, landing a blow to a scaly thigh.

"Be careful, sister," the one holding me said. "They have that cloaking device."

"I'm not afraid," Medusa said. "You wouldn't hurt me, would you, child?"

At the moment, I couldn't have hurt her if my life and the whole planet Earth depended on it. It was as if I had lost all sense of my free will.

"Stop wriggling about like a fish on a hook. Stheno, put her down."

My feet touched the ground. I wanted to run, but I couldn't see anything with my blindfold on.

"Take off your blindfold," Medusa said. "I just want to talk."

My fingers itched to do as she said, but I balled them into fists. "No. I know what you can do. You turned all those people into stone. You haven't even asked us why we're here."

"Now I am curious. Tell Medusa why you invaded her home."

"He sent me."

"Who?"

"Poseidon."

She sucked in a breath, and the snakes around her head all let out an excited hiss. "Poseidon?" Her voice had a breathy note to it.

"Yeah. He has a message."

"Why would he send children?"

"Because all the sailors he sent you turned into stone."

"He sent? But they never said!" Her voice was rising.

"Medusa, she lies." That voice was definitely Eury. "She is distracting you. Get on with it, and let us find the others."

"That's fine," I said. "Turn me into stone. Poseidon just wanted to know how you were feeling."

"Why?"

"You know, because you're having his babies."

The next thing I knew, a hand was at my throat, and my blindfold was ripped off. Snakes hissed in my face, rubbing against my skin and touching my hair.

"Open your eyes but do not look into mine," she said. "I will know if you are lying."

I kept my eyes squinched tight, and the tips of her nails dug into my skin as her hand tightened. "Do it now."

I couldn't resist. My eyes fluttered open, but I kept them pointed straight ahead. I was inches from her face. Her nostrils flared, and she smiled, revealing fangs at the corners of her mouth. "How do you know I am with child?"

The snakes moved in front of my eyes, their tongues flickering out.

This would be the perfect time for Perseus to strike, but if he takes her head off, he'll take mine off. I had to get her to let me go.

"Take your hands off me, and I'll tell you," I said.

She lifted her other hand, using her index finger to tilt my chin up. I kept my eyes down, but she kept pressing. Forcing my head back. "Tell me or I will make you look."

"Let me go so I can show you."

She slowly released her grip. "Do not be a fool and try to run, or I will let Euryale tear you limb from limb."

"I'm just going to walk over there toward the edge." I jerked my head at the water. "There's something you have to see." I took a careful step and then another step. When I was at the edge, I gave the signal.

"Poseidon has returned." I raised my hand to point. "Look, his trident appears."

"Poseidon? Here?"

"Medusa, it is a trick!" Eury screamed.

But Medusa stepped forward. "His trident is there! See, Euryale? He came back for me as promised."

I could hear hissing as she moved closer. She was only a few feet from the edge.

"They have the power of cloaking," Eury reminded, prowling and flinging white powder in the air. "They could be hiding anywhere. They carry a blade sharp enough to remove our heads."

"Poseidon would never hurt me." Medusa drew closer to the water.

One more step and she would be in range.

"Poseidon is not here, you fool!" Eury raged.

"Wait, there he is," she said, sounding breathless as a girl coming face to face with her crush.

The water in the center rippled, and then the tips of Damian's fake trident appeared. It was working!

I looked down at the water. Medusa's image flickered as one hand went to her mouth, the snakes a cloud around her head.

And then the sticks on the trident fell apart and floated on the surface, and Damian bobbed up, gasping for air and flailing at the water.

"That's not Poseidon." She whirled on me. "You lied to me."

"Now, Perseus."

Behind Medusa, the bushes rustled. I ducked, putting my arms over my head. I heard a swishing noise as the sword sliced through the air, and then there was a sickening thud.

Her head bounced on the ground and then rolled toward the water.

I dove for it, praying I didn't accidentally look into her eyes, and grabbed a handful of snakes before it rolled over the edge. They writhed and twisted under my hands, snapping at me. I kept her face turned away and jammed it into the bag, careful not to let any of the blood touch me.

Perseus ripped off the helmet. He hovered a few inches off the ground in Hermes's sandals. "I did it!"

"Here." I tossed him the bag. "Put the helmet back on and go."

The shrieks of the gorgon sisters filled the cavern.

"I can't leave you."

"You promised. Just go—help Mom. Be a hero."

He didn't argue, putting the helmet back on and disappearing from sight. Then his arms went around me, squeezing me tight. "I'm going to miss you," he whispered, and then he was gone.

I put two fingers to my mouth and whistled.

Time for part two of the plan.

CHAPTER 22

"You murdered our sister!" Eury the Fury fell to her knees by Medusa's side, her wings arched up behind her. She cradled her sister's body in her arms. Stheno stood over her, tilting her head back to let out a mournful wail that echoed off the walls of the cavern. Strange white liquid pooled around Medusa's body, seeping into the water where Damian floundered.

"Phoebe, I can't swim—I've got a cramp," he shouted.

Problem was the gorgons were between me and the water. "Give me a sec, D. I'm kind of busy."

Eury let Medusa fall back to the ground and advanced on me, the red centers of her eyes burning like flames. The wound on her chest seeped green blood, and the snakes growing from her head curled around her body and arms, heads up, jaws open, ready to strike. Stheno prowled closer, the two of them penning me in on either side.

"We will pull your limbs from your body one at a time," Eury rasped.

"We will watch you suffer until you don't know your name," Stheno added with a hiss.

I edged around them, inching toward the water.

"You cannot escape this island alive," Eury said.

"Phoebe!" Damian sounded desperate, his hands slapping at the water. "I've got a cramp. Please."

"Come on, Angie," I whispered. "Any day now."

There was the sound of flapping wings overhead. Eury looked up as a boulder came crashing down, hitting her square on the head. Another boulder hit Stheno on the back, breaking her wings and pinning her to the ground.

I turned and dove in. There was no sign of Damian. I swam hard and fast to where I'd last seen him and dove down, feeling everywhere until my fingers touched his arm. I grabbed it and hauled him up to the surface.

He wasn't breathing. I slapped him, trying to keep his head up. "Damian, breathe. I really don't want to have to do mouth-to-mouth."

I shook his chin, and he finally roused, lashing out with his arms and dunking me under.

I held him back, struggling to calm him down and keep him from drowning me. "Damian, stop it. I've got you."

He blinked at me, stilling. "I thought I was going to drown."

"You know I wouldn't let that happen."

"I was literally drowning. Another minute and it would have happened."

"But it didn't. Come on, we have to get out of here before the gorgons wake up. Can you swim?"

He nodded, and we swam toward shore as Angie landed the pegasuses. That strange white blood was spreading on the surface. We carefully avoided it and climbed out.

"Nice job, Angie!"

She rolled her shoulders. "The pegasuses did the heavy lifting. There was no shortage of statues to choose from."

"Let's go before something else goes wrong." I wanted to shout with glee. Not only had we fixed everything we'd messed up, but I wasn't going to be erased from existence.

"Check it out," Angie said, looking over her shoulder.

I turned, fearing the gorgons had revived, but it was something else entirely.

The white blood pooling on the surface misted, the particles lifting and swirling about. The water rippled, and then a pair of white pointed ears broke the surface, then the tip of a wing, and then a fully formed pegasus burst out of the water and landed next to the body of Medusa. It was magnificent, snow white with deep blue eyes and a full mane it shook out. Behind it, a golden sword pierced the water's surface, and then a giant of a man strode out of the water, leaping onto the shore next to Medusa's body. He knelt down, placing one hand on her chest, and bowed his head briefly before leaping onto the back of the pegasus. The pair took flight, quickly winging up out of the chasm until they were out of sight. If they saw us, they paid no attention to us.

"Was that really a pegasus?" I asked.

"Not a pegasus. *The* Pegasus," Damian said, sounding giddy. "That was mythology happening right before our eyes."

One of the gorgons groaned, and the boulder resting on her began to move.

"Time to go," I said.

We winged our way up and out of the chasm. When we broke free from the spire of rock, a surprise awaited us.

On the flat spot below us were a pair of figures. One was Perseus on his knees. The other was a red-haired statuesque woman wearing a golden crown and holding the glittering sword of Hermes, ready to bring it down on his head.

"No!"

The word ripped from my throat, and I practically flung myself off Nero to get to Perseus. Angie urged the pegasus down to the plateau, and when we got close, I leaped off, tumbling once before getting to my feet.

"Get away from my brother," I said.

The woman didn't even look at me, flicking a hand and sending me flying backward into a rock. "I'll deal with you in a moment." She raised the sword again. "This one is not going to be remembered as a hero while my son rots in Tartarus."

"Ares got what he deserved. He tried to destroy Olympus."

She whirled, her gray eyes flashing fire. "It was you who was the perpetrator, not him. He was simply doing what all gods do—seeking power."

"No. He wanted to enslave the people of Olympus. That's not what gods do. That's not what Zeus does."

"You think your father is so high and mighty," she scoffed. "He is not."

"I'm sure he makes mistakes. We all do. But I know he tries to do right. I have seen that. If you strike down his son, he will never forgive you."

She laughed, but it was a mirthless sound. "You think I want his forgiveness? I want him to suffer, as I suffer. If I cannot have my son, then he cannot have this one."

She turned back to Perseus, ready to bring the sword down. I tackled her, knocking her off her feet. Damian sat on her chest while Angie pried the sword from her fingers. With a sweep of her arm, she flung us off and got back on her feet, trembling and white with rage.

I held the sword out, guarding my friends. "Just leave us alone."

"You have no idea who you're dealing with," she spat. "None of you will leave this place alive. I don't need a sword or a weapon to kill you, not when I have you to do it for me."

Her gray eyes turned calculating and cold, like a shark sighting its prey. She waved her hand toward me. "You hate your friends, and you always have. You despise them. They lie to you. They turn your stomach. You would give anything to get them out of your life. They are nothing but cheats. You want to take that blade and rid the world of their vile presences, then turn it on yourself."

My heart froze in my chest, and I couldn't breathe as a wall of hatred slammed into me. I could feel its fingers curl into every pore, fill every inch of me with black tar, blocking out any other thought.

I didn't just hate my friends; I loathed them. And my brother? He was slimier than a sewer rat. It made my flesh crawl just thinking of them living and breathing. I gripped the sword tighter, ignoring the sly look in Hera's eyes, and turned to face them.

Angie and Damian took a step back, but Perseus didn't budge.

"Are you tired of me already, sister?"

"You are disgusting." I hardly recognized my own voice. "I hate your very face."

He laughed. "That's too bad, because it looks a lot like yours."

I held the sword out, pointing it at his chest. "I can't believe the gods cursed me with such a stupid, idiotic, worthless, lowlife, scum-sucking brother."

He didn't flinch at my words, just laughed again. "And I can't believe the gods cursed me with a weak-willed sister who can't fight off a simple enchantment spell."

Spell? I wasn't under any spell. In fact, for the first time ever, I could see clearly. Angie was a two-faced liar, and Damian the know-it-all knew nothing. They were all plotting behind my back. Roaring, howling pain ripped a hole in my chest. I had trusted them, befriended them, but all along they had plotted to bring me down.

Use the sword and all this pain will go away, a voice in my head whispered.

Yes, the sword in my hand. I would use it to rid the world of these useless, vile creatures. Before I could act, Perseus took the tip of the sword and placed it over his heart. "Go ahead. Take my life. Our mother will cry tears all the way to Olympus."

My arm wavered. I wanted to ram it in. The same way he'd rammed it into Eury the Fury saving my life. My arm shook. *He'd saved my life.* How could that be true? I must be remembering it wrong—he was a traitor. Resolved, I prepared to strike when Damian pushed Perseus aside, taking the blade and putting it over his own heart.

"No, take me instead. You know I'm not really your friend. All those times I let you use me as bait prove you can't trust me."

Bait. Damian was always the bait. I'd used him so many times, and he'd saved me—again and again.

My head hurt, and the tar boiled in my veins. I had to make it stop.

Get rid of him now! the voice in my head roared. My arm shook as I tried to force it to do as my brain asked.

Then Angie was there, shoving Damian aside.

"If someone's getting the pointy end, it's me. When have I ever saved your life? If you count the time in the bathroom when that hydra came out of the toilet, I think it's six, or is it seven times? Some friend I am. I can't even keep track."

The hydra. Angie covered in goo. Holding her little switchblade. Bravely fighting for me.

I let the sword drop, hearing it clang on the stone.

I blinked, clearing my vision, and saw my friends and my brother before me, and I wanted to weep because I saw how much they cared about me.

I turned to face Hera, who was white-faced with fury. She snatched up the sword and held it at my chest.

"Fine. I will do it myself and blame you for it." Her face twisted with determination as her grip tightened, and then a voice rang out.

"Hera, strike down my sister, and you will have me to deal with."

Athena. At last.

Zesto landed, his hooves clattering on the stone, and Athena leaped down, kitted out in her helmet, shield, and golden sword. My heart soared even higher as Argenta landed with the slender figure of Hermes.

I would have cheered, but Hera still had Hermes's scimitar pointed at my chest. The tip nicked my skin, and I sucked in a breath.

"Hera, I do not speak lightly." Athena drew her sword. "Step away from her, and we can discuss this."

Hera wavered and then let her arm drop. "What business is this of yours, Athena?"

"You know why I am here."

"This girl deserves to be punished. I have every right to take her life after what she did to my tree."

"And she will be punished when she is brought before the gods and stands trial."

"You think they will give me the justice I seek?"

"This is not justice, Hera. This is revenge. Zeus will not stand for it."

Her eyes narrowed to slits of rage. "Zeus lacks the courage to lead as he should. He's too soft by far. It is I who should rule this world, not him and his miserable offspring."

"That's something for you to discuss with the council of gods. I will escort Phoebe to Olympus myself. While there, we can discuss how it is my *Athenoi* became so intent on destroying me that I nearly forgot who I was."

Hera's face tightened. "If you do not appear with them, I will find other ways to take my revenge." She vanished in a puff of air.

Athena came to my side and clasped my shoulders. "Are you all right, sister?"

"Yes." I flung my arms around her waist. "Thank you for coming."

"I'm sorry I was so late. Argenta found me and led me to a rather grumpy Hermes."

"Sorry about that," I said to the god who sat on my horse with his arms folded. "But we really needed your sandals."

His face finally cracked into a smile. "A taste of my own medicine. It is usually I who do the robbing. However did you get Geryon to give you the Argus Slayer?"

"We traded him a feisty goddess of war," I said.

Damian handed him the lyre. It was a little worse for wear from our travels, but when Hermes ran his fingers over the strings, sweet notes trickled out.

"I'll take my scimitar back." He held his hands out, and I picked up the curved blade and passed it up to him. "And my winged sandals."

"But how will Perseus get home?" I asked.

"We can take him," Athena said. "On our way to Olympus."

My heart soared. That meant I would get to see my mother.

Perseus toed off the sandals and handed them over to Hermes. The messenger god put them on and, with a small salute, winged off into the air.

"Come, we must not delay," Athena said briskly. "Phoebe, with me on Argenta. Perseus can ride Zesto."

She leaped onto Argenta's back and held her hand out to me. I gripped it and let her tug me on.

"I must warn you," Athena said once we were up high, "Hera is very powerful, exceeded only by our father. Burning her tree is a great offence. They will have to punish you."

"It's okay," I said. "As long as Perseus is okay, I can take it."

"I don't know if you can," she said. "They may demand your life."

"Still worth it." I yawned. My eyes were getting heavy. I couldn't remember the last time I'd slept, and there on the back of Argenta, leaning against my sister, I fell sound asleep.

CHAPTER 23

I awoke to the sound of a seagull shrieking and bright sunlight over a dazzling turquoise sea. A small island with pristine white sand along the beach lay beneath us.

"Is that Seriphos?" I asked, rubbing the sleep from my eyes.

"Yes."

"I thought it would take days to get here."

"I gave speed to the pegasuses."

We flew over the town square where I had first met Perseus, on up to the small fishing village on the bluff. We set the pegasuses down, raising a cloud of fine dust. Perseus ran to the door of his small hut.

"Mother! I have returned."

"She's not here," a gruff voice said.

A man with a weathered face and a fishing net thrown over his shoulder came out of the shadows.

"Dictys." Perseus ran and threw his arms around the man. "Where is my mother?"

"Polydectes has taken her to his palace. They are to be married this day. I was just preparing to go."

"But she can't marry him. She hates him!" Perseus cried.

"She had no choice. No one expected you to return, and without the head of the gorgon, you have nothing to bargain with."

"But I do have it," Perseus said. "And I'm going to stop the marriage." He jumped onto Zesto's back, and the little red pegasus took speedy flight.

Wordlessly, we jumped back on the pegasuses and flew toward the top of the island, where an imposing palace stood surrounded by tall gates. The inside courtyard was packed with people.

We landed the pegasuses in the center, scattering the assembled guests. Guards ran forward, holding lances out, but Athena—her sword in one hand and her shield in the other—gave them a quiet stare that dared them to stop us. Perseus ignored all of them, dodging between the crowd and heading for a steepled building with large double doors. From inside, we could hear an organ playing a wedding march.

Perseus rattled the handles. "They're locked!"

Athena brushed him aside and kicked the door open with one strike of her boot.

The place reminded me of a cathedral, with stained glass in the windows and rows and rows of pews packed with guests. In the center, an aisle laid with red carpet and scattered rose petals led to a dais, where a woman in a white dress stood next to a familiar man. King Polydectes wore a heavy gold crown and red military tunic with gold braiding. Next to him stood the little toad who had beaten me up, looking sullen and unhappy.

The king turned, looking shocked. Our mother's face took on a look of joy and relief at the sight of Perseus.

"King Polydectes, I have returned with the head of the

gorgon," Perseus announced, striding confidently down the aisle.

The king looked less than happy at the news. "Guards, remove them."

Athena took up a fighting stance. "You all know who I am. I dare any of you to come near." We made our way forward unhindered as the guests whispered and murmured.

As we reached the head of the procession, Perseus stopped. "Release my mother now."

"What proof have I that you've accomplished the deed?" the king sneered. "And who says I can't marry her? I said your sentence would be reduced. You can spend ten years in prison instead of life."

"No! You said my sentence would be erased and that my mother and I would be free of you."

"Prove it," he said, his eyes glittering. "Now, if that is all, you can show me this head later. Today is my wedding day."

I couldn't take my eyes off my mother. She hadn't really noticed me—her eyes were locked on Perseus, hungrily taking in his features, searching for injuries, showing him so much love with just her eyes it made my heart hurt.

"I must take the head of Medusa with me for safekeeping, so we will deal with this now," Athena said with that bossy goddess voice of hers.

"Fine, fine," the king muttered. "Show me the head, and then be gone, all of you."

"Mother, please shield your eyes," Perseus said. "You mustn't look at it. It's too horrible."

Our mother nodded, placing her hands over her eyes.

"No matter what, don't look."

Athena held open the bag, and Perseus stuck his hand in, grimacing a bit before pulling up the head of Medusa.

We took a step back, averting our eyes from it, but Perseus made sure to hold the face toward Polydectes.

We knew the mythology, so it was no surprise when Polydectes let out a scream. "Her eyes! They're open! How is that possible? Put it away! Put it awaaaaa—"

And then with a rippling crackle, Polydectes turned to stone.

There was silence in the room, then gasps of horror and shock.

Athena turned to the crowd, her sword and shield at the ready. "No one move, lest you meet the same fate as your king. Perseus did what was asked of him to the letter. He has been exonerated. He and his mother are now free to live their lives. If any interfere, they will have me to deal with."

The assembled throng remained silent, too stunned to react or too scared they would be next. Athena took the head of Medusa from Perseus and carefully replaced it in the bag. She addressed the crowd once more. "Now you must search for a new king. I know of no kinder man than his brother, Dictys." She nodded at the kindly man in the back of the room.

The old fisherman looked uncomfortable, but the crowd began to applaud, and soon there were shouts of "Long live King Dictys."

Perseus rushed forward and hugged our mother. I continued to hang back, not sure what to do.

Athena's hand landed on my shoulder. "Come, we must go," she said softly, motioning to Angie and Damian.

"But . . ." Surely she didn't expect me to leave without even saying hi to my mom!

"The Erinyes are here," she explained.

She dragged me backward as Perseus recounted the

story of his adventures to our mother. It wasn't until we were at the door that he realized we were gone.

"Phoebe! Wait! Come back."

I wanted to stay more than anything, but Athena's grip was ironclad. I caught one glimpse of our mother's face turned toward me with hope and excitement before the door was slammed shut.

Alekto waited with her two sisters, their eyes grim.

"I will bring her," Athena said. "You have my word."

"We trust you, Athena, but it is our sworn duty. Forgive the insult, but we must escort you."

Athena lifted me behind her on Argenta, and we swiftly took flight. Tears burned my eyes. Below me, I could see Perseus shouting and waving at me. Next to him, our mother stood with her hand shielding her eyes as we left Seriphos behind.

"Why couldn't I just say hello?" I asked, wanting to jump off Argenta.

"Because you wouldn't have wanted to leave. You want a mother's love too badly."

"What's wrong with that?" I said in a thick voice, wanting to bawl my eyes out.

"It will be harder for her when she finds out her daughter is out of reach."

"What if I stayed?"

"What if the gods decide to send you to Tartarus? Her heart will be broken all over again."

Tears slipped down my cheeks. "I just wanted to say hi—give her one hug." It would have been enough. I could have wrapped it up and held on to it forever.

"There will be another time. If the gods see fit to let you live."

"What about Angie and Damian?"

"I'll make sure they are held blameless."

My throat was so thick I could hardly breathe as I recalled every inch of my mother's face. Athena's powers carried us fast, as if an invisible wind pushed us along. The Erinyes kept pace, one on either side and one behind us. In no time, the white-rimmed peak of Olympus came into view. We flew over the golden gates that had been repaired since our last visit, when Typhon had ripped through them. Athena's palace was restored, but we didn't stop there, heading straight for the large round building at the top.

Zeus's temple and the Hall of the Gods. The place where I had saved my father's life that night and nearly lost my own when Ares had impaled me with his lightning scepter.

I was nervous to see Zeus again. Mostly I was scared about what was going to happen. Spending eternity in Tartarus wasn't appealing in the slightest.

We left the pegasuses outside. I turned to Angie and Damian. "You guys should wait here."

"Oh, please," Angie said. "I'm not going to let that red-haired witch take you down without a fight."

"You'll need us," Damian said. "We stick together."

The Erinyes were waiting impatiently, but I ignored them, putting my arms around my friends and drawing them in to form a tight circle. "No matter what happens, I want you guys to go home. You can't be stuck here with me."

"We're not leaving you behind," Angie said.

"Yes, you are. You have families that need you. Your mom's going to get better soon, Angie, and if you're not there, then what?"

Her lip wobbled.

"And, Damian, your family needs you even if they aren't always there. Family is here, in your heart. I love my mother so much even though I've never spent more than a minute with her. I would give anything to be back with her, so I can only imagine what it's like for you guys."

"I don't want to leave you," Damian said. "I can't imagine it."

"It might not come to that. I just want you to be ready. If Athena gives the word, you go with her. No arguing. Agreed?"

It took a moment, and then they nodded their heads in agreement.

"I'm ready now," I said to Alekto.

Athena touched my arm. "I will do my best to gather support for you."

The Erinyes led me up the steps and past the columns. There was no sign of the destruction Typhon had wrought. The twelve thrones were arranged in a semicircle, and all of them were full. Enyo lounged on Ares's throne, throwing daggers at me with her eyes. Apparently she had escaped Geryon's advances.

Zeus sat on the largest throne in the center, holding his lightning scepter in one hand. He didn't smile at me as we walked to the center of the room. He looked pensive, worried. Hera sat to his right, staring straight ahead as if I were invisible.

Alekto began. "We have brought you Phoebe of Argos, daughter of Zeus, who has confessed to committing a crime against the gods. Phoebe of Argos knowingly took actions that caused significant damage to the sacred tree of Hera whilst a fatal injury was inflicted on the guardian of the tree, Ladon."

I searched for a friendly face. Each god's throne was engraved with their name. To the left of Zeus sat Athena, then Apollo. Macario's father looked worried, whispering in Athena's ear. Next was Hephaestus, the lame machine worker who'd built the chains that sank Typhon, then Dionysus, who drank from a chalice in his hand and seemed to be laughing at some private joke. Hermes sat on the end, quietly watching me, his lyre resting on his lap.

On the other side of Hera, a dark-haired man dressed in a sea-green robe held a golden trident.

Poseidon. God of the seas.

His eyes were scorching as he stared at me, as if he wanted to run his trident through me. Damian had said something about him being the father of Medusa's children. My gut tightened a bit. *Not an ally.*

Next was Enyo. Her dark hair was tied back, and she wore her black leather armor. She looked as fierce as Athena, and her raptor eyes burned with hate. My heart sank further. Next was a simpering goddess named Demeter, who was casting side-eyes at Poseidon, hoping to get his attention, and Artemis and Aphrodite, who were busy chatting, seemingly ignoring the drama playing out in front of them.

Poseidon rose, pointing his trident at me. "I say she should be put to death. Thrown off the top of Mount Olympus. This is not her first offence. She is reckless and has no regard for the laws of Olympus."

"It was just a tree," I said.

All twelve gods swiveled their heads to stare at me in shock.

"You are not allowed to speak," Poseidon said.

My temper was rising, which probably wasn't good, but it was all I had to keep me going, so I let it rip. "Too bad. This is my trial, and you all seem to have decided I'm guilty, but none of you have asked me why I did it."

"Let her speak," Zeus said.

Thanks, Pops.

I shook off the hands of the two Erinyes holding me and stepped forward. "You all know about the prophecy that led me to be exiled from this place when I was only a baby, so forgive me if I don't know all the sacred laws here. I'm still new to all this. But when Olympus was threatened, I did everything in my power to save it."

"You nearly destroyed it," Hera screeched, hands clamped down on the arms of her throne.

"Yes, and where were you when that happened?" I asked.

She hissed. "How dare you speak to me like that."

"This is my trial. I get to dare say what I want, so I'll ask again. Where were you when Olympus was threatened? Where were any of you besides Apollo and Athena?"

"We were busy with our own matters," Poseidon said, dismissing me with a wave of his hand.

"Exactly. Too busy to save your own home. So if you don't like my methods, tough. I did the best I could."

"That doesn't excuse what you did to my precious tree," Hera said shrilly.

"No, it doesn't," I agreed. "I have a habit of making excuses for what I do because the ends justify the means. Herk didn't need our help, not really. He just needed to know we believed in him. I burned the tree because it was easier than getting the nymphs to see reason, and I was impatient to get to my brother."

"So you admit it was your fault."

Was that what I had just said? Before I could argue, Poseidon rose.

"I say we put it to a vote. All in favor of executing Phoebe of Argos?"

"You will not execute my daughter," Zeus thundered.

Poseidon simply shrugged. "Fine. All in favor of sending her to Tartarus for eternity?"

He raised his trident. Hera's hand went up, as did Enyo's. Hera glared at her son Hephaestus, and the kindly machine worker raised his hand, sending me an apologetic glance. Hera turned to her right. Demeter shook her head, folding her arms, but Artemis and Aphrodite raised their hands.

Six votes to exile me to Tartarus.

"All in favor of releasing her back to the human world?" Zeus asked, raising his hand. Athena quickly raised hers, as did Apollo, Demeter, and Hermes. Dionysus raised his glass in a toast. "The vote is split six to six. In the event of a tie, the deciding vote goes to Hades. Alekto, did you bring his vote?"

The winged avenger nodded, carrying forward a sealed scroll. She broke the seal and unrolled the parchment, then turned the page around.

Guilty.

CHAPTER 24

Zeus rammed his scepter into the ground. "No. I will not stand for a daughter of mine to be sent to Tartarus over a tree. Hera, see reason."

"I see justice," Hera spat. "For all that you have cost me, let you now feel the pain of losing something you care about."

"You are a hateful woman." His words were coated with regret, and I knew, right then, he wasn't going to fight for me. I wasn't sure what hurt more, seeing my mother for only a moment, or having my father turn his back on me.

"I am sorry, young Phoebe," he said to me, "but the council has spoken. I cannot go against it, even though I wish it were me that paid the price."

Alekto's sisters took me by the elbows, ready to escort me down into the dark pit of the underworld.

"What about what she did?" Angie suddenly shouted, pointing at Hera. "This is all her fault."

"You have no voice here," Hera said, "so be quiet, unless you want to join in the fate of your friend."

Damian stepped up beside Angie, his fists clenched at his sides. "Why don't you tell everyone what you did to Hercules? It makes for a great story."

"Silence!" Hera shouted, rising from her throne. "Take them all away, or I will execute them myself."

"None of this would have happened if you hadn't caused Hercules to go mad," Angie shouted.

"You can't blame me for that murderer's actions," Hera spat. "He should have been executed, not given labors to redeem himself."

I shook free of the Erinyes' grip. "No. I've met him. Herk is a great guy. He would never hurt anything unless he had to. He swore he was enchanted by a voice that told him to murder his own family. Like the voice I heard when you tried to get me to do the same thing to my friends."

"Is this true, Hera?" Zeus asked, his voice edged with anger. "Did you cause Hercules to be enchanted into madness?"

Hera dismissed it with a wave of her hand. "The girl knows nothing. She lies to get herself out of this predicament. The council has spoken. Take her away to Tartarus, or I will throw her off the top of Olympus myself."

The Erinyes grabbed me, but I lunged forward. "Admit it. You enchanted Athena into throwing away her armor, then impersonated her and gave Perseus a cheap sword so he would fail and get turned into stone."

Hera leaped to her feet, her face white with anger. "Liar! You cannot prove it was me."

"Hera, explain yourself," Zeus ordered sternly.

The queen of the gods silently breathed in and out until her face settled into a mask of contempt. "Explain myself? To you? That's a laugh. You never answer for anything. But tell me, why is it always the children of Zeus who are the great heroes? What about my children?" She clamped a hand to her chest. "Does anyone tell great tales of them? Is Enyo even mentioned in these heroic myths you speak of? Does Hephaestus get a great tale? Meanwhile, my beloved son Ares rots in Tartarus like a common criminal for doing nothing less than what every son of Olympus has done throughout time: overthrow the overbearing father. So do not expect me to explain myself to you."

"Look, I know you don't like the children of Zeus," Damian said. "But you have to get over it. Hercules and Perseus are important to this whole place. Without them, no one would much care about Greek mythology, and you all would cease to exist."

There were outraged shouts from the council of gods.

Zeus rammed his scepter into the ground. "Silence!" He waited for the talk to die down. "What makes you say this?"

"An oracle told us," I said.

"An oracle? Who?"

"The one you sent me with when you exiled me."

"Phenicia?"

"I don't know her name. She goes by Miss Carole."

"And what did she say?"

"I said this place would crumble to dust if the great legends of Olympus didn't rise to meet the challenges." The crisp voice carried in the domed room as Miss Carole, aka the oracle known as Phenicia, strode into sight. Her high heels clicked on the marble floor. She was still wearing the prim gray suit she'd been wearing when we left.

"Phenicia? Is that really you?" Zeus rose to greet her.

She bowed her head. "It is I, Zeus. So good to be home after so many years away. I can see nothing has changed for the better." She eyed the council of gods with disdain.

"Dionysus is still drinking away his troubles. Apollo looks like the sun rises and sets on him. And Poseidon looks angry enough to raise the seas."

"Sassy as always," Hermes said with a wink.

"And you, Hermes, letting your lyre fall into the hands of mortals." She *tsked* him. "Do you know how much grief it has caused me?"

Miss Carole turned back to Zeus. "I am taking this girl and her companions back to earth with me."

"You cannot do that," Hera said. "She must be punished."

"Trust me, being related to the lot of you is punishment enough," I grumbled.

"There has been much said today that has muddied the decision," Zeus said. "Hera, your jealousy has caused a great deal of trouble."

Hera drew herself to her full height. "My jealousy is what drives Hercules to become a great hero, so who has the last laugh? The fact remains the tree was given to me by Gaia herself." A calculating look came over her face. "Release our son from Tartarus, and I will consider forgiving her crime."

"Fine. Send me to Tartarus," I said quickly. "I'd rather go than have that scumbag Ares released to cause more trouble."

But Zeus rapped his scepter against the ground. "It is a fair and equitable exchange. Ares will be released and Phoebe's crime wiped clean. Are we in agreement?"

Hera nodded, and the rest of the gods agreed. "Then it has been decided. Alekto, please send word to Hades of the council's decision. I will expect Ares to be returned forthwith."

Alekto bowed, and the Erinyes backed away.

"Not so fast," I said, holding my hand out.

Alekto gave me a rare smile, then drew the bolt from her quiver and placed it in my hand. "I almost thought you'd forgotten."

"Not likely."

As soon as my hand touched the bolt, it sparked to life. A jolt ran up my arm as the power that had been encased in the bolt refilled my veins, charging my inner batteries back to life until the lightning bolt glowed as bright as the sun.

Miss Carole went over to Hephaestus and asked for a word.

Someone tapped me on the shoulder. I turned to find Zeus standing behind me, his brow deeply furrowed.

"I sense you are disappointed in me."

I shrugged. "No big deal. All's well that ends well."

"You wanted me to stand up for you."

I said nothing.

"You will find that when you are in charge of all this"—he waved a hand—"every decision is more complicated than you can imagine, and there is always a price. I knew Hera wanted Ares released very badly, and it was the only thing I could do to make peace between you and her. I would have never let you be sent there. I want you to know that."

I nodded, but I wasn't sure I believed him.

He sighed. "I don't deserve your trust, or your loyalty. You have already done far more for Olympus than I have ever done for you. Just know that I will not let you down again, I promise." He squeezed my shoulder and then moved away.

Miss Carole returned from speaking to Hephaestus, looking satisfied. "Time to depart, children."

"How are we getting home?" I asked.

She held up a small mechanism that looked like a pocket watch. "I spoke to the master himself. We have what we need to return. We'll have to stop in Athens first."

We walked out of the temple. From behind a pillar, a figure emerged.

Athena.

My sister waved me over and pulled me into the shadows.

"Phoebe, are you all right?" she asked.

I nodded, but tears spilled over.

"I'm sorry." She pulled me in close. "Family can be trying at the best of times, but when your father is the king of the gods . . ."

"It's complicated." I wiped the tears away.

"Yes. But he cares deeply for you. And Perseus."

"I don't suppose I can see my mother before I go?"

"There is no time. It is not wise for you to linger here in Olympus."

Disappointment stung, but I smiled at Athena. "Take care, sis. I hope to see you again."

She clasped my arm in hers. "And you, Phoebe. Be well. And stay out of trouble."

I laughed. "Like that's going to happen." I started to walk away and then stopped. "I almost forgot." The magic bag was still strapped to Argenta. I unlatched it, and she reached her hand inside.

"Avert your eyes," Athena said.

I covered them with my hands. I could hear the snakes hissing and then a *gloop*, and everything went silent.

"You can open your eyes now."

I lowered my hands. Athena held her shield, Aegis. Where there had been a plain gold center, now the head of Medusa pressed outward, encased inside the shield. Her snakes stood up in a circle around her face, which was locked in a permanent grimace.

"Now my enemies will think twice before approaching me," Athena said, giving me a wink.

We stepped onto our rides for the last time. Miss Carole sat with her legs primly crossed on the back end of Nero, not the least bothered by the windy ride. I wrapped my arms around Argenta's neck as she winged us south toward Athens. As the Parthenon came into sight, my eyes clouded. I would miss Athena. Miss my crazy family.

We landed near Athena's olive tree. The plaza was deserted—no crazy Athenoi hanging around to attack us.

"Time to say goodbye to your friends." Miss Carole nodded at the pegasuses, who pranced in place, looking confused.

We each wrapped our arms around the neck of our rides.

"Oh, Argenta, I wish I could take you home with me." I buried my face in her silky coat.

She whickered at me, then nudged me with her head.

"Until the next adventure, okay?" I scratched her ears, then stepped back. Angie had tears running down her cheeks, and Damian wiped his face with his sleeve as the three pegasuses raised their front legs in the air, flashing their hooves in unison before taking flight. We watched them go until they disappeared from sight.

"Now to see a man about a machine," Miss Carole said.

We followed her down the long set of steps into the narrow alleys that made up the marketplace.

I stopped at a familiar alley. "Hold on a sec." I darted down the narrow lane. The three old hags sat at their table with their broken loom, muttering and bickering with each other.

I slammed Calypso's loom down on the table. Their eyes flew up at the sight of me and then settled on the loom.

"Where did you get this?" the crone with the broken loom asked.

"From a sea witch named Calypso."

"Calypso?" the one with the needle asked. "But she makes the finest things in the world."

"And now it's yours. Are we even now?"

"You destroyed our loom," scissor-wielding crone said. "We will never be even."

"Fine." I snatched the loom back, but the crone holding the loom held on to it.

"All is settled," she said eagerly. "The Fates will smile kindly on you."

I made my way back to my friends. Angie waved me into a small shop filled with the oddest mechanisms and robots. There were statues with moving arms, and dog statues with tails that actually wagged. On the counter, an old yellow rotary phone sat, similar to the one in Miss Carole's office.

"What is this place?" I asked Damian.

"This is the shop of Daedalus," he said, his eyes shining with excitement. "He's an apprentice of Hephaestus and very clever. Look what he's done."

He stepped aside, revealing Hilda, his robotic housekeeper who'd broken into a million pieces when we'd traveled here. She looked fully repaired with a new screen and reattached arms, but the screen was blank.

A man with frizzy gray hair was fiddling with her midsection. He inserted the pocket watch Miss Carole had gotten from Hephaestus and then straightened.

"All better?" Miss Carole asked.

"That should get it restarted." He tapped on the screen, but nothing happened.

"Why isn't it working?" Damian asked, looking worried.

"I don't know. It could be there was too much damage," Daedalus said. "I would need a powerful source of magic to fix it."

My eyes widened. "What about this?" I quickly rummaged in Calypso's bag, pulling out the golden apple Herk had left behind.

The tinkerer's eyes grew wide as he reached trembling fingers toward it. "Is that what I think it is?"

"One of Hera's apples. I know they're sacred, but I didn't mean to steal it. Will it help?"

He took the apple, holding it up to the light, then polished it with his tunic until it shone brightly. "If this doesn't restart her, nothing will."

Quickly using a screwdriver, he opened her midsection. There was a glowing energy core in a glass case. Using a pair of tongs, he inserted the apple into the energy core. It hovered there and then began to spin, slowly at first, then faster and faster until it was a blur. Hilda's eyes suddenly flew open.

"Hello, how are you, I am fine," she said, her eyes large circles on the screen.

"Hilda, you're back!" Damian shouted, throwing his arms around her.

"Master Damian, I feel so funny. Like I can fly!" She took off, zooming around the shop as we laughed.

Daedalus wiped his hands on a rag. "I must say, I've never seen a machine like this. Are you sure I can't keep it and study it a bit longer?"

"No, Daedalus," Miss Carole said. "We must be returning." She passed him a small bag of coins. "Our transport has been repaired?"

"Yes, it's out back."

"Children, shall we?"

We followed her out the back door of the shop, and our jaws dropped. The Titan's Tacos truck was parked in the dirt alley. The side panels were battered, the windshield cracked, and one tire was low. Damian lifted Hilda inside, and we followed, only to find a glum-looking Tony in manacles sitting in the passenger seat.

"Tony, what happened?" I asked.

Miss Carole glared at him. "Tony is going back to serve an extended sentence."

"Just let me go to Tartarus, please," he said. "Anything but that horrible city of New York."

Miss Carole turned the engine over. It backfired once, then coughed to life. "Phoebe, I don't suppose I could borrow some lightning?"

I grinned, twitching my fingers and calling up a bolt. "You mean like this?"

"That will do nicely. If you would just insert it in that round opening on the floor."

At our feet was a round valve. Damian twisted it open and lifted a small hatch. Inside a small chamber, sparks flew in a swirling vortex. But before I could drop the bolt in, there was a knock at the back door.

Miss Carole checked the side mirror, then her face creased into a smile. "Phoebe, I think there is someone here to see you. We don't have much time, dear, so make the most of it."

Confused, I set the bolt down, climbed past Angie and Damian, and opened the back door. My heart dropped to my toes.

There in the road was Zesto, tossing his yellow mane at the sight of me. We had left the flame-colored pegasus back in Seriphos. Then from behind him, Perseus stepped forward, dragging a woman by the hand.

Mom.

Her eyes were bright with tears as she held her arms out. I didn't hesitate—I ran. I'll never forget that moment as long as I live. The feel of her arms, the smell of her, the soft press of my face to her chest.

"Phoebe, darling." She pressed a kiss to the top of my head. "I have missed you so much."

I couldn't speak. I held on to her as though my life depended on it.

"I never wanted to let you go," she whispered. "And I have thought of you every day since that day. I am so proud of what you have done. Perseus has told me everything, how brave you were, how you saved him, saved me. Please—tell me that you will stay here with us and be a family."

Tears ran down my cheeks. I had waited my whole life to hear those words. I wanted to say yes with every fiber of my being.

Slowly, I pulled away, wiping my eyes with my sleeve. "I wish I could. But it's too risky. I have a habit of getting into trouble and causing things to change. If I stay, I could risk this whole place."

There was a tug on my elbow. Damian and Angie stood waiting. "It's time, Phoebe," Damian said.

I nodded. "Just give me a sec."

Perseus looked angry, his eyes shiny with unshed tears. "I can't believe you are just going to leave."

"You know I'll just mess things up again. Besides, you're going to do great things without me."

"But it won't be as much fun." He threw his arms around me and squeezed me so hard I thought my ribs might break. "I am so proud that you are my sister. I will never forget you."

"Nor I you." I let him go, stepping back.

"It's been real, Big P." Angie held her hand up for a high five.

"Back at you," he said, slapping her hand with his.

Damian extended his hand, and they shook. "You will do great things, Perseus. I'm sure of it. Just don't forget to go save Andromeda."

He grinned. "She better be beautiful if I'm going to fight that sea lobster."

"Trust me," Damian said. "She's worth it."

Miss Carole honked the horn twice.

"We have to go." I looked at my mother, memorizing her face, and then gave her one last hug. She tucked something in my pocket, and then Damian dragged me away.

Perseus and my mom stood by Zesto until we shut the door.

I picked up the lightning bolt and dropped it in before I could change my mind. It briefly exploded in light, and the sparks flew faster. Damian quickly screwed the hatch back on.

"Hold on." Miss Carole threw the car into gear. We bounced down the road, faster and faster, until the truck bent like Damian's kitchen, and we were rocketed through space and time.

It was only a few seconds before we landed on a tree-lined street with brownstones on either side.

"This is my block," Damian said.

The truck rolled to a stop.

"Are we really back?" I asked.

"Yes," Miss Carole said. "It's time for you to get off. I've informed your parents about an extended absence. You'll find them not terribly worried." Tony reached for the door, but she gave him a cold glare. "Not you, Tony. We still have your punishment to discuss."

He sighed, folding his arms.

"See you at school?" I met her eyes in the rearview mirror. She shrugged. "I suppose being a counselor isn't so bad."

"Thanks. For everything," I added. "You're not so bad for an oracle."

We piled out the back of the truck. Damian and Angie helped Hilda up the steps and opened the door.

"Hilda is happy to be home," the robot sang. She spun in a circle, waving her arms in the air. "Home. Home. Home."

We laughed, following her into the kitchen.

"So, do you think we fixed everything?" I asked.

"One way to find out." He opened up the mythology book that he'd left on the table, thumbing to Perseus's story first. My brother was proudly holding the head of Medusa out. "Looks like he's restored as a hero."

"What about Herk?"

He flipped the pages. "Yes, the order has been changed, but Herk rises to become an immortal hero like he was supposed to. You did it, Phoebe."

"We did it," I said. "Do you think we'll ever get to go back?"

"I don't see how," he said. "Not without messing things up again."

I hid my disappointment behind a smile. "At least I got to meet my mom this time." I blinked back tears. "I should be going. Carl will be wondering where I am."

"I'm going straight to pop's restaurant and ordering the biggest pizza he's got," Angie said, rubbing her stomach dreamily. "After I call Ma and tell her how much I miss her."

"Damian, will you be okay?" I asked.

He smiled. "I've got Hilda to take care of me."

The housekeeping robot pinched his cheeks. "What a good boy. Let's have spaghetti and meatballs for dinner. And cookies. Hilda will bake cookies."

Just then, the front door burst open, and a tall couple dressed in ski caps and heavy parkas came bursting in, dropping bags of luggage.

"Damian, we're home!"

"Mom! Dad!"

They engulfed him in hugs. "We're sorry we missed your birthday—we did everything we could to get here."

"It's okay. Mom, Dad, these are my friends." He introduced us, and they offered to have us stay, but we were eager to get home.

We left Damian with promises to come back and have more of Hilda's cookies.

I waited with Angie as she hailed a cab. "You okay?"

She nodded. "Yeah. I think my mom's going to be okay. I have a good feeling this time. Maybe if I tell her that, she'll feel it to." She hopped into a cab and waved through the window.

As I rode the train home, I relived every moment of my meeting with my mother. Then I remembered—she had tucked something in my pocket.

I pulled it out, and my eyes widened. It was a detailed drawing of her and Perseus. She had her arm around my brother and they looked happy. I ran my fingers over her face and then his, memorizing every line before carefully tucking it away in my pocket. They were with me now always.

I opened the door to Carl's apartment to find him pacing the room. His face had that worried look that vanished at the sight of me. In two steps, I was in his arms, sobbing my heart out.

"Hey, kid, you okay?"

"No."

"Do you wanna talk about it?"

"Not today." I let him hold me, savoring the smell of lemon polish and the fuzzy warmth of his sweater. It was the closest thing to home I had ever felt.

I didn't have my mother, or much of a father, but my brother was safe. And right now, that was enough.

THE END

FROM THE AUTHOR

Dear Reader:

I hope you enjoyed reading *The Medusa Quest*! After so many years writing about Norse mythology with my *Witches of Orkney* and *Legends of Orkney*™ series, I was so excited to share a story set in Ancient Greece. I loved creating a strong female protagonist in the sassy Phoebe Katz and hope you enjoyed reading about her as much as I did writing her story.

A couple of author notes I'd like to point out:

In order to write books with characters from mythology, authors have to do a lot of research into the ancient myths, and many of the stories differ depending on the source. For my research, I relied heavily on two resources: *Who's Who in Classical Mythology* by Michael Grant and John Hazel, and *The Greek Myths* by Robert Graves.

The timeline in Greek mythology has been "flattened" in the Legends of Olympus series. For example, the great Perseus was believed to be the ancestor of Hercules, so they would not have been able to be in the story at the same time.

Due to the current pandemic, I was unable to include illustrations inside the book.

As an author, I love to get feedback from my fans letting me know what you liked about the book, what you loved about the book, and even what you didn't like. You can write me at PO Box 1475, Orange, CA 92856, or e-mail me at author@alaneadams.com. Visit me on the web at www.alaneadams.com and learn about starting a book club with my free book club journals or invite me to visit your school to talk about reading!

Keep reading!

—Alane Adams

ABOUT THE AUTHOR

Alane Adams is an author, professor, and literacy advocate. She is the author of the award-winning Legends of Orkney and Witches of Orkney fantasy mythology series for tweens and award-winning *The Coal Thief*, *The Egg Thief*, *The Santa Thief*, and *The Circus Thief* picture books for early-grade readers. She lives in Southern California.

Author photo © Melissa Coulier/Bring Media

SELECTED TITLES FROM SPARKPRESS

SparkPress is an independent boutique publisher delivering high-quality, entertaining, and engaging content that enhances readers' lives, with a special focus on female-driven work. www.gosparkpress.com

Caley Cross and the Hadeon Drop, J. S. Rosen, $16.95, 978-1-68463-053-0. When thirteen-year-old Caley Cross, an orphan with a dark power, is guided by a jumpsuit-wearing mole into another world—Erinath—she finds a place deeply rooted in nature where the people have animal-like powers and she is a Crown Princess—but she soon learns that the most powerful evil being in any world is waiting for her there.

Witch Wars: The Witches of Orkney, Book 3, Alane Adams, $12.95, 978-1-68463-063-9. Orkney is on the brink of war now that the witches have destroyed Odin's Stone—the powerful talisman that kept the balance. With the evil he-witch Vertulious returned to his full form (thanks to Abigail's help), nothing will stop the witches from taking over Orkney—unless Abigail and Hugo can find a way to balance the power. Can Mjolnir, the hammer of Thor, do the trick?

Eye of Zeus: Legends of Olympus Book 1, Alane Adams. $12.95, 978-1-68463-028-8. Finding out she's the daughter of Zeus is not what a foster kid like Phoebe Katz expected to hear from a talking statue of Athena. But when her beloved social worker is kidnapped, Phoebe and her two friends must travel back to ancient Greece and rescue him before she accidentally destroys Olympus.

The Rubicus Prophecy: Witches of Orkney, Book 2, Alane Adams. $12.95, 978-1-943006-98-4. As Abigail enters her second year at the Tarkana Witch Academy, she is up to her ears studying for Horrid Hexes and Awful Alchemy. But when an Orkadian warship arrives carrying troubling news, Abigail and Hugo are swept into a puzzling mystery when they help a new friend go after a missing item—one that might spell the end of everything they know.

ABOUT SPARKPRESS

SparkPress is an independent, hybrid imprint focused on merging the best of the traditional publishing model with new and innovative strategies. We deliver high-quality, entertaining, and engaging content that enhances readers' lives. We are proud to bring to market a list of *New York Times* best-selling, award-winning, and debut authors who represent a wide array of genres, as well as our established, industry-wide reputation for creative, results-driven success in working with authors. SparkPress, a BookSparks imprint, is a division of Spark-Point Studio LLC.

Learn more at GoSparkPress.com